This book is a work of fiction. Any resemblance to actual persons, living or dead, events, or locales is entirely coincidental.

The Final Women
Copyright © 2022 by Pardeep Aujla

Cover art copyright © 2022 by Hardeep Aujla

All rights reserved. No part of this book may be reproduced or used in any manner without written permission of the copyright owner except for the use of quotations in a book review.

ISBN: 9798802816080

THE FINAL WOMEN

PARDEEP AUJLA

1

Camp Haven Cove, 1986.

"The following is a tale of murder, witchcraft, and revenge."

The campfire's snapping radiance lent a ghoulish aspect to Stan's normally friendly face, the corner of his mouth quirking with the satisfaction that the spell he sought to weave this mild June night held those gathered around enthralled.

A stifled snicker on his right pissed on the shoe of that spell.

Stan shot narrow-eyed annoyance at Booger, who pinched his jest-reddened face in a bid to stifle further outbursts.

Beside him sat Nell, with her voluminous black curls, vibrant makeup, neon hoop earrings, and a sweatshirt hanging off dark brown shoulders. Sharing in her boyfriend's annoyance, she shoved at Booger's mop of tangled hair, prompting him to raise his hands in apology.

"Doofus," said Ryan from across the licking flames, clothed in little more than a cropped football jersey and jean shorts. Cradled within his muscular arms and bundled in his large varsity jacket was Nikki, her whale-spout ponytail swaying with each disapproving shake of her head.

Booger returned with a childish pull of his face.

"C'mon, you guys," said Alex, knees updrawn on Stan's left, swaddled in an oversized denim jacket, her face untouched by makeup. "Let Stan tell the story."

"Thanks, Alex." Channeling the charismatically ominous stylings of Vincent Price, Stan continued to spin his yarn. "The tale of the phantom of Haven Cove. The tale . . . of Silas Crowe."

A hulking silhouette lumbered to a halt between the bare and palsied pines making up the dense yet lifeless forest surrounding the abandoned summer camp. Breath crackled through a sputum-choked trachea as they observed the trespassing teens.

Merged as this figure's profile was with the deep dark of the forest, little could be discerned of their form beyond the frightful size. Though, if one were to look closely, to parse the shadows and separate the arthritic angles of barren branches from the smoother curves of flesh, one might be struck incredulous by the suggestion of an abnormally large head.

The figure communed through labored thought with the slithering whispers that haunted their perpetually fogged mind, seeking the forgotten answers to questions they asked each time trespassers entered their domain, drawing them forth from a void they could not comprehend.

Where?
Here.

"Legends say this campsite was once home to a coven of witches," Stan continued, light and shadow playing upon his features. "And that here, on these very

The Final Women

grounds, the wicked threesome would perform ritual sacrifices to their unholy gods."

Nikki nestled deeper into the reassuring security of Ryan's linebacker physique, and he in kind closed his arms tighter around her.

"Their last and final ceremony involved the murder of six young women." Stan turned to Alex. "Virgins."

Alex frowned at his insinuating look.

Booger released his toke with a "Sweeeeeet." He passed the joint to Nell.

"Six throats slit," said Stan. "Their blood spilled upon the hexed earth."

"Freaks," said Ryan, accepting the joint from Nell and taking a hit before holding it to Nikki's mouth so she could do likewise. Alex took the joint and handed it off to Stan, not partaking herself.

"After some incantations, an inhuman baby crawled up out of the blood-soaked ground, screaming like some hell-born horror. That baby . . ." Stan took a toke, letting the expelled smoke crawl over his face as he eyed each member of his captive audience, granting a theatrical pause before the revelation. "Was Si—"

"Silas Crowe!" said Booger.

Stan threw up his arms. "Booger! You're fucking up my story, man!"

Booger plucked the joint from Stan's hand. "Sorry, sorry." He took a hit, croaking out his next words. "Pretty obvious, though. I mean you said—"

"Can I continue?"

Booger once again raised his hands in apology, a can of beer in one, the joint in the other. "Continue, continue. Jeez."

Stan took a breath to reset himself. "Silas was to be the earthbound vessel for the vilest of the witches' demonic deities, The Great Eater."

"Why'd they call it that?" asked Nikki with childlike sincerity.

"I'm guessing it didn't stress too much about counting calories," said Nell through a smoky exhalation, drawing a chuckle from everyone except Stan, who looked frustratedly between the bunch.

"Guys!"

"Sorry," groaned the others in unison.

"However . . ." Stan reset himself again, his put-on voice frayed by his rising frustration. "However, the ritual was interrupted by enraged townsfolk, come to avenge loved ones taken and killed by the demon-worshipping trio."

Though scared, Nikki was eager to know more. "Then what happened?"

Firelight perverted Stan's smile. "The witches were tortured and buried alive for their crimes. Right here. On this very campsite."

Looks of doubt and unease passed over the group's faces as they looked about the fire-ochred ground on which they sat.

"But," said Stan, reclaiming their attention, "that demon baby? It disappeared without a trace."

"Far out," said Booger.

"It is foretold that on the centenary of that night, Silas Crowe will rise from the earth once again, butchering anyone foolish enough to enter these accursed grounds. His purpose? To resurrect those witches, six lives for theirs, so that they might finally finish the ritual they started one hundred years ago. One hundred years ago . . . tonight."

Nikki straightened with wide-eyed alarm. "But wait, there's six of us, and we're right here!"

Stan's brows bounced with his smile. "Exactly."

The revelation was met with silence from all but the crackling fire. Stan looked between the unmoved faces, his smile straining.

Booger caught Ryan's eyes, and as one, they burst into hysterics.

A frowning Stan pushed Booger over. "You guys suck." Nell caught Booger as she too joined in the laughter. Stan gave his girlfriend a hurt look. "Et tu, Nell?"

Nell let a cackling Booger topple as she moved behind Stan and looped an arm around his neck. "I'm sorry. You're just so cute and sincere." She kissed his cheek and ruffled his hair, loosening him up. "Anyway, the way I heard it, Silas Crowe was just some kid who snapped and went psycho after being bullied by the other campers here."

"I heard the camp was built on an ancient Indian burial ground," said Alex. "And Silas Crowe is the physical manifestation of those angry spirits, punishing all who trespass."

"I heard this Silas guy was the last survivor of some super-inbred cannibal family who lived in an old mine around here," said Nikki.

Ryan nodded as he gulped a swig from his beer. "I heard he was a counselor back when this place first opened. He fucked with a Ouija board, got possessed, killed a buncha people, then disappeared, but he keeps coming back here"—he tickled Nikki, startling her to laughter as she fought him off—"to kill agaaain!"

"I heard he was your mom," said Booger, provoking a middle finger from Ryan.

"It's an old story." Stan sulkily threw a handful of dirt into the flames to little effect. "Gotta be like a bazillion versions of it."

Free from the obligation of having to listen to Stan's story, Ryan and Nikki proceeded to unabashedly suck face. Alex knit her brows and shifted away as they inconsiderately leaned into her. "Guys, c'mon. Get a room, seriously."

A Cheshire cat grin spread across Booger's face. "If they wanna put on a show, let 'em put on a show." He gave a lewd waggle of his eyebrows. "I don't mind."

Ryan threw his empty beer can at him without a glance, though Booger was quick to dodge. "C'mon, Nikki, let's go for a walk."

Within the forest, the dark figure watched as two of the teens stood and broke off from the others.

When?

Soon.

Wet, wheezing breaths hastened with perverse excitement.

"Suuure, a 'walk,'" said Booger with air quotations. "A long, *hard* walk."

Nell jabbed at his arm.

"Ow!"

"You're such a skeeze."

Stan upended his beer can, draining the last few dregs. "Cashed out."

"You brought more, right?" asked Nell, palpable concern in her voice.

Stan nodded. "In the van. Booger, you wanna go fetch?"

"I most surely do not."

"You wanna keep smoking my weed?"

Before the word "weed" fully left Stan's mouth, Booger sprang to his feet, hand outstretched. "Keys."

Stan tossed them over.

"Booger away!" The joker of the pack sped off toward the van, leaving the others to laugh at his sudden, though predictable, change of heart.

Alex looked around at the desolate camp.

The eight log cabins—one of which was little more than a disordered stack of charred wood—were arranged in a horseshoe formation: four dorm cabins, a counselor's cabin, the mess hall, showers, and the cabin housing the office, infirmary, and game room. There was also an outdoor sports area, and between the cabins and moonlight-speckled lake shouldering the camp was an obstacle course, complete with raised platforms connected by rope bridges and a zip line.

The entire assemblage was in dire disrepair, with most of the cabin windows broken and the exteriors tagged with graffiti ranging from crude to cryptic—here a dick-nosed face beside an eye with a knife down its middle, there a disembodied butt farting out an indecipherable speech bubble beside a "Hail Satan," the T being an upside-down cross.

Alex sighed at the sight. "Hard to believe this place used to be a summer camp."

Nell cozied up to her boyfriend. "What really happened here?"

Stan curled an arm around her. "Some counselors got murdered last year, and the year before. Not to mention a buncha disappearances."

"You don't really buy into what that crazy old coot at the gas station said?"

"Sounded pretty convincing to me."

"Cuckoo for cocoa puffs is what he sounded to me."

"No, I remember the stories," said Alex, eyes on the fire. "There was a survivor from each of those incidents. Both swore they killed the guy responsible."

Stan huffed sardonically. "I guess that first survivor didn't do too good a job."

Alex shrugged. "Cops said the second killer was a copycat. Still, kinda creepy to know people actually died here."

Nell hugged herself, chilled by the thought. "Remind me why we came here again?"

"A notable lack of authority figures," answered Stan.

"Well." Nell stood. "We're here now. Might as well check this place out." She turned to Stan. "You coming?"

"With you?" He jumped eagerly to his feet. "In about five seconds."

"Being a little generous there, aren't we?" Nell mocked, to which Stan gave a sarcastic chuckle. Nell turned. "Alex?"

"I'm gonna stay here, wait for Booger. Make sure he doesn't glom all the weed."

"Good idea," said Stan. "Can't trust that putz with anything."

Nell smiled. "He'll behave if Alex is around."

"What's that supposed to mean?" asked Alex, trying to suppress an embarrassed flush of her cheeks indicating she knew exactly what it meant.

"Oh c'mon, isn't it obvious? He's in luuurve with you."

Alex's blush deepened despite her efforts. "What? Get out."

Stan's face drew up in playfulness. "More like in lust with her. I heard him practically chanting your name once when he was jerking off."

Alex recoiled at the thought.

"Ugh, gross!" said Nell, voicing Alex's thoughts. "And why in the hell were you watching him jerk off?"

It was Stan's turn to flush. "I—We were—I didn't—"

Nell pulled on Stan's arm. "C'mon, pervert, let's take a look around."

"Babe, I swear!"

"Oh, I'm so sure!"

Two more left the fire, leaving one of their number alone. Defenseless. All the watcher need do is tread carefully, close the distance, approach at just the right angle, and then—a garbled breath caught in their throat. They shifted behind the cover of a tree as the girl by the fire turned their way. The confusion was uncertain, then quick to fade when a cawing crow flapped free of the tree, returning the girl's attention to the flames. Did they speak to her like the whispers spoke to them?

Who?
All.

There came a scream.

Nikki ran playfully through the moon-mottled forest, either oblivious or unconcerned by the gnarled, anguished forms of the dead trees appearing to reach yearningly for her from all directions.

Ryan gave chase, his athletic prowess quickly catching him up to his quarry. He grabbed and pinned

Nikki to a tree beside the camp's sports area. "Gotcha!"

Nikki reached down and squeezed at the expanding bulge in his shorts. "Gotcha more." Their mouths met in impatient passion, hands groping hungrily.

Tilting her head as the kiss deepened, Nikki opened her eyes at a weird wheezing sound.

There stood a man, or a grotesque approximation of one, for he looked like a child's exaggerated drawing. Towering over the pair, the abomination was seven feet tall at a modest estimate. The head—resting on the excessive hump of his left shoulder—was too big, even upon this huge frame, and cocooned in dark, thorny vines offering no hint of the features beneath. His arms were a mismatched pair, the left apishly long with a trio of large, rusted nails sprouting from the back of his hand. His naked body—rangy, though sinewy—was an eyesore of filthy, scar-strewn meat, corpse-gray beneath the grime, and betoken of inhuman power despite the obvious scoliosis. A lumpen, sunken whorl of tissue occupied the space where genitals ought to be.

Nikki shivered in wide-eyed shock, a thing Ryan misread as a sign of heightened arousal, spurring him to slip his hands beneath the waist of her pants for a rough squeeze of her ass.

Silas Crowe shrugged his head upright off his hunched shoulder, then raised a javelin. In a single motion, he rammed it with a sharp crunch through the back of Ryan's head, through his and Nikki's mouths, out the back of her head, and deep into the trunk of the tree.

He hovered a moment as the young couple struggled limply upon the javelin, sputtering on the blood pouring from between their locked lips.

Why?

. . .

The ill-fated lovers were left to expire in their final kiss.

Stan and Nell pushed through a creaky, loosely hinged door, entering the dark, mildew-reeking mess hall.

Probing around the side of the entrance, Stan found and flicked the light switch. "Ta-da!"

A series of overhead lamps blinked to life, a couple blowing out with pops loud enough to startle Nell and Stan into each other's arms, the pair laughing with relief.

It was a large space, with tables and chairs stacked neatly in one corner and a DJ and disco light setup in another. These, coupled with wall-mounted streamers, bunting, and a centrally hung mirror ball, indicated the hall was last used for a party. Signed double doors at the rear led into the kitchen, and a fire exit led out the right side of the building.

Stan nodded. "Well, this sure is . . . uh . . ."

"I think the word you're looking for is skeevy," said Nell. She approached the dust-rimed audio equipment and began haphazardly flicking switches, bringing red and green LEDs to life. "Hey, this stuff still works!" Another button press sent festive disco lights in a cheery merry-go-round about the hall. The turn of a dial phased the sound of "Cruel Summer" by Bananarama into existence, widening a smile on Nell's face, her body bopping as the hall filled with the song's perky beat thanks to several wall-bracketed speakers.

These speakers weren't confined to the inside of the mess hall. Two more on the outside broadcast the song to the rest of the camp.

Sitting alone by the fire, Alex lit up with surprise as the music borne on swirling beams reached her. She looked up at the starry sky above, her mind weighed with thoughts of the future, of life after graduation. That's what tonight was: their official end-of-high-school blow-out. Chances were they'd all be going their separate ways soon enough. At least, she knew she would be.

These were good friends, no doubt there, but they were all so different from her. Even Nikki, with whom she'd shared a juice box on their first day at kindergarten, had changed so much. In truth, she couldn't see herself remaining friends with any of them long after tonight. As cold as it sounded, they were just the people she was meant to navigate high school with, temporary allies through the tumultuous trials of teenhood before the siren call of adulthood, with all its glittering possibilities, pulled them in different directions.

Flicking off the overhead lamps and leaving the disco lights to swim through the air, Stan shucked his Members Only jacket to the paneled floor and strutted into the center of the hall, spinning to Nell with a dramatic dance pose. "Let's do it, girl!"

Nell raised an eyebrow. "Excuse me?"

Stan swayed and dipped his body mostly-but-not-quite in time to the beat. "Dance off!"

The traveling disco lights reflected off the mirror ball and capered across Nell's face as she laughed at the efforts of her goofball boyfriend.

Undeterred, Stan completed his clumsy jig with a spin, hand outstretched and inviting Nell to dance.

Stepping up to him with more rhythmic aptitude than he'd showcased in his entire sorry attempt, Nell pushed Stan back and proceeded to bust moves like a pro despite her loosely whipping shoelaces, leaving her boyfriend awed and more than a little turned on.

He took her in his arms.

"Giving up already?" she asked.

Stan pulled her close. "You got me at a disadvantage."

Nell smiled as she felt his erection press against her. "I can see how that would impede your performance."

They kissed.

The song from the rec hall was muted but discernible out on the moonlit dirt road, where a buzzed and agitated Booger kicked up a small dirt cloud as he approached Stan's van. It was a sight, with its duct-taped bumper, wire hanger antenna, and airbrushed Frazetta-esque mural depicting a bronzen-thewed barbarian posed upon a fiery mountaintop. A pair of buxom babes in scaled bikinis on either side fawned over the glistening sword held suggestively between the barbarian's legs. "'Hey, Booger, you wanna go fetch?' Hey, Stan, you wanna suck my nuts?" He sighed deeply.

Time was slipping away from him. The wider world beckoned, and he knew Alex was eager to answer. If he wanted to confess his feelings for her, it had to be tonight, while the weed and the beer still coursed through him, giving him both courage and a viable excuse for his out-of-the-blue profession when she inevitably rejected him. *Hey, Alex, I just wanna apologize for last night. All that weed and beer really did a number on me. Had me all muddled and thinking totally random shit. I mean, you're real nice and all, but you know I only date Play-*

mates. Cool and casual, a good laugh to break any lingering awkwardness. His rejection speech was better rehearsed than the declaration of his feelings.

A resplendent moon cast Booger's shadow upon the van's side door as he slid it open, unwittingly ejecting a heap of trash. "Fucking—" Booger kicked at the pile, hurting his foot on a crowbar among the mess. "Fuck!" Sighing in frustration, he turned to the van's cluttered interior. There, nestled among the assorted detritus of carefree youth like a treasure chest surrounded by lesser booty, was the cooler.

"Come to papa!" Booger leaned in to retrieve a sixer, helping himself to a sly seventh as reward for the task, and to further pacify his nerves. *I totally should've asked her to come with me, gotten her away from the others.* He shook his head at such an obvious missed opportunity. "Stupid."

A startling caw caused Booger to hit his head on the van's ceiling. "Ow!" Leaning out, he came nose to beak with a crow upon the roof. "Wah!" The crow departed by Booger's fright, mimicking his outcry perfectly as it left him to steady his spiked heartbeat. "Fucking feathered fuck!" Beer was employed to restore his equilibrium. As he chugged the can and slid the side door shut, he failed to note the large shadow now smothering him.

Turning mid-chug, Booger had all of a second to register the huge fist that hammered the beer can down his upturned mouth and into his esophagus, where it lodged, bloating the mass of his neck. Gagging, suffocating, and unable to tilt or turn his head due to the rigid beer can, Booger did not see the rudely wrought blade that opened his throat with the sound of tearing tin, releasing a fizzing froth of blood and beer that gushed pinkly from the ragged mess of flesh and metal. Booger pawed uselessly at his ruined neck as he fell against the van's side door and slid down, the heels of his sneaks scraping furrows in the dirt.

Silas watched as the curly haired teen toppled and shuddered on the ground; the hiss of the beer and blood concoction fading out into the distant song from the rec hall.

Why?

. . .

Nell and Stan screwed hurriedly against the DJ's table, their breaths coming fast and heavy, their moans and groans uninhibited. Leaning back for purchase, Nell inadvertently mashed a hand upon the sound equipment, flicking a switch that turned off the music and turned on the mic.

Poking at the fire, Alex found herself all of a sudden subjected to the live audio of Stan and Nell's climactic finish. At first horrified, Alex couldn't help but crack up at the copulating couple.

"Ooh—ooo—aah . . ." came Stan's voice over the speakers. "So . . . How many seconds was that?"

"Y'know," said Nell. "I think that might've been six."

"Well, how about that, a new personal best! Hey, what's this light mean?"

"Ah shi—"

The broadcast ceased, switching instead to the next song in the DJ's playlist: "Life's What You Make It" by Talk Talk.

Alex shook her head in amusement, hugging herself as she took in the dismal camp.

This place definitely had bad energy. Crooked cabins surrounded by a lifeless forest where not even leaf-rot littered the ground, with not a chirping bird nor buzzing insect to be seen or heard, only the odd crow. It was summer, yet the twisted trees looked winter-dead. The smell of the place was off too, with none of the piney richness one might expect but rather a nose-furling mustiness. The overall effect gave these woodlands an air of drear antiquity, of belonging to another time and place entirely, a place where things died. The cherry atop Alex's unease was the disquieting feeling she'd had since they'd arrived of being watched.

She looked down the path leading to Stan's van. "What's taking you so long, Booger?" Boredom and loneliness winning out, Alex stood and headed out in search of her friend.

Nell straightened her mini skirt. "I'm gonna freshen up. Meet you back outside?"

Stan zipped up his pants. "Sure, right after I perform my customary post-coital victory jig."

"I thought we agreed you weren't gonna do that anymo—"

Stan was already silly-dancing. "Sorry, can't hear you over the roar of the crowd."

Nell rolled her eyes. "You're such a dork."

"A dork who just rocked your world," Stan corrected with a satisfied smirk.

Nell raised her hands in defeat and made for the bathroom, leaving Stan alone to do his dance.

Alex approached the van, the music from the rec hall taking on a haunting quality with the distance. "Hey, Booger?"

Something about the scene pricked at a deeper part of her, the part that warns not to cut through that too-dark alley or stop for that overly smiley hitchhiker. "Where are you?"

Her steps slowed the closer she got, that deeper part of her loudening its concern. Her nerves won out, bringing her to a stop. "Booger, quit goofin'."

She hesitated with the decision to go closer or to turn and leave the clown to his prank, which this was, right?

"Boog?"

No answer came, only the distant song, whose plaintive melody continued to add an eerie edge to the situation.

She took a breath. She was being silly, her inner child affected by Stan's story and pulling on the sleeve of her older self out of fear, a fear she knew to be irrational. And so, settling on bravery and a fully justifiable kick to Booger's nards should he jump out at her, Alex stepped closer.

She stopped.

Was that . . . blood on the ground?

"Booger?" Alex rounded the van's front, then rent the night with a scream.

Booger lay slumped against the side of the van, wearing a bib of still-flowing blood.

Alex raked quivering fingers through her hair. "Oh God! Oh God, no! No!" She stepped toward her friend, reaching out a hand that quickly retracted to cover her mouth. Her thoughts were pure noise—loud, confused.

Some instinctual part of her took over as her bleary eyes fixed on the crowbar by her feet. Her hand grasped it without knowing exactly what she would do with it, but her feet seemed to know, turning her about and beating a frantic pace back to the camp.

Sitting on the toilet, Nell read the plethora of doodles and notes scrawled upon the side of the stall, among which was a heart with the initials JJ and MK at its center. She popped the top off her candy-red lipstick and began to add to the declarations with a heart of her own. She paused midway through the '&' of Nell & Stan, hesitating a moment before putting her lipstick away and making a rosy smear of the avowal with the sleeve of her sweater.

Flicking disapprovingly through the DJ's abandoned cassette tapes, Stan jumped at a loud bang. "Shit—Fuck!"

The fire exit door banged again, swayed by a mounting breeze, giving glimpses of the murky night beyond.

Stan sighed with relief. "Friggin' door." It banged once more as he headed over, humming along to the song beating through the speakers.

Gripping the push bar, Stan was perplexed when it didn't budge under his pull, then alarmed when it was instead thrown open further, yanking him roughly into the doorway, where he bumped into the unyielding barrel chest of someone very big.

Stan couldn't look up immediately, his eyes fixed on the rusty pitchfork head gripped in the frightful stranger's meaty mitt. With trembling breaths, Stan lifted his gaze, and as his face stretched in shock, the stranger uppercut him under the chin with the four-pronged weapon, raising him off his feet as the tines popped through the top of his skull and stabbed into the door's head jamb, which held the entirety of his weight. Blood sluiced down Stan's face, highlighting eyes rolled back to their whites and painting the front of his clothes red. His jaw clamped to a molar-cracking tightness, and his arms flapped about like a pair of

hysterical eels strung up by their tails before settling with limp finality.
Why?
. . .

Nell touched up her makeup in the grimy bathroom mirror, beside what must've been the only unbroken window in the entire camp, though its frosted film had long since degraded to a frayed mess. Her hand moved mechanically as she applied eyeliner, her gaze somewhere distant.

She sighed at the bittersweetness of the night. What would become of her and her friends? Of her and Stan? As far as she figured, college was the move. Makeup artist or fashion designer, that was where her passion pointed. For Stan, the move was going full time at his dad's hardware store. *Few years and I'll be running the place, babe*, he'd tell her. *Then, expansion. Imagine it, a chain of Stan's Hardwood and Nuts! We'll be set for life!* She'd humor him, laugh at his jokes, even when they weren't all that funny, but his vision for the future wasn't one that interested her at all, especially considering they'd only been going steady for a few months.

What annoyed her most was the way Stan spoke about his plans like she was naturally a part of them—a thing she found sweet at first, but quickly came to dislike due to him never showing any interest in discussing *her* dreams and aspirations, making her feel as if she were just another piece on the board of *his* life, to be moved around to fit *his* ideal design.

She wanted no part of it.

Travel, adventure, to leave this Podunk town and not look back, that's what she wanted. The world was big, full of sights and wonders and experiences, and she wanted to chase them all. And she planned to, even if it meant going it alone. She just needed to find the courage to tell Stan that.

Her eyes drifted down to her boots and their loose laces. Stirred by Talk Talk's suitably poignant lyrics, her mind sought to create meaning between the sight and her present headspace. Something to do with tying up loose ends, maybe? Pulling yourself up by your bootstraps? That one was a stretch. She shook her head at the dumb train of thought, deciding that sometimes a loose lace was just a loose lace, and kneeled to tie them. At that exact instant, Silas swept past the window, glancing inside, a great white scanning for prey.

Time may have slackened for that second, the music from the dance hall stretching across the moment, or what was nearly a moment. Silas felt almost a confluence of some significance, but, seeing no one, he continued, the feeling slipping away.

Nell stood and turned to the window, unsure if she'd heard something, then deciding it was probably just some fluctuation of the speakers. She appraised herself one last time in the mirror before putting on a smile and heading back into the hall.

Disco lights passed over Stan's red-splashed sneaker, blood dripping and expanding the puddle beneath his suspended feet.

"You done with your—"

For a moment, Nell wasn't sure what she was looking at, then came the thought that this must be some practical joke. Stan and Booger loved those, but how was he hovering like that? And what was that dark stuff pooling beneath his feet? Looked like . . .

Her hands went to her mouth as realization hit, muffling a confused and heartbroken wail. She moved toward Stan's body, then stopped, her shaking head denying the truth her widened eyes could not. She heard a scream outside. A sound that didn't just confirm that truth but underlined it with blood.

"Help!" screamed Alex as she broke through the tree line. "Somebody help!"

"Alex!"

Alex saw Nell running out of the rec hall. The look on her face, tremor in her voice, and stumble in her step telling her Booger wasn't the only one dead.

And then she saw him.

Silas Crowe came purposefully around the side of the rec hall, practically dragging his longer, weightier arm; a lumbering figure out of nightmare. A felling ax winked silver in his hand as he made for Nell, who was unaware of the monster closing in behind her.

Alex pointed with the crowbar. "Look out!"

Nell turned with the sincerest scream she would ever release at the sight of the malformed giant approaching her with ax raised.

"Run!" yelled Alex.

Nell did so, putting the whole of her being to the purpose.

The world seemed to slow as Alex watched Silas shift his grip on the ax's handle, rearing it back. Then, with an awe of force that violently tore the air, he hurled it end-over-end at Nell's retreating form.

Nell tripped on her insistently loose laces, falling face-first to the ground beside the waning campfire. She felt a chill whoosh over the back of her neck as she tumbled and, looking up, saw a flung ax hit Alex full in the face, splitting her head with an outward blast of blood, knocking her off her feet and dropping her splayed upon the dirt, the crowbar thudding beside her.

A scream was all Nell could offer her fallen friend, for the monster was on her heels. She scrambled to her feet and ran beyond Alex's corpse, out into the forest of leafless, crooked trees.

Silas stopped to look down at the girl. Not his intended target, but a kill was a kill. He regarded her split, blood-splashed face: the broken mouth, distended eyes, and deeply embedded ax head between them.

Why?

. . .

"Help!" Nell screamed as she pelted between the twisty-limbed trees, their bare, overhanging branches a vast net above her, sure to fall at any moment and hand her to the killer.

She dared a backward glance but saw nothing, though every shadow and vaguely humanoid tree was a potential threat.

Turning back, Nell barely managed to swerve her step, falling as she avoided the end of the javelin nailing two more of her friends to a tree through their heads. She cried at the sight of Nikki and Ryan, the couple dangling from the javelin like loose meat on a skewer.

A twig snapped in the near distance.

Nell spun and saw him, advancing toward her with an urgent need to deliver the long, pointed object held by his side. Regaining her feet, Nell was once more running for her life.

Breaking through the tree line, she came upon Stan's van, wasting no time in going for the driver's door.

Locked.

She ran around to try the passenger's door.

Locked.

"Come on!"

She went for the side door and was met by an open-throated Booger, whom she greeted with a startled cry.

All of her friends—whom only a short while ago she'd been talking with, laughing with, enjoying one last night of togetherness with—were dead. Slaughtered. Cut viciously from the cloth of existence.

Doomful footfalls from the forest told her now was not the time to mourn. Hurrying into the van, she began patting Booger down in search of the keys, eyes averted for fear she might retch or else succumb to paralyzing panic if she were to look at him. The coppery tang of blood, mixed with the acrid reek of her dear friend's posthumous shit, was doing a fine job of pushing her in that direction without the added visual accompaniment.

She found the keys in the pocket of his blood-drenched jeans and hurried into the van.

Wet, fumbling fingers caused her to drop the keys in the footwell as she tried for the ignition. "Fuck!" Scrabbling madly, she retrieved and hurriedly smacked them home, bringing the van to life with an unhealthy sputter that transitioned into an angry growl.

Flicking on the headlights brought the nightmare man back into reality, standing several feet ahead, his features etched in frightening relief by the light.

Nell's mind strove to make sense of what she saw: A man? A monster? He was pale and filthy, his proportions wrong, his body crooked. His huge, slanting head was wrapped in a dead thorn bush or something. And his arms, one looked way longer than the other. And what the fuck was that situation between his legs?

The blade he held was a singular length of sharpened metal similar in size to a machete, honed to a razor, albeit uneven, edge and tapering to a penetrating point that surely guaranteed tetanus with the smallest of nicks.

He pushed his head from off his enlarged shoulder and started toward the van.

"Oh yeah?" Nell revved the gas and shifted into gear. "Fuck you!"

The vehicle launched at Silas, who advanced despite its rushing approach; defiant, or else certain of his survival at the meeting.

The van struck the monster, and as he seemed to go under, Nell cheered through her tears. "Take that you—"

A large hand slapped upon the hood of the moving van. The other stabbed the unrefined blade through metal. Silas pulled himself up over the front.

Adrenaline superseding fear, Nell pulled the seatbelt across her body. "Okay" She increased the van's speed. "Okay, motherfucker!"

The van swerved abruptly from side to side, but the killer held on, pulling himself up before the windshield, blocking Nell's view with his bulk.

"Just die, you—"

Silas smashed his weapon-wielding arm through the windshield, catching a screaming Nell in the shoulder with his primitive weapon, white-hot pain shocking her entire body.

An involuntary jerk of the wheel flung the weapon from Silas's hand as he reared it to stab again, and so he instead punched his longer arm through the penetrated glass, grabbing a handful of Nell's curls and tugging her head sharply to one side.

Nell's foot instinctively slammed on the brakes, throwing Silas frontward—a chunk of her hair gone with him—as the van came to a skidding halt on the gravelly road.

The monster pitched and rolled away in a cloud of dirt, but returned to his feet with unhindered urgency, heading straight for the van with not a stutter in his step as he charged like an enraged bull.

Watching his approach through the punctured windshield, Nell pushed through her pain and once again set the van in motion, her foot a cinder block on the gas pedal.

The sight of Silas expanded and brightened rapidly through that hole in the glass as the van ate the road between them.

Nell bucked in her seat at the jolting impact.

This time Silas did not go beneath the van, staying pressed against the front, trying once again to reach his prey.

Seeing a large tree, Nell screeched the van toward it, bracing herself with a scream.

The resulting crash was mighty, crumpling the front of the vehicle with a detonation of glass and a flying hubcap.

The van's horn blared unbroken. Smoke spewed from the ruined hood. Shattered glass glittered in the surrounding area.

For a long moment, such did the scene remain.

The driver's door groaned open, vomiting out Nell, who landed in a wheezing heap pained, bloody, and disoriented.

After crawling away and taking in a few hard-fought breaths, she seemed to regain herself. A hand to her injured shoulder sent a shock of sobering pain through her body, sitting her upright. An instant of confusion had her looking about herself, then she saw the wrecked and shrilly hooting van, and the lifeless body of Silas Crowe sandwiched between it and the unyielding tree, his huge head and shorter arm unmoving upon the demolished hood.

With his body unresponsive and darkness claiming his senses, a single, lonely thought drifted through Silas's mind.
Why?
. . .

2

Thirty years later.

"I ask myself that question every day," said Nell, sitting in the plump patient's chair of her therapist's bright office.

Her appearance had changed much in the intervening decades. Her once big hair was shortened to a cheek-length bob. Gone too was the loud makeup, or any, and her sense of style had subdued, sitting as she was in a simple marl-gray sweater, jeans, and black-framed glasses. New, though, was an edge in the eyes behind those lenses: the hardness of one who knew devastation and lived in its unrelenting shadow.

"Why?" asked the rapt therapist sitting across from her, whose sincerity and unmasked horror at her story had Nell thinking he might need therapy of his own after this.

"Why'd it happen? Why'd it happen to me and my friends? Why'd I live? I've never come up with any . . . any profound answers, y'know? No big, philosophical revelations. It happened, and it happened because . . ." Nell shrugged. "It happened just because."

The therapist shook his head. "Tragic. Just tragic."

Nell pulled her mouth into a thin line and drew a semicircle with her eyes as she waited for him to say more, until it became apparent more wasn't coming. "Hoping for a ray of light here, doc. That's kinda why I came."

The therapist straightened himself in his chair, remembering his purpose. "Uh, well, what more could you have done?"

Nell sighed and shook her head.

"Silas Crowe . . ." The name seemed to physically weigh the shrink down. "I remember the stories. We'd scare each other as kids with—" He shook himself back to professionalism. "Anyway, they never caught him, right?"

"There were suspects, arrests. Some high schooler gone stab-happy 'cause he got pranked on prom night, or a transient vet who thought he was still in War Zone C. None stuck. Local law, state police, even the FBI looked into the murders and disappearances. None found him. No body. No trace. Only the victims. What was left of them."

"I see . . . And is this your first time seeing a therapist since that incident?"

"Tried it before. It helped some, up until the exposure therapy part anyway, then I checked out. I . . . I just couldn't."

"But you're here giving it another go. Why?"

"I heard the camp's being reopened. I guess hearing that . . ."

"Reopened your wounds, so to speak?"

Nell cringed. "Dumb, right?"

"No, not at all." The therapist sat forward in his seat. "Have you ever considered volunteer work?"

Nell furled her face. "Like petting mangy puppies and slopping out soup to the homeless?"

"Sure. Or helping others who've been through a similar ordeal. It's good for the soul. Help others and be helped in turn. There were others, right? Survivors of Crowe and his imitators, I mean?"

Nell nodded. "Three. One in eighty-four, another in eighty-five. The third was a few months after me, but no one knew about her until way later."

"Ever try reaching out to any of them?"

"My publisher contacted them for interviews when I was working on my first book, but they weren't interested. Can't say I blame 'em."

"Well, maybe if you approached not with the intent to exploit, but to understand."

Nell jerked back, insulted. "Exploit? I wasn't trying to exploit—"

The therapist raised placating hands. "What I mean is, if you contacted them expressly with the intent to empathize, to just talk."

Nell turned the idea over. "I dunno. It's been so long."

"And yet, here you are, still struggling with the trauma."

Nell couldn't deny that truth. She *was* still struggling, couldn't remember a time when she wasn't, or imagine a time when she wouldn't be.

"Who better to understand that trauma than those who share it?"

Nell's feet pounded the polyurethane surface of her local athletics track. She ran here daily, ritualistically, never a session missed come rain or shine. Here she meditated, contemplated, but mostly escaped.

Completing a run each day gave her a feeling of having hit reset on some internal timer counting down to the abrupt unraveling of her life, stalling it for another twenty-four hours. That it kept her fit and her weight in check was also of great importance. Diabetes and heart disease had run wild in her family, and she was determined to outrun both, to outrun everything.

Coming to a gradual stop as she caught her breath, Nell checked the fitness tracker on her wrist to measure her heartbeat, loud and furious in her ears. A self-approving nod indicated she was pleased with her performance.

Relaxing the keys habitually clutched between her fingers, Nell checked all around herself to ensure she was alone, then unlocked the three separate deadlatches on her apartment door, checked around again, then entered.

It was a tidy, ordered, one-bedroom deal. A mostly white interior with splashes of yellow and plenty of houseplants gave the place a fresh and airy feel. Everything seemed placed within its own strict, invisible border, from additional pairs of shoes to the toaster to unopened mail on the kitchen counter. An over-filled bookcase beside the door held several books with her name along their spines.

She'd made a career penning books on the bloody history of Haven Cove, its myths, its phantom, and its victims. It was Silas, though, not the victims, who captured peoples imagination, becoming a figure of modern folklore, one that Hollywood Hollywooded, turning real world pain and trauma into a cash grab series of slasher flicks. The latest in the *Teenage Wasteland* series pitted a wholly inaccurate Silas

Crowe against the titular killer from the *Bloodglutter* films—another long-running horror series Nell had neither the interest nor stomach to watch.

Supplementing her books with editing and ghost-writing gigs just about kept her refrigerator stocked, allowing her to hide away from the world, rarely needing to leave her apartment. Some days that suited her just fine, other days not so much. There was no one to say hello to here. Not even a furry companion to greet her with a pattering of excited footfalls. Relationships had been few, far between, and short-lived. As for friends, well, those she could count on one hand and have enough fingers left over to high-five herself with.

Fear of loss kept her alone, and a hesitance to trust, to allow others in, drove all potential friends and partners away sooner or later, mostly sooner.

In the aftermath of the incident, people would often tell her that time was what she needed. *Give yourself time. Time heals all wounds.* But it doesn't. At best, it inures you to your pain. In Nell's case, time allowed her paranoia, anxiety, and reclusive tendencies to take deeper root, such that they were now the default.

Nell performed her customary securing of the door: unlocking and relocking each latch three times, being sure to hear the telltale clicks, sliding home the heavy-duty bolt locks at the top and bottom, fastening the chain, testing the door with three firm tugs, placing the designated drinking glass over the handle, and completing the routine by toeing a rubber wedge beneath it. No one was getting in here without significant and clamorous effort, by which time she'd be ready with her pistol and high-power, triple LED flashlight, poised to startle and blind from around the cover of her open bathroom door, exactly as she'd drilled.

She brought up her phone's voice mail, switching to loudspeaker as she placed the device on the kitchen countertop along with a bag of groceries before removing her shoes and coat.

"You have one new message," said the automated voice. "Received today at seven forty-two a.m."

"Nell, it's Linda."

Nell pulled a face of mock puzzlement. "Linda? Lin-daa?"

"Your agent, remember?" said the pre-recorded Linda, as if hearing her.

"Nope, doesn't ring a bell."

"I know, I know, it's been a long-ass time."

Nell went into her fridge—as neatly ordered as the rest of her place—and grabbed a bottled protein shake. "That's one way of putting it."

"But I return to you bearing good—no, great fucking news!"

"Spill it already," said Nell, massaging the shoulder bearing the scar from Silas's stab as she took a swig of her shake.

"You see the news? I've got publishers going absolutely bug nuts! I swear my phone hasn't stopped ringing all morning!"

Confused, Nell took the remote to her TV and switched it on to the news.

"I'm talking a full-on bidding war with you at the center, girl!"

Nell's protein shake hit the white-tiled floor, splattering its milky-pink content.

The headline on the news channel read, 'Counselors missing one week before Haven Cove reopening.'

"I smell a sequel!" Linda sing-songed.

Nell stumbled back as if struck in the gut, hand on her shoulder as if feeling the bite of Silas's blade all over again. She caught herself against the countertop. The TV, Linda's voice, the world. Everything became a distant, indistinct rumble in her ears. Her unblinking eyes read and re-read the news headline until the words blurred through the sheen of her welling tears.

"Call me back pronto!"

Nell rushed into her small bathroom, throwing off her glasses and flinging up the lid on her toilet as she collapsed before it, head thrust inside to purge the contents of her quivering stomach. After a horrid retch, a heavy slosh, and a hasty flush, Nell slumped back against the wall, breaking off an excess of toilet paper to wipe at her mouth as she caught her reeking breath. Her returning senses picked up the ongoing report on the TV.

"—live as we speak to Mayor Leeman about these disappearances."

Mayor Leeman appeared beside the reporter, looking like a low-rent oil tycoon, complete with an obvious and mismatching toupee. "These disappearances are—are of course, uh, highly distressing to all concerned. But I want people to know—no, I want them to rest assured, that finding these—"

The crustiest of old men shoved himself into the cameraman's frame, yanking the microphone away from the mayor's face and before his snarling own. "I warned 'em!"

The abashed mayor worked his mouth for a couple of seconds before words began to flow. "C-Clem, please, this is—"

"Things've been just fine all these years," continued Clem, undeterred, "but now you done woke him up again!"

The reporter went with the unplanned interview. "Woke who up, sir?"

"Silas-fucking-Crowe!"

The words were a blast of icy air over Nell's body, shuddering her airflow and threatening to bring up more puke.

"Sir, please don't swear," the reporter admonished.

"Just leave the camp be! Can't you dumb fucks understand that?"

Nell drew up her knees and hugged herself tight, hands shielding her head against what felt like a falling sky. Her thoughts came in a rushing squall. She began rocking back and forth, striving to level herself out enough to process what was happening.

A bird squawked somewhere close by. The sound was enough to startle Nell out of her fearful trance.

It came again.

Where's that coming from? Reclaiming her glasses, she rose and left her bathroom. It wasn't unheard of for a bird to stray into the building through an open window in the summer months, flustered and rowdy until someone shooed it outside.

Sun-stealing clouds gloomed the entire apartment as she drifted toward her door, the agitated caws loudening as she drew near.

Leaning to the peephole gave her a view down the length of an empty corridor, empty save for a lone crow standing a few feet from her door, facing her door, cawing *at* her door. It turned and took to wing, its gliding retreat leading Nell's eyes to the hall's farther end, where it was lost in an emerging shadow belonging to someone turning the corner.

The wall-mounted lamp there flickered out before the shadow's source was revealed, though an indistinct bulk could be glimpsed. It moved toward her apartment with slow, calculated purpose, each successive lamp blinking out the instant before its light could illume the large figure.

Nell's breaths hastened as she double-checked the integrity of her locks.

The crow's increasingly excited caws drew her eye back to the peephole. The corridor was darker, the figure closer. Somewhere, a phone rang, its shrill clangor mingling with the unseen corvid's cries, and yet, through all that discordance, the dark shape's thumping footfalls were clearly discernible, and became increasingly so as it loomed ever closer.

Its outline became more defined with the shrinking distance, bringing with it a gut-plummeting familiarity as the disproportionate dimensions of its slanted head became apparent.

The last lamp to die flashed off a length of metal gripped in the figure's hand.

Nell jerked away from the door with a sharp breath. *How? How could he be here? How could he have found me?*

She couldn't move, her feet rooted by terror.

The crow's squawk signaled it was right outside the door.

She couldn't move.

The phone rang as if encased within her skull.

She couldn't move.

The door shook and split as something struck it from the other side, the glass over the handle shattering at her feet.

Gun! Get the gun! her mind screamed.

She couldn't move.

All commotion ceased at once.

In that silence, with tremulous breaths, Nell leaned back to the peephole.

There was nothing but stark blackness, until that blackness opened a single, livid eye, blood leaking from the pupil into the crimson nebulae of the iris and pooling above the lower lid.

Silas's blade tore through the door and into Nell's abdomen, punching out of her back as she gasped—

Waking with a start, Nell snapped her pistol and flashlight up to catch a target that wasn't there, her chest rising and falling rapidly, her frantic eyes scanning the darkened space in a blur, which she hastily corrected by retrieving her glasses.

A nightmare, she realized, remembering she'd locked herself in the bathroom after hearing the news. The realization did nothing to stop the tears from falling, however, because the nightmare was real; the phantom stab in her stomach morphing into a gut-souring awareness that her sanctuary had been breached, her bubble pierced.

Silas Crowe was back.

Who else could be responsible for the disappearances? He was back, and more people would die, and there was nothing anyone could do about it because no one had ever been able to do anything about it.

And now that he was back, would he be coming after her? What was she supposed to do with this knowledge? Run? Hide? That's what she'd been doing. Should she try to convince the authorities? What would be the point? They wouldn't hear her out. No one would believe her, just like they didn't believe her thirty years ago.

Nell emerged shaken from her bathroom. Looking at her front door, she saw it remained locked and intact, the glass still in place.

Night had fallen, making her question how long she'd been asleep, though that word implied intentionality. No, what she'd done was shut down.

The only light in the apartment came from the TV, still on, its steely hue creating sharp panes of light and shadow. Nell was drawn to its cold glare and saw the same news interview from earlier being replayed.

"Silas-*bleep*ing-Crowe!"

"Um, sir, please don't swear."

"Just leave the camp be! Can't you dumb *bleep*s understand that?"

No, thought Nell. *No one understands what they're dealing with at that camp.*

She recalled the parting words of her therapist: *Who better to understand that trauma than those who share it?*

Shit . . .

The idea had been planted now, Nell hating herself for having seeded it.

No one understands what they're dealing with at that camp . . . except those who do.

Her anxiety spiked sharply.

But what does that mean exactly?

More people will die unless he's stopped.

And you'll die.

I'm not some badass with the skills or know-how to do anything.

But no one else is going to do anything.

*And you'll die.
But—
No one.
And you'll die.
But the others wouldn't want anything to do with this.
You have to try.
Try and you'll die.
But they're just as scared as I am.
But you have to try.
Try and you'll die.
But I'm too scared.
More people will die unless he's stopped.
You'll die.
I'll die.*

Nell stared into space for several long minutes as the mental see-sawing continued.

Turning without purpose, she caught herself in a wall-mounted mirror, though the image within was of her younger self checking her reflection in the camp restroom as she had that long-ago night, wondering on the paths laid out before her. Nell blinked, and the illusion was gone, the reflection of the path taken laid bare.

Little by little her expression changed, slackened, firmed, hardened, though the fear never left her eyes.

Her fists clenched at her sides.

In the kitchen now, phone held before her face, Nell paced restlessly back and forth, the fingers of her free hand tapping a frantic beat on her thigh. "C'mon, you—"

"Nell?"

"Linda! It's—Yeah, Nell—I—"

"Where've you been?"

"I—"

"Never mind! Can you believe this?"

"Yeah—Listen—"

"We're talking 'fuck you' money here—"

Nell clenched her eyes, reminded now why she rarely spoke to this parasite and making a mental note to fire her. "Dammit, Linda!"

"What? What'd I say?"

"Do you still have contact details for the others?"

"Other whats?"

Nell hesitated using the instinctive word, deciding instead upon "Survivors."

The word sounded hollow and ill-fitting to her ear. Being the sole 'survivor' of that night meant Nell had to face the poorly concealed animosity of her friends' parents alone. Their pained, wet-eyed looks that screamed, *Why did you live and not my child? Did you do all you could to try to save them? Did you have a hand in their death?* And she would in turn ask herself these questions, replaying and dissecting her trauma in hopes of finding some peace of mind that she *had* done all she could have, that she *hadn't* caused any of their deaths, if even inadvertently. But there was no peace to be found in such reflection, because maybe her friends *would* still be alive if she'd done things differently. If she hadn't left Stan alone in the rec hall, if she hadn't tripped on her laces and fallen when the ax meant for her struck Alex instead. If right from the get-go she'd suggested they go somewhere else, anywhere but that godforsaken camp. And so, she accepted the blame foisted upon her, because a part of her felt it was deserved.

Her dreams reflected that belief, frequently playing out the deaths of each of her friends as if she'd watched them like a ghostly spectator, unable to stop or influence the horror playing out before her. Worse, though, where the dreams where her friends were still alive, carrying on as normal, but shunning her, as one does those who wronged them.

No. She hadn't 'survived.' She'd been dealt a pernicious blow: a slow death by guilt, the kind of guilt that tricks you into thinking you've processed it, accepted it, surmounted it, only for it to strike when your guard is lowered, twisting its cold blade in your gut once more, leaving you enfeebled and tainting every day to your last with its poison.

"Forget it, I already tried," said Linda. "They're not interested, same as before."

"Gimme their addresses. I'll try them myself."

"Listen. Money, fame, they ain't interested. The hell're you gonna offer to get 'em on board?"

Nell looked to the TV. The faces of the five missing counselors were on screen. Young, smiling faces, their life stories written upon them. Nell fancied she could see sadness behind one or two of those smiles, while others projected fully the brilliant light of the individual. Each one of them was gone now. All their tomorrows wiped away. Just like her friends' had been.

How much more was Silas Crowe going to be allowed to take from the world? How many more lives would he gut, leaving those left behind to fester with grief?

No more.

"Revenge," said Nell, at a near whisper.

"Huh?"

"Uh . . . Closure, I guess."

"Sounds like BS, but okay. Lemme see here . . . Um, remember Ana Gómez?"

"The one from eighty-four, right? Who's like, a—"

"Paranoid prepper. Yeah, that headcase. Let me pull up her address."

3

Having set out early, Nell's Prius—garish orange on account of her reading that brightly colored cars were less likely to be involved in traffic accidents—pulled up outside of an austere bungalow. It was defended by a seven-foot, electronically locked steel perimeter fence crowned with anti-climb spikes, surely in violation of several HOA regulations. The place was a miniature fortress, in stark contrast with its neighbors with its entirely paved lawn, cold and unadorned exterior, steel-reinforced front door, barred windows, solar-paneled roof, and security cameras no doubt covering every square inch of the property from multiple angles.

"Oh yeah, this is the place all right." Nell took a deep breath. Her agoraphobia had lessened over the years, though some days leaving her apartment still felt like a perilous expedition. Today was such a day. Another breath. She opened her door, anchored a foot on the sidewalk, drew it back in, and did this two more times before committing to exiting the car with a frustrated sigh.

The Final Women

Motion sensor security lights blinked on—uncomfortably bright despite the daylight—as Nell approached the gate and knuckled the buzzer. She waited for a response.

None came.

She tried again, depressing the buzzer longer this time. Again, nothing.

Nell looked around at the neighboring houses, catching a swiftly drawn curtain across the quiet street.

Frustration mounting, she abandoned politeness and pressed the buzzer repeatedly. She stopped when its aggravating clamor was drowned out by a series of loudening barks, heralding the biggest pair of Rottweilers Nell had ever seen as they came bounding from around either side of the house.

"Shit!" she yelped, jumping away from the fence not a second before the beasts threw themselves at it, froth flying from their snapping maws as they berated her from the other side.

"Whoa there, doggies! Good little monster doggies!"

A shrill whistle pierced the dogs' hubbub, settling them in an instant and turning both their and Nell's heads to the front door.

Ana Gómez stood in the doorway, exuding the aura of a legit, no-nonsense badass with her shaved head, eyepatch, and black tank top showcasing brown arms that spoke of many a slain chin-up. That she was barefoot and wore checkered pajama pants did nothing to lessen her intimidation factor.

Unnerved by the icy glare she was receiving, and also the Glock 9mm Ana held, Nell smiled and gestured amiably to the dogs. "Some mean mutts you got here."

Ana let the silence stretch for a long, uncomfortable moment before asking, "I know you?"

"We've, uh—" Nell took a cautious step toward the fence, the dogs' throats rumbling in response. "We've not met before, but—"

Ana turned around and shut the door.

"Wow, okay, rude." Nell looked at the dogs who, though calmer, continued to eye her with hunger. She returned her attention to the door. "Ana, I really need to talk to you."

No response.

"It's urgent."

Silence.

Nell pushed the buzzer again, holding it down for several seconds in hopes of bringing Ana back out in anger if nothing else.

The Rottweilers once again grew agitated, barking at Nell's flagrant misuse of the buzzer, which she released upon their warnings.

Unable to bypass the barriers of Ana's gate and stonewalling, Nell succumbed to her frustration. "Fucking—Silas Crowe's back!"

The dogs went silent, as if they understood the portent of those words.

The gate buzzed and clicked open an inch.

Nell looked to the house and saw the front door do likewise, though Ana herself did not reappear. She eyed the dogs nervously as she stepped to the open gate. "Your dogs aren't gonna eat me, are they?"

Silence. Of course.

Nell steeled herself, touching and retracting her fingers from the gate three times before braving on through as non-threateningly as possible. The dogs—Kull and Kane by the tags on their collars—watched her with restless intent, their desire to rip out her throat straining against the taut leash of their strict schooling. "Good doggies. Good, gentle, friendly doggies. Please stay the fuck there."

The inside of Ana's home was as utilitarian in design as the outside: tidy and uncluttered, the sparse furnishings positioned and upheld with military efficiency—something Nell found reassuring. The only real flavor came from the numerous pieces of framed fantasy art by the likes of Sanjulián and Boris Vallejo, depicting fierce warrior women.

Scanning farther inside this ascetic abode, Nell saw a desk with a multi-monitored computer setup sat in the corner of the living room, the screens currently showing live feeds from the security cams. A heavy bag—duct-taped about its middle—and weights bench occupied an adjacent room, and there were boxes from a health food delivery service stacked by the kitchen door. These signifiers—when added to the pajama pants at a quarter to noon—pointed to someone who, like her, worked from their home and rarely left. Nell didn't doubt there were also hidden weapons placed strategically throughout, maybe even a trapdoor leading to a vat of acid. She scanned the laminate floor beneath her feet for irregular joins.

"Talk," said Ana, arms crossed, though with the gun—fitted with a tactical light Nell noted with an *I gotta get me one of those* look—still gripped firmly across her bicep.

Now that they were face-to-face, Nell became aware of the burn scarring running up one of Ana's arms, the fibrous, irregular tissue climbing her shoulder and reaching up the side of her neck, leading to an eye like that of a wolf primed to lunge at the slightest provocation. Deeper, though, beneath that edge,

Nell could see pain, the same she tried to avoid seeing each day in the mirror.

Hoping to build rapport, Nell tried for friendly sarcasm. "Words with more than one syllable really aren't your thing, huh?"

Ana's face remained stone-cold. "Actually, I do know you." She walked past Nell to a large shelving unit filled with books on survival, self-defense, DIY, serial killers, and an impressive collection of pulp sci-fi and fantasy novels. Nell tilted her head. Was that a *Star Trek* Blu-ray box set behind a line of painted tabletop gaming miniatures? Ana pulled down a particular book and dropped it onto the coffee table.

Summer of Silas, by Nell James. Nell's first book. She'd always found that title cringy, but the publisher had insisted.

"Amateurish writing, prone to exaggeration and with the kind of hackneyed emotional manipulation you'd see in a daytime soap opera," said Ana pointedly.

Nell smiled. "Want me to sign it?"

"You already know I'm not interested in being a part of any book."

"That's not what I'm here for."

"Then skip to what you are here for."

"I . . ." Nell sighed, not sure of what to say or how to get through to someone coming at her with such palpable hostility.

"Yeah." Ana stepped aside, gesturing to the front door. "Best you don't look the dogs in the eyes on your way to the gate."

"You still have nightmares, right?" asked Nell, sincerity and more than a hint of desperation in her voice. "Still check all your doors and windows twice or more before you sleep? If you even can. Like me,

The Final Women

you're probably still afraid to even close your eyes. Probably have a lock on your bedroom door even though you live alone." Ana recrossed her arms and set her jaw. A sign she was getting through? Nell pressed her point. "Shit, I can't even remember what a good night's sleep feels like. What it was like before every tick and creak in the dark had me jumping in my skin, convinced every time—*every single* fucking time—that there was someone creeping in my home. I can't tell you the number of times I've woken up with my hands wrapped tight around a baseball bat, or . . . or slept in the closet because that was the only place I felt even a little . . ." Nell struggled to think of any other word but, "Safe?" She huffed. "I know the word, know what it means, but I couldn't tell you what it feels like." Ana's jaw seemed to be loosening. "It's like . . . it's like we got sucked into a black hole, and we've been living at the center of it all this time."

Ana gave a curt shake of her head. "Not the center."

"Huh?"

"First off, you'd cease to exist because the laws of space and time are absent there, but even so, if you were sucked into a black hole, you wouldn't be able to reach the center, you'd just be trapped forever in the moment of hurtling toward it. For you, that moment would never end, but for everyone else outside the black hole, the moment ended before it even started."

Nell took a blank-faced moment to process that.

Ana gave a terse shrug and turned away. "It's a better metaphor when you think about it."

Nell shook her head. "You know what I'm saying. I mean, look at this place." Nell gestured to the home at large. "You're living inside of one big panic room. This is the home of someone living in constant fear."

Ana's expression conveyed her clear displeasure at that statement. "Spare me the psych eval—"

"I'm the same," Nell stressed. "I am. And I dunno about you, but I'm *tired* of it." She paused a moment to let that tiredness show, and was heartened when Ana's expression softened almost imperceptibly with recognition of it. "I'm gonna take my life back."

Ana scoffed, her guard back up. "And how're you gonna do that?"

"By killing Silas Crowe."

"Tried that already. So did you, if your book's to be believed."

"So you do think he's still alive?"

"I watch the news."

"And you think it's him? Not just some copycat?"

Ana looked away, answering instead with another question. "Supposing it is. Hard to kill a thing that doesn't wanna stay dead."

"So we do it for good this time. I'm talking overkill. Whatever it takes."

Ana raised an eyebrow. "We?"

"I can't do it alone. I need your help. That's why I'm here."

"And what makes you think I need *your* help?"

"I . . ." It was a question Nell had no answer for, making her feel like she'd just been checkmated.

"*You* can't do it alone, doesn't mean I can't."

"Fucking do it then," Nell snapped.

Ana looked away with the tiniest of smirks. "Why me?" she asked.

"'Cause you believe me—and I know you do."

Ana said nothing.

"'Cause you know what we're up against. 'Cause you want him dead just as much as me. And 'cause you look like you can hit things real hard."

Ana's expression lost more of its edge. She turned and stepped away, looking out of her barred window for a long moment.

Yeah, she'd seen the news. It sickened her to her core. Not that Silas Crowe was back; that detail came as little surprise at all, perhaps because he'd never been far from her thoughts. Despite his apparent demise and the passage of time, he never stopped being a threat.

What sickened her was her reaction to the news. Fear. Something she thought she'd overcome, had gone to extreme lengths to master. But she hadn't. Not entirely. Not when it came to him.

Ana realized she was kneading her pistol. She stopped, not wanting to project her anxiety, to be seen as weak, because she wasn't, and she knew that. She knew that. No, what she was, was angry. That's what she'd learned to channel fear into over the years, into anger, into action. That's what she needed now, and had already been planning before Nell's arrival: going to the camp, tonight, fear be fucking damned, knowing full well she might not come back alive and feeling like maybe that wouldn't be so bad, just so long as she took that fucker with her.

Nell wondered whether Ana was looking out of the barred window or at her own reflection within it. The thought made her reassess this home as less of an impenetrable fortress and more of an inescapable prison, which in turn made her wonder if the same could be said of her apartment. She didn't like the apparent answer.

She desperately needed Ana to be in on this. She knew that from the first look. Nell had no idea what the other two survivors were like, but she couldn't imagine either of them being as seemingly tough and capable. She realized these were big assumptions to make about someone she'd just met, but Nell had always fancied herself a quick and accurate reader of people, and everything she'd read about this woman since arriving—her cold demeanor, her tightly muscled physique, the strictness of her home—told her she was sharpened steel. A weapon.

What am I doing? she thought, catching herself. This woman, Ana, wasn't just some weapon to be wielded on her personal crusade. It wasn't even *her* personal crusade, it was Ana's and the others' too. They each had just as much reason to want Silas dead as she did. She just hoped she'd be able to convince them of that, because she really didn't want to go it alone.

"Y'know . . ." Ana turned to Nell. "You talk a lot better than you write."

4

Home after shabby home passed by Nell's driver's side view, a slideshow of broken and boarded windows, overgrown or outright dead lawns, and decrepit cars.

Ana sat beside her, pajama pants swapped for black cargoes, a khaki military-style jacket, and combat boots. Venturing out was a rarity for her these days, online shopping and no real friends to speak of making it easy to fall into the whittled-down life of a recluse. Plus, she didn't much care for the stares she got on account of her scars and eye patch. Still, something about this outing gave Ana a certain buzz. "So, who else we recruiting for this hit job?"

Nell's eyes flitted between an address on her phone and the houses drifting by her window. "Josie Jedford."

Ana nodded, recognizing the name. "The one who killed the first copycat."

"We both know that was no copycat."

Ana knew indeed. She'd read the reports, Josie Jedford's statement. The description she gave of Silas Crowe matched her own. You don't forget such an uncanny figure as that. You certainly don't mistake such a monster for the frail, malnourished vagrant the authorities had so lazily pinned it on, dismissing any plea to the contrary. "They try to make you feel crazy too?" Ana asked. "After you told them what you saw, I mean?"

Nell nodded. "I heard it all, that I was drunk, or high, or both. No one believed what I saw—well, most people, anyhow."

"Yeah?"

"Some religious nuts believed me, like *really* believed me. Telling me Silas was a sin-eater, punishing the wayward youth who engage in premarital sex and consumption of *the devil's weed*, et cetera. Puritanical asshole types, y'know?"

"Oh, I know." Ana turned to the passing houses. "Was raised by one."

Nell's interest piqued at that personal disclosure. Now they were officially a team, she wanted to know more about Ana. "So whe—"

"Ever been to this part of town before?"

It was a hastily asked question, delivered without eye contact, signs Nell recognized as a desire to change the subject. "Uh, no. You?"

Ana shook a no.

Silence was closing in.

"Y'know I half expected you to be living in, like, some underground bunker or something. Gotta say I was pretty surprised to see you living among regular folk—not that you're irregular or anything, just, uh . . ." Nell chuckled. "Help me out here?"

Ana huffed amusedly. "Elderly neighbors are like free security cameras. My street's mostly retirees. A cat can't cross the street without one of them kicking up a storm about it online."

"Clever thinking."

"Security's what I do."

"For work?"

"Right."

Nell had to prompt for more. "So, what's your job exactly?"

"Cybersecurity analyst."

"Fancy."

Ana shrugged.

"What drew you to that line of work?"

"It pays well, and I can do it from home."

Nell nodded. "I hear that."

"Same reason you're a writer?"

"Kinda. I mean not at first, no."

"Then?"

"I guess I started to write because . . . well it was the only way I could get any of what I was feeling out, y'know?"

"Sure. That probably makes sense."

"Then, when I found I could make money from it, I stuck with it. Nothing else really took."

Ana nodded. "You found your thing."

"Yeah . . ." said Nell with a wistful bent. Being a writer hadn't exactly been 'her thing' as a teen. Hell, at that point she hadn't even read a book beyond those foisted upon her in high school English. To work in fashion had been her dream growing up. A life of style, art, travel, and adventure. To date, she'd never left her home state.

The rising clamor of a speed-metal track brought the car curbside of a run-down abode. A supercharged sixty-eight Dodge Charger was parked out front, cobalt blue and polished to a photoshoot-ready sheen.

Ana gave the house a questionable look. "This it?"

Nell replied with a nervous nod as she eyed the place. "You brought a weapon, right?"

"Weapons," Ana corrected. "Plural."

"All right." Nell took a deep, steadying breath, the presence of another not allowing her to appease her anxiety with her usual tics for fear of being thought a weirdo. "Let's go say hi."

The front door was ajar and led into a dingy, hazy living room, extra murky on account of the thin curtains that didn't so much block the light as tint it, casting the interior in brownish twilight. The pervasive skunkweed stink and music blaring from a large stereo system were an arresting combination on the senses.

Facing the far wall, unmoving upon a tattered couch whose arms were pocked with cigarette burns and shuddersome stains, was a pasty, lank-haired man in ratty attire, doped out of his mind as evident by the fact he was staring zombie-like at a TV that wasn't on and the assorted drug paraphernalia on the table before him.

From the kitchen came the shouts of a highly agitated fellow, though who or what he was so thoroughly scolding remained unclear.

The riotous noise, foul smell, and seedy atmosphere had Nell feeling keyed up in the worst way. She strove to fight through despite the fact. "Hello?" Her voice was lost beneath the music. She walked over to the stereo and turned it off.

"The fuck?" came the angry voice from the kitchen, followed by the imposing frame of a bald, bearded man, looking like that one felon all the others politely give up the weights bench for mid-set. A denim vest showcased thick arms adorned with faded ink, while camo shorts revealed bullish calves.

Nell froze, rigid, as the man pulled a switchblade. Violent eyes fixed on hers, a wolf staring down a rabbit.

She couldn't move.

Ana moved for her, interposing herself between Nell and the brute with a blur of hands that left him disarmed and clutching at his croaking throat in shock, followed by a whooshing spin to power an elbow that laid him out, his eyes lost in their upper lids. Then her pistol was in her hand, aimed for the execution shot.

"Stop!" cried Nell. "He's out!"

The zombified dope fiend snatched a gun from the coffee table as he sprang from the couch and turned on the women.

Ana jerked her aim up.

BANG!

The man's head snapped to the side with a spurt of blood and dusty pop in the drywall behind him.

BANG!

His half-raised weapon blasted the floor as he fell back and through the table.

BANG!

Another errant shot hollowed the TV screen as he crashed.

Semi-crouched with her hands over her head, Nell slowly straightened, her heart thumping and ears ringing with the echo of gunfire. A dog complained from somewhere not-too-distant.

What the fuck just happened?

Her eyes goggled at the carnage. "Holy shit . . . Holy shit, you—you killed him. . . . A-a-and I'm an accessory!"

Her weapon still aimed at the doped-up goon, Ana shook her head. "I got him through the cheek."

"You sure?" asked a worried Nell.

"I always hit an inch or two to the left of what I aim at when I quick-fire like that." Satisfied neither of the men would be posing any further threat, Ana holstered her gun. "I was aiming for his nose."

Ana's word not enough, Nell cautiously approached the man to see for herself. Sure enough, she saw a ragged red hole through his cheek, the blood from the wound spreading beside his head. He was alive, but solids would be a frustrating memory for the foreseeable future.

Nell *whewed* internally, then turned to Ana with a relieved smile. "I'm real glad I came to your place first."

A woman appeared in the kitchen doorway—limped, Nell noted—her demeanor suggesting indifference to the violent eruption that had just taken place. She wore a nicotine-stained robe over a faded Poison Idea T-shirt and sweatpants. A near-spent cigarette dripped ash from between her fingers. Her drawn face, listless graying hair, pallid complexion, and darkly circled eyes suggested she was no stranger to whatever the dopehead was currently on.

Nell and Ana exchanged a look before turning back to the woman. "Josie Jedford?" asked Nell.

Josie stared unemotionally at the big man on the floor, who was making a strangled snoring sound as he choked on his tongue. "Is he dying?" she asked with cold disinterest.

Ana pressed her foot against him, pushing him onto his side, which seemed to dislodge the blockage. "He'll be fine." He made a choked gasp. "Probably," she added.

Josie took a drag of her cigarette as she surveyed the rest of the damage in the room, again with minimal interest. "You here to rob us?"

"No," said Nell.

"So, this was what? A message? From who? The Druid? We already agreed to—"

"Silas Crowe's back," said Ana, cutting to the chase.

The till-now dispassionate Josie came alive with fear, shunted into the wall behind her by the force of that name, one hand grabbing for the door frame while the other moved to her lower abdomen. "Where?"

Witnessing such a sudden attack of fear made Ana turn away in deep discomfort.

"Haven Cove," Nell clarified. "Haven't you seen the news?"

Josie shook her head as she shrank in on herself.

"The camp reopened," said Ana. "Counselors are missing. Read: dead."

Confusion and terror wrestled across Josie's features. "I-I—" She plunged a hand into the deep pocket of her robe, pulling out a rattling bottle of pills.

Nell stepped toward her with calming hands. "Hey—hey, you okay?"

She clearly wasn't, trembling as she broke off a quarter of a scored bar of those pills and swallowed it dry. She took a moment to work it down and catch her breath, taking several long draws on her cigarette before attempting to speak again. "W-who—who're—"

"Nell James. I was . . . he . . . back in eighty-six."

Josie turned to Ana.

"Ana Gómez. Junior Camp Counselor. Eighty-four."

Josie hugged herself, all of a sudden feeling terribly cold, saying nothing, looking at nothing, lost within herself.

Nell and Ana exchanged another look, Ana shaking her head. Nell moved a step closer. "Josie?"

"Why're you here?" Josie asked, though her unfocused eyes were to the floor.

Nell took another step toward her, causing Josie to shrink further into herself. Nell stopped. She understood Josie's reaction, but part of her, the part that had spent the years since that night demanding strength and courage from herself, felt revulsion at such a display. Looking to Ana, she saw the feeling was shared, though her one-eyed ally seemed less inclined to mask her dislike.

Nell remembered her purpose here. "You still have the nightmares, right? Still check all your—"

"We're gonna kill him," interrupted an impatient Ana. "Figured you might wanna kill him too."

Nell turned a frown on Ana, annoyed at not being able to give her speech, refined since she'd last used it. "Yeah. That."

Josie scowled as if she'd just heard the most astoundingly absurd thing ever. She pressed a hand against the wall, the world turning too fast. "Stop. Just—" She took a hasty puff of her cigarette. The silence stretched before she spoke again. "W-what do you mean he's back? How? How could he be back?"

"We don't know," said Nell.

"Then how do you know it's even him?" Josie's tone was beginning to take on an edge of hysteria.

"It's him," Nell affirmed, and the assurance in her voice halted any further debate on the matter.

"You in or not?" Ana asked without a hint of sympathy.

"No!" said Josie, resolute. "No. I-I can't."

Nell was finding it increasingly difficult to witness such a reaction, such defeat, perhaps because a part of her wanted to just hide and deny all this too. "Don't you wanna—"

"No!" Josie practically shouted. "I don't! So leave me alone!"

Nell hesitated with what to say, feeling terrible for having upset another so. "Look, I'm real sor—"

"I'm not a fighter, okay!" said Josie, tears welling in her eyes.

"Bullshit," said Ana. "You wouldn't be alive right now if you weren't."

Josie wiped her eyes and shook her head. "I can't . . ." She looked directly at the pair, an angry, spiteful look. "You can't just come into someone's home and drop something like this on them, expecting them to . . ." The news of Silas's return seemed to hit her all over again. "No . . . No, I-I can't. I can't."

Nell nodded in acceptance, though her disappointment was obvious. She needed Josie to say yes, needed her to be strong, like Ana, needed it because she felt weak and afraid and wanted to surround herself with strong people, then she could at least pretend to be too. But Josie wasn't strong. Josie was the person Nell had spent the last thirty years trying not to become. "I get it. It's okay. We'll leave you alone. Sorry."

Unlike Nell, Ana was little affected by Josie's refusal, heading for the front door without hesitation. There was no place for someone so fragile on this mission, which is exactly how she thought of it. Better for all of them if this woman didn't get involved.

They're leaving? thought Josie. *Just like that? Drop a bomb on me then leave like it's fucking nothing?* But then, she wondered, what more could they say? "Why?"

Nell stopped and turned to her. "Why what?"

Josie moved away from the wall, though still hugged herself. "Why are you doing this?"

"Because no one else will," answered Ana, hand on the door handle.

"You'll die," said Josie.

Nell felt a foreboding chill at those words, delivered with a look of such absolute certainty. Her own thoughts parroted Josie's warning. Nell pushed them down. "We survived before. Beat him before. Each of us. If we team up, go back there knowing what we're getting into, armed, alert, ready, he doesn't stand a chance."

Josie took another drag on her cigarette, taking in all that had been said along with her inhalation. *What is this? How could this be? How could he be back? How the fuck could he be back?*

There were no answers, only the apparent facts before her. These two women, whose names she recalled from reports and interviews all those years ago, were here, in her home, telling her *he* was back, and they were going to kill him. Were they crazy? They looked a little crazy. Dangerous too. Look at what the one with the eyepatch and shaved head did to Lugg and Scud. But then again, if they were telling the truth—and she couldn't figure why they'd be lying—then dangerous is what they'd need to be if they were going to do what they said. "You're really gonna stop him?"

"Try fucking murder him," said Ana with supreme confidence. She immediately wished she

The Final Women

hadn't, worried they might actually be getting through to this woman.

Nell saw hesitance on Josie's face, could maybe see the slightest something catch. A foothold.

Josie needed to sit down. To think. To run. To hide. Her eyes caught sight of something on the other side of those thin, brown drapes. A green Volvo station wagon with tinted windows, one she recognized all too well by the Dara Celtic Knot spray-painted upon its side. "Shit!"

"What?" asked Nell, following Josie's gaze.

Ana was already beside the window, furtively peeking with both hands around her Glock. "Take it these guys are bad news?"

"It's The Druid," said Josie, edging away into the kitchen. "Lugg must've pissed him off bad this time. I-I gotta—"

"We need this to be over," Nell blurted, snatching Josie's attention back in an attempt to not lose that foothold.

"What?"

"You asked why we're doing this, it's because we just . . . We just need this to be over. An end to it all, y'know?"

Josie searched for but found no response, instead finding herself looking at the general state of her surroundings. Lugg, Scud, drugs, scary Druids, a busted TV, and a pocketful of pills. Her life. The path she'd stumbled down ever since that night at the camp; the only path that bastard had left her. She wanted—needed it to be over too. This scant existence where she was either exhausted from the endless dread or else numb and apathetic from self-medicating. A ghost.

This is crazy, Josie thought. *This is so fucking crazy. How can I even be thinking this? Why am I still thinking this?* The phrase 'an end to it all' repeated in her mind in answer to every question.

When she turned back to Nell and Ana, her face spoke still of profound doubt and fear, but looking between the two, feeding off the determination and confidence they exuded, and hurried by the imminent wrath of Druidic drug lords, that doubt and fear gave way to a firm decision.

5

"I've changed my mind," said Josie, sitting in the back of Nell's Prius and dressed in slightly more suitable attire, her robe and sweat pants traded out for a pink hoodie and faded jeans, hastily snatched in their flight from her place. "Take me back."

"Back to what?" asked Nell. "That big asshole and his zombie sidekick?"

"Lugg might be an asshole, but he makes me feel safe."

"Really?" asked Ana, scanning the houses they passed. "Coulda swore I saw him get knocked the fuck out by a chick earlier." She turned to Nell with mock puzzlement. "You saw that, right?"

"Oh, I most definitely saw *that*."

Ana returned her gaze to the houses. "Thought so."

Josie shook her head at the pair.

"What're you gonna do back there, anyway?" asked Nell. "Your TV's busted, remember?"

Unable to find a convincing counter, Josie sank into the seat, pulling the same pills as before from her pocket. She broke off another quarter and popped it into her mouth, swallowing it dry.

She'd smoked, snorted, shot up, popped, and huffed just about everything at one time or another, but it was the benzodiazepines that really took hold. She'd been on and off them for years, going long stretches sober, leaning heavier on weed and alcohol to stay afloat, but then a random sound, image, or scent would unearth a previously suppressed memory so horrific she would relapse, taking refuge in Xans or Vals, desperate to forget, to not fear, to not think or feel a fucking thing.

Therapy hadn't done shit. How can you rationalize something like Silas Crowe? You can't. Family, friends, lovers, how could they ever hope to grasp the sheer terror of that night? A terror that had stained every aspect of her life since. They couldn't. Drugs, however, had taken her to places where he was unable to haunt her. Wiped her mind and all the horrors it contained clean, like a shaken Etch-A-Sketch. All they demanded in return were large swathes of unremembered time and a heavy toll on her health.

Looking up, Josie caught Nell's eyes in the rearview mirror, and the question within them. "Xans," she answered.

"Are you, uh . . . Are you like—"

"I need 'em. That's all there is to it."

Nell thought she glimpsed part of a scar on Josie's wrist as she pocketed the pills—barely perceptible, but highly suggestive.

Josie pulled her sleeve down to hide the scar.

Nell returned her eyes to Josie's, and the look exchanged between them answered the next unspoken question. Nell nodded—"Sure, okay."—and left it at that. She understood. She'd had a long spell on SSRIs and anti-anxiety meds herself, and though she was off any pills now—except for the occasional sleep aid—

she knew how easy it was to become dependent on them, and how hellish withdrawal could be. As for the scar, well, she'd have been lying if she said she'd never contemplated similar alternative remedies.

Josie's addiction was nowhere near as bad as it once was. At one time she was popping six bars a day, but over time she'd weaned herself off, bringing that daily dose down to half a milligram. Today required extra, though, and she wasn't going to beat herself up about that because of course it fucking did.

"Hey, uh, are you gonna be okay?" Nell asked Josie. "We kinda left a bad situation back there."

Josie dreaded the thought of returning. She'd left the house in haste, grabbing a change of clothes and not even closing the back door behind herself while Lugg and his human suckerfish pal Scud counted stars and dealt with whatever form The Druid's wrath took. "I—"

"The two of you can stay at my place tonight," said Ana.

It was a suggestion Nell found surprising. "You sure?"

Ana nodded. "Makes sense. We wanna hit the road as early as possible."

Nell wondered if Ana's gesture was born more out of guilt than any practical considerations. Nevertheless, it was a kind and welcome gesture. "Little old for a slumber party, aren't we?"

"It'll be my first, actually."

"Oh, well, in that case we absolutely accept your gracious offer! We can play Truth or Dare, Light as a Feather Stiff as a Board, Never Have I Ever, talk about our crushes."

"It'll definitely be my last, in that case."

Nell caught a slight smile on an unaware Josie's face.

The combination of a lighter mood, rare change of scenery, and most significantly the meds taking effect, eased Josie's jangled nerves somewhat. She looked out at the homes of the affluent gated community they'd managed to tailgate into: lavish abodes with pristine lawns, sculpted hedges, gleaming SUVs, and long driveways. A whole other world from her neighborhood. "What's her name again?"

"Cassy Phong," said Nell, also regarding the impressive digs, imagining herself owning one, then deciding that was far too many doors and windows to worry about.

"It's Cassandra Rafferty now," Ana corrected. "Married some tech mogul named Blake Rafferty. Keep your eyes out for a red Ferrari convertible, license plate 8L4K3."

Nell turned a questioning eyebrow on her one-eyed passenger.

"It's called doing your homework," said Ana.

The car rolled to a stop outside of an expensive white stone house with a porticoed entrance. In the large bricked driveway were two vehicles, a red SUV and the red Ferrari convertible they sought, as indicated by the vanity plate.

"Guess this is it," said Nell.

Josie self-consciously touched at her clothing. "Feel like I shoulda made more of an effort or something."

"You're fine," said Nell, inwardly questioning her own appearance now.

"I'm still bringing my gun," said Ana as the three of them exited the car.

Walking up the driveway to the house, Nell once again noted the hitch in Josie's gait, and couldn't help wonder which monster was responsible for it.

Ana and Josie flanked Nell as she rang the musical doorbell. Nell made a quick practice smile, pushed her glasses back up her nose, and touched up her hair, then touched at it again, then again, then ceased when she realized what she was doing. Ana scanned suspiciously out at the road and surrounding houses. Josie scratched at her neck and arm. Glancing furtively at the lavish houses, luxury cars, and moneyed residents tending to them prompted her to pull up her hood and retrieve a pair of pink-framed shades from her pocket, shrinking in on herself as she slid them on.

The door opened.

There before the trio stood Cassy Rafferty, formerly Phong. Her pricey attire, imperious expression, and the half-drunk cocktail she held despite it being three-thirty in the afternoon spoke of her existence as a spoiled lady of leisure. Out of sync with her tailored beige blouse, pencil skirt, and patent heels was a rather common white-patterned, red neckerchief. She stared back at the three, sniffily inspecting each in turn.

The awkwardness stretching, Nell thought to break the silence. "Hi—"

"Cassandra?" came a woman's voice from behind them.

Nell turned along with Ana and Josie, with Cassy herself peering over their heads to see another well-to-do housewife at the mouth of the driveway, in the middle of a power walk judging by her tracksuit, sweatbands, and the tiny pink dumbbells she gripped.

"Erika!" Cassy greeted back.

Erika appraised Cassy's three visitors with thinly veiled disgust. "Friends of yours?"

Cassy glanced at the three women with entirely unveiled disgust. "Goodness, no! From one of the many women's shelters I donate to, no doubt."

"No doubt," echoed Erika doubtfully. "Oh, will you and Blake be joining us for our soiree this Friday?"

"We wouldn't miss it." Cassy smiled, a gesture that somehow confined itself to her lower lip, the rest of her face rigid from a recent bout of Botox.

Erika smiled in a similarly Botoxed fashion. "Oh good! You can bring more of that cute Chinese-y dessert like last time."

Cassy exhaled through her smile at the comment. "Actually, Erika, that was a Vietnamese dessert. My mother's recipe—"

"Well, the dogs couldn't get enough of it!"

Nell and Josie looked on uncomfortably while Ana openly smirked at the entire passive-aggressive display.

"Oh, how sweet of you to say," Cassy replied with a twitchy smile. "And I'll be sure to bring some Four Loko too. I know how fond you are of a can, or twenty."

Erika gave an embarrassed chuckle before quickly continuing with her power walk, working out her ire with exaggerated sways of her hips.

"Ta-ta!" Cassy waved. Then, so only Nell and the others could hear, added, "Cunt."

Nell cleared her throat. "Um, Cassandra Rafferty?"

Cassy didn't seem to hear as she took a large gulp from her cocktail, speaking before fully swallowing.

"She cheats on her husband, ya know. Makes out she goes to a Jazzercise class three times a week."

Nell strived to continue. "My name's Nell James—"

"But she's absolutely screwing her trainer." She gave Josie a gape-eyed nod. "Oh yeah." Another sip of her drink. "Jazzercise my ass."

"This is Ana Gómez, and Josie Jedford—"

"More like jizz—"

"We're here to talk to you about—"

"—ercise"

"Silas Crowe!"

They finally had Cassy's bewildered attention.

Cassy's living room was as big as Nell's entire apartment, and markedly more sumptuous in its furnishings, brighter too, and not just inside, like clouds never marred the sky here.

"Are you people insane?" asked Cassy, seated across from Nell on a plush chaise lounge, eyeing Ana and Josie dubiously as the former stood at the window watching the street like she was in the secret service, and the latter limped around the room, admiring the decor as if she were in a fine art gallery. "Like clinically?"

Josie stopped before a framed picture of Cassy with her husband and two children, a son and daughter who looked to be in their teens, though the picture itself seemed at least ten years old. They were arrayed in the standard cheesy-family-portrait pose, the same affected smile on each of their faces; regardless, Josie couldn't keep the melancholy from her eyes.

"We're serious," said Nell.

Cassy kept watching the other two, making sure they weren't pocketing anything. "Silas Crowe is long dead and long g—" She spotted Josie about to touch an antique figurine on her mantel. "Donttouchthat!" she snapped. Josie pulled her hand back like a scolded child. "Or anything else, thank you please," Cassy requested.

"That's what the rest of the world thinks," continued Nell, frustration growing as she struggled to hold Cassy's attention. "But we all know that's bull."

"How do I know *you're* not talking bull? Because that's what it sounds like, like a big, huge, stinking pile of bull . . . shit."

"But if we—"

"What? Hm? If we—*you*—do what, exactly? Seriously, what are you actually thinking of doing?"

"I—"

"I'd really like to know too," said Josie.

"See!" said Cassy. "This one's on board—for some reason—and doesn't even know your plan!"

Nell was becoming flustered. "We're gonna—"

"Arm ourselves to the teeth and take the fight to him," said Ana. Then, with a look to Nell, said, "Overkill. Whatever it takes."

Nell smiled appreciatively.

Cassy shook her head as she glanced between the two of them. "I just—" She turned to Josie. "Are these two holding you against your will? You need me to call the cops? Blink any number of times for yes."

"What's it gonna take to convince you?" asked Nell.

"Nothing, because I don't need convincing. There's nothing to be convinced about." Cassy pointed to her mouth. "See my lips?"

"Hard to miss with all that filler," Ana semi-mumbled.

Cassy scowled as best she could. "Read them—Silas Crowe is dead."

Nell sighed. "Look, you still have the nightmares, right?"

Ana smirked and shook her head.

"Still check all your—"

"I see what this is." Cassy's expression took on a slant of bitter amusement. "You can't stand to see someone like me doing well for myself."

Nell jerked back. "What?"

"I mean, look at you all." Cassy thrust her chin at Ana. "A pirate." Josie. "A junkie." Nell. "And a hack writer."

"Pirate?" Ana quizzed.

"Hey," said an offended Josie, though her outrage came out paltry and unconvincing.

Cassy continued. "I'm sorry none of you were able to recover from what happened, but I did. I've got it all now. Money, family, a big-ass cellar full of wines I can't even pronounce, money."

"You said that already," said Josie.

"Yeah, but I got a lot. Like *a lot* lot."

Nell understood Ana's anger, empathized with Josie's fear, but this indifference from Cassy was straight-up insulting. "Don't you wanna see this bastard put down for good? To put an end to this—this dark cloud that's hung over us all these years?"

Cassy lifted her cocktail. "Honey, my life is nothing but blue skies and woo-woos. Now, I think it's time you and your she-goons returned to your cave or swamp or whatever the fuck." She took a sip of her drink.

Nell huffed and shook her head, incredulous at what she was hearing, but as she thought about it, looked around the house, the money, the family photos, she came to understand. Cassy *was* doing better than all of them, really did have it all. Where they had each been shaped irrevocably by their encounter with Silas Crowe, Cassy seemed to have shrugged it off and left it in the dirt like a soiled shirt. Nell couldn't blame her for not wanting to risk all she had to face him again, though, a part of her did resent Cassy, because why had she been the only one allowed to move on?

Ana moved away from the window. "I've heard enough. Let's leave *her majesty* here alone so she can get back to warring with the Joneses and her, what, third or fourth liquid lunch of the day?"

Cassy's face clouded as she self-consciously put down her drink. "Out! All of you ho-skank tramps! Out!"

Josie deliberately knocked a wall-mounted picture askew as she limped her way to the front door.

Nell stood and offered a slip of paper to Cassy. "If you change your mind, this is where—"

Cassy snatched the scrap and threw it to the floor. "Get out!"

Nell gave Cassy a disappointed nod. "Sorry for wasting your time." She left after the others, closing the front door behind herself.

Cassy retrieved her drink and necked it. *The fuck do these bitches think they are? Coming here—to my home—insulting me like that? The fuck should I care about some dead counselors, anyway? It's obviously—clearly just another Crowe copycat. Or some sick internet prank. Yeah, just a buncha squirts tryna make bank on a viral video that'll come out soon enough. Little shits need to grow the fuck up and get real jobs, instead of . . .* The realization that she was a lady of leisure clipped her line of argument shorter than intended.

In any event, there was no way the Silas Crowe she'd encountered was back. That fucker was dead. Definitely, *definitely* dead . . . he had to be.

She lifted her glass for another sip but found it contained only disappointment.

She looked around at the lush living room and was struck by the emptiness of it, of the house. Her life. With the kids having long since left the nest, and Blake only making what felt like the occasional guest appearance, she'd essentially become a hermit, albeit a filthy rich one.

Sure, she had her weekly hot yoga, spin, and body pump classes, and attended the bi-weekly social gatherings with the neighbors, but those events felt more like endurance trials than friendly get-togethers, where everyone was looking for you to slip up, to find and exploit some crack in your armor, for such things were currency amongst the shallow and vain. To Cassy, it was like entering into a snake den each time, constantly on guard so as not to get bit. She knew she was no better, though, and played her part in maintaining the game. Played it damn well if she did say so herself.

She ambled over to the crooked family picture Josie had knocked, smiling softly at the faces of Dale and Dakota, her son and daughter, her pride and joy, the only good that had ever come from her as far as she was concerned. Her smile faded with the knowledge of how long it'd been since they'd last spoke.

Her smile fell away entirely when she looked next at Blake. He was still handsome in an increasingly artificial way, but then he could afford to be, for both of them to be, the surgical "touch-ups" becoming more frequent and seeming to touch more of them each time.

There were no real feelings between them. Lust had brought them together. She was young and made a concerted effort at being hot, and he had the money to afford hot.

A brief fling, that's all it was ever meant to be. Another fleeting shadow through the bedroom door for the both of them, but a drunken lapse in due diligence had gotten her pregnant. That brief fling had stretched on for twenty-seven years, on account of Blake not wanting to bring what his high-handed father insisted would be shame upon the family name, a name that held sway among elite circles, and if he ever wanted a piece of that eye-popping inheritance, he'd "do the right thing." And so he proposed, and she said yes, because when you're young, alone, and pregnant with twins, and a man with a lot of money offers you those things you've never known—stability, security, comfort, wealth—that's what you do, right? Love? That was just something invented by Hallmark.

Cassy knew Blake screwed around. Of course he did. It was an open but unspoken secret between the two of them at this point, one neither of them had the energy nor interest to address.

She'd cheated too in the past: the cliché pool boy affair, various delivery men, and one best-forgotten dalliance with a Jehovah's Witness who'd come knocking one particularly dull afternoon. Nowadays, she was mostly content with drinking her husband's booze and spending his money on luxury yoga retreats. He never complained, perhaps thinking it somehow absolved him of his continued extramarital fuckery.

Cassy straightened the picture, catching her reflection as she did. She brushed lightly at the fringe of her short hair, then her fingers found her red neckerchief. A memory stirred at the touch, threatening to rise from its decades-long slumber.

She turned away from her reflected self, afraid of what a prolonged look might reveal, of what the woman looking back might be thinking or wish to say. She brought her glass to her lips and again found it empty. With a frustrated sigh, she went to make herself another drink. A stiff one.

6

"Is it on?"

"Hang on, just gotta—"

You open your eye. A blurred face sharpens in your vision. A young man. Noah. He steps away to join two others. It's dark. Night. Outside. The one to Noah's left looks nervous in his neon pink beanie and camo jacket. The one to Noah's right looks excited in a skeleton print hoodie, thumbs hitched in the straps of a backpack. You've seen them before. Justin and Sean. Justin sniffs wetly.

"Dude, blow your fucking nose, what the hell," Noah moans.

Justin rubs at his nose. "Allergies, man. You know I have a delicate system."

Noah makes a quick adjustment to his hair and persona before addressing you. "All right, guys—" He looks displeased with something, looking down and mumbling to himself. You wait patiently, accustomed to the process. He looks you in the eye and smiles with bigger energy. "All right, guys! You asked for it, so here we are . . ." He approaches, lifts you from off the roof of his car, and turns you around to get a better look at the surroundings. A gravel road within a forest of dead trees. The flashlights held by Justin and

Sean, and the light from you, are the only sources of illumination. Noah shows you a rainbow-lettered sign hanging high between a pair of branchless trees on either side of this road. "Camp Haven Cove!" Noah announces. A trio of crows perched atop the sign stare back at you.

Back on Sean and Justin.

"Joining me, as always, are Spooooky Sean . . ."

Sean throws up a pair of Vs. "Sup."

"And Big J." Justin is too busy scanning the surroundings with his flashlight to catch his prompt. "Yo, Justin!"

Justin turns, looking over your head with wide eyes. "Huh?"

"You good, man? You look a little . . ."

"Yeah, yeah. Just . . . People really got murdered here, huh?"

"A lot," says Sean. "With five more gone missing."

Justin shakes his head. "Remind me again why we came here?"

"For the views." Sean makes stabbing motions in your face. "So y'all better murder those like and subscribe buttons."

"All right, let's do it," says Noah, turning you to look down the gravel road. Sean and Justin are up front, the crunch of gravel beneath their feet loud in the otherwise mute surroundings, absent as it is of all the nocturnal music that ought to haunt a forest at night. "This place is giving me major Blair Witch vibes."

Justin turns his flashlight on Noah. "Dude, for real—" He stops and lifts his light. "Uh, guys."

Sean turns to what Justin's found. "Whoa!"

"What?" Noah turns you around. Your vision blurs for an instant, but you correct it, seeing some graffiti on the rear of the Camp Haven Cove sign that reads *Teenage Wasteland*. "Nice!"

"How are you guys not more nervous about this?" asks Justin.

"Relax, it's just from those shitty movies."

Sean steps into your field of vision. "Um, I think you mean great fucking movies."

"And how comes there's no cops here?" Justin grouses.

"How comes?" Noah mocks.

"It's late," says Sean. "Maybe they left for the night."

Justin grumbles to himself.

Noah turns you back to the path ahead. "Sean, how about dropping some history on our viewers?"

"The infamous Camp Haven Cove," Sean begins as he continues down the road. "First established in the early eighties as a summer camp for kids, this supposedly cursed site has been a hotspot for unexplained disappearances, grisly murders, alleged hauntings, creepy Satanist shit, *and* UFO, Bigfoot, Elvis, and Loch Ness Monster sightings since way before it ever opened."

"Loch Ness?" says Justin. "That's not even— That's just dumb."

"No one knows the real number of people who've gone missing or been found dead here over the years, and I do mean *years*, like centuries."

"Shit."

"But most folk credit all those deaths and disappearances to a figure of local lore and legend. The infamous—"He looks you in the eye for a dramatic "Si- las Crowe."

"Sketch as fuck, yo," says Noah as he gives you an unsteady look of the eldritch forest.

"Emphasis on 'as fuck, yo,'" says Justin, warily scanning the environment with his flashlight. "Why would anybody build a summer camp here if all that were true?"

"You know the answer. Starts with 'capital,' ends with 'ism.'"

"The place is a major tourist attraction for weirdos," Sean explains. "Like a Halloween haunt, only for real. I read they even had some morbid tours thing running here in the nineties, but those stopped when some tourists went missing. The cops thought they caught the guy responsible way back, but people keep going missing to this day."

"Some X-Files shit, yo," says Noah.

Justin nervously sweeps the trees with his flashlight. "Seriously, what're we doing here? Especially after that old whackadoo at the gas station told us—like *really* fucking told us—not to come."

A dizzying blur as Noah spins you to himself. "Which is *precisely* why we had to!"

"Let the record state I think this is a dumb—"

A noise.

Noah turns you to where the others are already pointing their flashlights into some unmoving trees on the left. The noise sounded close.

"Probably just a broken twig," says Noah.

"Yeah, or a—a fallen rock?" offers Sean.

"Or a snapped neck," says Justin.

Sean frowns at him.

You find yourself moving closer.

"Hello?" says Noah.

Nothing.

Sean looks to Noah. "Must've just been—"

A dire groan rends the night. The four of you jump back in startled fright.

"Yo!" says Noah.

The groan comes again. Louder. Angrier.

"Fuck this!" Sean declares.

The world shakes and bounces as Noah hurries after Sean, distancing you from a back-peddling Justin, who trips and falls on his ass.

"Justin, c'mon!" Noah yells.

A pale figure emerges from out of the forest with a crescendoing wail. You can't quite make it out, but get the impression of some bipedal, single-horned horror.

Justin screams.

The figure's wail transitions into mocking laughter.

The world steadies. You look closer at the cackling figure: someone in a blue and white unicorn onesie.

"The fuck?" says Noah.

The horror pulls back their alicorned hood. It's a young woman, her hair mussed by the unveiling. Her laughing face grows in your vision.

"Macy?" says Noah.

Macy points at a still-frightened Justin. "Somebody throw Justin a life preserver before he drowns in his own shit!"

"Fuck me," says Sean, coming up alongside as you return to Justin. "We thought you were some hillbilly psycho!"

"You're half right," says Noah.

Macy gives her best redneck impression: "Darn tootin', by gum!" She helps Justin to his feet. "You guys are too easy."

"Real fucking funny," says Justin unamused. "What's with the onesie?"

"I needed a costume to scare you guys with. This was all I had."

"Well, it's stupid," Justin sulks.

Macy laughs. "Says the guy wearing a high-viz hat with a camo jacket! What's up with that? Doesn't one just defeat the functional purpose of the other?"

"Shut—You don't know shit."

"Thought you couldn't make it," says Noah.

"I wasn't gonna miss this. Besides, I know one of the missing counselors."

"Who?" asks Sean.

"My cousin went to elementary with one of them. Said she was a real bitch, so."

"So you couldn't pass up the chance to find her corpse?"

"Exactly." Macy pulls up her hood and flicks on her flashlight to under-light her now-skullish face, putting on a spooky voice as she says, "So let's go find us some cooorpses, woooo—ha ha!" You all follow her down the road.

You spot Justin's cell phone on the ground where he fell.

"Justin," Noah calls. "Your phone." He lowers you by his side as he bends to retrieve it, giving you an upside-down view of the road behind, including the large, half-hidden something behind one of the trees shouldering the camp's sign. A figure? You strive to focus on it, but a flicker of blocky distortion hampers the effort.

Righting you as he stands, Noah holds the phone out to an approaching Justin.

"Shit, thanks," he says, reclaiming it. "Don't wanna be stuck out here without—" His gaze fixes on something behind you. "Dude, what the fuck is that?"

You turn with Noah, observing the same view as before, right-side-up. The thing that caught your attention before isn't there. Was it ever?

"What?" asks Noah. Back to Justin. "I don't—"

"YAAH!" screams Justin, right in your face.

Noah jerks you back with a startled "Fuck!"

Justin laughs as he walks away. "Serves you right for pranking me, assholes."

You follow.

"Dude, that was all Macy."

Macy steps into view with a lit joint, proffering it to Justin. "Here, peace pipe."

Justin waves it away. "I don't smoke that shit."

Noah jiggles his fingers before you. "Shit, I'll smoke that shit."

Macy insists the joint upon Justin. "C'mon, one toke won't kill you."

Justin sighs and takes it.

"Yay, peer pressure!" Macy cheers.

Justin inspects the joint like it's an alien object. "Okay, so what am I—"

"Just breathe it in deep, let it out slow."

Justin does so, cheeks puffing and eyes clenching at the harshness. The exhalation comes out as a hacking cough, doubling him over and dislodging a wriggling rope of snot that refuses to drop.

You close your eye as the others "Ewww!" collectively.

Eye open.

"—ucking ditch!" Macy wipes mud off the leg of her onesie while the others laugh.

The newly refurbished camp grows closer as you near.

"Hey, Justin," Noah calls. "What's this?" A giant finger creeps in from the right side of your eye, taking up half your vision, the other half on Justin farther ahead. He looks back at you.

"No."

"C'mon," Noah chuckles.

Justin turns to you again. "Nope!"

"Here it comes!"

"It's a dumb bit! I'm not—" The giant finger prods at Justin, who stumbles aside in response. "Damn giant finger!"

Noah laughs. "The fans love that gag!"

"Do they though?" asks a sardonic Macy. "Do they really?"

You're all entering the camp.

Sean crosses your path. "Here we are."

"Shouldn't there at least be like, police tape or something all over this place?" Justin asks. "People *were* murdered here."

"I guess it is kinda weird," says Noah as you look between the first few cabins. "I thought we'd for sure have to sneak in."

Macy continues to nurse the joint. "Backwoods places like this have lousy cops."

Sean appears from the side. "I think my mom used to live around here."

"She ever mention Silas Crowe or any other spooky shit?" asks Justin.

The windows of these cabins give a view into solid darkness.

"No, just that people mostly kept away from this place."

"What's up with that hick-ass name?" Macy chuckles. "Silas Crowe."

"I read that Silas means like, man of the forest," Sean explains. "And Crowe is because for as long as anyone can remember, there's been nothing living here 'cept for crows. So when you have a murderous boogeyman haunting a dead forest full of crows, what else do you call him?"

"A frickin' loon?"

A passing glance at the next cabin hurts your eye. Noah stops and forces you to look again, though the pain does not repeat. "Weird." Noah carries on. But you know something he doesn't—that if some future and more scrupulous person were to check your memory of this night, pause on the window of that distorted cabin, and study the image for a moment, they might well see the fuzzy figure of a person on the other side of that glass.

"What was his deal, anyway?" asks Justin. "What was he, just some serial killer?"

"I heard he's the kid of some woman who got abducted and impregnated by aliens way back," says Sean. "And that he ate his way out of her womb and developed a taste for human flesh."

"I mean, have you tried it?" asks Macy, punctuating with a chef's kiss.

The rec hall is ahead.

"I heard his crackhead parents dunked him in a barrel of toxic waste as a baby," says Noah. "Fucked him up inside and out, turning him into a homicidal mutant."

Macy moves ahead. "I heard he was born in some traveling freak show-type thing. Like his daddy was a super-strong dwarf and his momma a bearded mermaid."

"So, he's half fish?" asks Sean.

"Do the math, dumb-dumb. He'd be a quarter fish."

"Gotcha."

"I also heard that if you say his name five times, he'll magically appear and give you a handy."

A fast turn to Sean, smiling impishly as he and Noah chant as one, "Silas Crowe! Silas Crowe! Silas Crowe! Silas Crowe! Silas Crowe!"

Laughter from everyone except Justin, whose jitters won't allow it. "Aren't you guys scared that he might still be here?"

"Killers returning to the scene of their crime is a mostly overblown notion," says Sean. "I wouldn't worry."

Justin looks worried. That his flashlight chooses that exact moment to cut out does little to help matters. He gives it a couple of resuscitating slaps. "Dude, I thought you said these things were new?"

"They are . . ." says Sean. "Or were when I bought them like five years ago."

A caw echoes through the trees.

"Was that a scream?" asks Justin with alarm.

"It was a crow, fucktart," says Macy.

"Sounded like someone screaming for help . . ."

You search the encircling forest, catching the occasional glinting eye of a crow perched among the gnarled and bony branches, each one watching in silence.

"What's with these creepy-ass crows anyway?" asks Noah.

"A lot of cultures see them as spiritual somehow," says Sean. "Like they—"

Macy blows air through her lips. "Fuck that. A bird's just a bird."

A close and irate caw startles all.

"Shit!" yells Justin, hand pressed to his chest.

Macy looks equally rattled. "Okay, I think I just peed *all* our pants."

Noah chuckles in relief while you take a closer look at one lone crow in particular. It stands unperturbed in the center of a small stone circle used for campfires, which is ringed by several shorn stumps for seating.

You follow the cawing corvid as it takes flight, disappearing into the inky blackness between the trees. Your vision spasms as you strive to look deeper between those trees.

Noah taps you. "Fuck is with this thing?"

"Well, this looks as good a spot as any," says Sean, bringing your attention back to the group.

"For what?" Justin whines.

Sean unslings his backpack and produces a Ouija board from within.

"No," Justin groans. "Guys, no, please. Are you fucking with me right now?"

Macy finds it funny. "Are you guys serious?"

"As a heart attack," Noah assures as he carries you over to the stones. "C'mon, everyone gather round."

Justin huffs and flails in protest. "Why you guys always gotta pull shit like this on me?"

Sean sets up the board within the circle of stones. "C'mon, Justin, don't puss out in front of our legions of fans," he says with a look to you.

"Dude, we're setting up a Ouija board in the middle of some spooky-ass forest where who-the-fuck-knows how many people died."

"Best place to try it out, right?" Noah reasons.

The Final Women

Justin gives him a candid look. "I'm not tryna piss off any evil spirits today."

Macy takes an eager seat beside the board. "I'll do it."

"Yes! See? Everybody else is in," says Noah to Justin. "C'mon, it'll be fun."

"If I had a dollar for every time a guy's used *that* one on me," says Macy.

Justin shakes his head—"Fuck."—then joins you all in the circle, begrudgingly asking, "So how does this work?"

"Sean?" Noah prompts.

"Okay, so we all place two fingers lightly on the planchette." Sean demonstrates and nods for the others to do likewise.

Noah complies. Macy waves her hands back and forth. "Wait, wait, wait. Gimme a close-up." You give your full attention to Macy, who looks deep into your eye as she says, "If someone finds this, if I don't make it back, please tell my mom . . ." She takes a weighty breath. "Tell her to stay outta my dresser."

She gets a laugh from the others.

Noah places you upon one of the seating stumps, ensuring you can see the four of them and the board. Everything beyond is murky darkness. All except Justin have placed their fingers as instructed, but a nod of encouragement from Noah, and an impatient elbow from Macy, force him to participate.

"Okay," says Sean. "Now that we're touching it, it's super important we do not—I repeat, *do not*—break contact until the session's ended."

"Or what?" asks Justin, sounding all the more nervous for this warning.

"Or I'm thinking those evil spirits you don't wanna piss off will be pissed off," says Macy.

"Right," Sean affirms.

"Okay, so everybody keep your fingers on this no matter what," Noah echoes.

You're having issues with your eye again.

"Next rule, one question at a time."

Noah nods. "We'll just take it in turns."

Sean looks between each of the others. "Ready?" The others return nods of varied content. "Okay, we make three circles with the planchette, then Noah asks the first question."

Three circles are made.

Noah takes a moment to think. "Are... Are there any spirits here that wish to communicate with us?"

Expectant silence falls.

Macy shudders with a stifled giggle, then, receiving Sean's severe look, mouths a sorry.

Distortion again, and within the window of that transitory fuzz you might have discerned the obscure semi-form of a fifth figure sitting among the others.

The planchette crawls to Yes.

Justin gapes his disbelieving eyes.

Macy looks between the others. "Okay, who did that?"

Noah shakes his head. "Not me."

"No one!" says Sean. "It's the board! It's working!" He moves the planchette back to center. "Macy, quick, ask it a question."

"Yeah, right," she says cynically. "Okay, um, o' hopefully benevolent spirit, what is thine'st name?"

Another suspenseful pause.

Another fluctuation of your sight that would startle those pareidolia-prone.

The planchette moves. B.

Justin gasps.

Moves again. O.

"Whoa," says Macy.

Moves to center, then back to O.

Begins to move to center. Justin pulls his hand away. "Fuck this!"

"Justin!" moan the others in unison.

"You can't take your hand away," warns Sean, deadly serious.

"Which one of you is moving it?" Justin demands.

"It's the board!" says Noah.

"Oh yeah, sure! The board makes you write 'boo,' and then what? Is that the signal for someone else to jump out and scare the shit outta me?"

"What?"

"Who else is out here? Huh? Who else came with you, Macy?"

Macy can't help but laugh at Justin's racing hysteria. "No one, you big—"

A particularly violent spasm of distortion addles your eye—though without a vague form to assign human shape to—as the planchette makes an abrupt circle around the board, startling the other three enough that they too withdraw their fingers.

"Whoa, okay," says Noah.

It moves urgently to R.

Macy edges behind Noah. "What the how?"

Zips over to U, then toward the bottom left of the board—

Justin flips it over.

"Dude!" Sean exclaims.

Justin runs his hand across the underside of the board. "This thing got magnets or something?"

"Magnets, no—"

"Then how did—"

A loud snap from the forest brings abrupt silence.

All humor drains from Macy. "What was that?"

No one speaks, only searches with wide eyes and frantic flashlights.

A startling caw.

A collective yelp.

All heads swivel up and to the right to something you can't see.

Sean calms himself. "These fucking birds, man."

Noah lifts you and focuses your gaze on the roof of the nearest cabin, atop which perches a single crow. It caws again, a noise that sounds uncannily like a shriek of "help," then flies low over the group's heads, almost hitting you as you all turn in the opposite direction, to a distorted sight that snatches breaths and freezes blood.

The crow alights upon Silas Crowe's lopsided, bramble-wrapped head, stark in the group's combined light despite your frenzied, glitchy eye. The poorly proportioned giant stares back at you—or seems to, his eyes unknowable through the withered, thorny encasing. His deformed wiry mass, ill-matched arms, and, most notably, bloated head bespeak of inhumanity, or humanity gone awry. His naked body is a filthy, sinewy tapestry of deep scars, the most disconcerting being the shallow, twisted crater of flesh where genitals are absent.

Abject awe seizes all.

"Is this a prank?" asks Justin shakily. No answer. "Guys, is this a prank?" The rapidity of his speech rises with his alarm.

Sean looks similarly fearful. "I-it's not us."

"Noah, who is that?" asks Macy, her voice is edged with panic. "Noah?"

"Should we run?" asks Justin.

Heretofore hidden behind his body, Silas brings his shorter—or rather, more conforming—arm fully into view, as well as the large, primitive-looking blade held in his meaty hand. The gesture agitates your eye further.

"Noah!" says Macy.

Silas lifts his leaning head from off his grossly hunched shoulder. The group holds a collective breath.

Silas comes at you in a lumbering rush.

"Fuck—Run!" yells Sean.

By the time the thought travels from their fear-choked minds to their jellied legs, Silas is already in the group's screaming midst.

You fall, your angled sight catching the instant Silas's nailed fist tears Justin's head from his body with a whooshing backhand, those nails keeping the head—its impacted side collapsed—pinned to it. Screams come from everywhere, raw, harsh, and breaking apart due to the distortion that afflicts you.

Macy and Sean scramble in opposing directions. Silas's longer arm arrests Sean's escape, forcibly yanking his screaming, thrashing body down beside Justin, pinning him prone with crushing weight. Silas pounds his knife between Sean's squirming shoulder blades, dragging it down the length of his spine with a protracted crack, opening him up to the night air as blood curdles his scream.

You're up in the next instant, twisting away from the sight of Silas—his hand still wearing Justin's stunned head—tearing Sean's spine out of his body, bloody tendons and pink connective tissue snapping with the gruesome extraction.

The world whips and leaps. Noah cries and whimpers in his terrified haste as he plunges into the dead forest, racing between the gaunt trees with no sense of direction or destination, distance the only objective.

The ground rushes up. Sky, trees, and dirt roll in your vision. Noah comes crawling at you, horror-stricken. You're up. Light off, night vision on, the world going green and black as you probe the enclosing trees. From which direction have the two of you come? Which direction will the monster come? The panic in Noah's breath is the only answer, turning into half-cries. "Oh fuck . . . What the fu—" A shuffle and snap spin the two of you around.

Macy's bug-eyed, tear-streaked face fills your sight. She throws her arms around Noah, the press of their bodies smothering you, her fearful gibbering unintelligible.

"Macy!"

She jerks harshly up and away, Silas's hand clamped atop her head, fingers spidering down her shocked face as it holds her aloft. Macy barely emits the first note of a scream before her head cracks in on itself with all the resistance of a soft-boiled egg, her eyes, shattered skull, and the bloody curds within mushing between the monster's thick digits and splattering over your eye, until he holds her up by little more than the gore-glutted hood of her onesie.

You're racing again, the trees a green-black blur, Noah's peal of panic shrill in your ear.

Breaking through the tree line. The lake, a still mirror to the moon and stars above. There's a small dinghy tied to the jetty.

A turn to scan the trees.

Nothing.

The Final Women

Some of Macy slides off your periphery.

Rushing for the dinghy. Noah breathing hard.

There's a pair of paddles within the small boat, no holes or leaks. Noah climbs in. Justin's ruined head gets in first. Noah gasps.

You turn.

Silas's body chokes your sight.

A struggle. You fall to the jetty's weathered boards and watch from a slanted, low-angled view as Silas lifts Noah by the throat with his longer arm.

Noah chokes out a scream, kicks, beats his fists against the monster.

Silas drops and extends a bent knee, snapping Noah's back upon it with a fatal crunch.

Rising to his full height, Silas casts Noah's backward-folded corpse before you, his face frozen in its final torturous moment of life.

You remain still.

The killer towers above you, a green abomination in the jumbled night vision, breaths audibly burbling in his throat.

In that moment he might be thinking, insofar as he's able. Perhaps asking a question, that question being, *When?* And perhaps he finds the answer in what sounds to you like the shush of wind through a hollowed skull that might well be interpreted as, *Soon* . . .

Silas turns sharply down to look at you.

There's nowhere you can run.

Nowhere you can hide.

Nothing you can do.

Your digitally disturbed sight freezes on his dreadful portrait before scrambling into black squares.

You cease to perceive.

7

"Authorities are now adding four young and prominent influencers to the number of those gone missing at Camp Haven Cove this week."

Nell and Josie were perched on the edge of Ana's couch, intently watching the report on the early morning news while the cups of coffee they held went cold.

Ana had woken the pair just before dawn, not with an alarm or gentle knock at their door, but with the sounds of her beating the sand out of her heavy bag. It'd been a restless night for all anyway, sleep achieved only with the help of a potent nightcap.

Ana was busy in the kitchen now, taking gulps from a protein shake between packing supplies into a large duffle bag: a ball of hemp twine, several cans of lighter fluid, a pair of folding shovels, and three lightweight body armor vests. The plan was to leave within the hour, stopping en route to drop Kull and Kane off at a boarding kennel.

The reporter on TV continued. "This follows the disappearance of five camp counselors two days ago at the same location. Local sheriff Dwight Pewson had this to say."

The footage cut to a pre-recorded interview with Sheriff Pewson, a man with a gray-speckled mustache and possessing all the authority of a reluctant eighth-grade hall monitor. "Uh, I-I mean—This is of course, just—just terrible. B-but rest assured we'll get to the bottom of this. No need for state police to intervene. Heck, this might all just be a case of—of—of youthful hijinks gone one beer too far! Yeah, I'm sure those youngsters'll show up hungover and feeling *pretty* foolish for all the fuss they've caused." His nervous chuckle hardly sold the theory.

"Thank you, Sheriff Pewson."

"Say, uh, w—what time will this be on? I wanna tell my mom—"

Nell turned it off.

"Four more." Josie's shoulders sank to match her dour expression. "He got four more."

Ana packed something that might have been a large machete into the same bag as the other supplies. "With Deputy Dingus on the case, expect a lot more."

"I remember Pewson," said Nell. "He was a pimple-faced deputy when I was . . . when it happened."

"Same." Ana hefted up the duffle bag and placed it near the door beside a couple of others, each looking full and heavy. "The man could barely walk without tripping over his own feet. Now he's the sheriff? No wonder we have to handle this ourselves."

Josie was a picture of pessimism. "You guys, what are we doing? We can't do this."

"We have to," said Nell.

"But there was supposed to be four of us." Josie shook her head at the floor. "I-I just, I just don't know."

"Don't you flake on us," said Ana with customary harshness.

Nell put a hand on Josie's arm. "We can do this. We don't need Cassy."

"Fuck no," said Ana, zipping up a backpack. "What does *Lady Rafferty* bring to the table, anyhow?"

A shrill buzz and pulsing red bulb above the front entrance signaled there was someone at Ana's gate. A clamor of barks outside confirmed as much.

"Now what?" Ana went to the door, Nell and Josie following as she swung it open, hand on the pistol forever holstered at her hip.

It was Cassy, dressed in a peach tracksuit and matching baseball cap, red kerchief around her neck, kicking through the fence at the loud and lively Rottweilers. "Back, you devil dogs! Back!"

A whistle from Ana stood Kull and Kane down, though they kept their untrusting eyes on Cassy.

Seeing the others, Cassy held aloft a pair of brown paper bags. "I brought sandwiches!"

The others exchanged looks—Nell surprised, Josie pleased, Ana annoyed.

"No crusts!" Cassy added.

8

"Your Love" by The Outfield blasted from Cassy's red SUV as she drove it down a country road beset on both sides by lush forest.

Cassy danced in the driver's seat, wearing driving glasses as she sang along to the pop-rock song. Nell sat next to her, glasses swapped for contacts, but it was to an amused Josie in the back to who Cassy shot a wink through the rearview mirror. An irritated Ana sat beside Josie, who couldn't help but smile and shake her head at the whole thing.

"Can you—" started Ana, though she was drowned out by Cassy's deliberately loudening voice. "Can you turn that off?" she tried again, loud enough to be heard.

Cassy frowned at her in the rearview. "Are you gonna be like this the entire trip?"

Nell turned the stereo off. "This ain't a *trip*, Cassy."

"Not with you miserable bishes, it's not."

"Why'd you even come along?" asked Ana.

A pall of seriousness overcame Cassy. "I heard about those kids on the news, and I just . . . You were right. We have to do something."

Nell smiled with sincerity. "Well, we're glad you changed your mind." She turned her head over her shoulder. "Right?"

Josie nodded. "Absolutely." A less enthused Ana offered only a vague sniff as she looked out the window.

"Did you tell your husband where you were going?" asked Nell.

Cassy gave a disinterested shake of her head. "I left him a note."

Hair stiff with product and body attired in tennis duds for an early session on the courts, Blake picked up a note from his marbled countertop on his way out, reading it aloud. "Gone to Camp Haven Cove with strangers to maybe slay a demon from my past. Might get arrested or die in the attempt. Tell the kids I love them. Sandwich in fridge."

He shrugged off his initial confusion and took out his cell phone, turning the note over as he dialed and waited for an answer. "Babe, where are you?" Opening the fridge revealed the aforementioned sandwich, plated and cut into triangles, sans crust. "Well, come over." Blake inspected the sandwich. "Better make it twelve." Cucumber. He squirmed. "I've got an investor circling the wagon . . . Yeah, just gotta tug their dick a little on the courts, that whole dance." He pushed the sandwich to the back of the fridge and shut the door. "She's gone . . . Fat camp or something . . . Whole weekend, from the sound of it." There was a knock at his front door. Blake went to answer, smiling at the response from the other end of the line. "Clamps *and* the paddle."

Opening the door, Blake was met by the surly countenance of Lugg, sporting two black eyes and a taped-up nose. Beside him stood Scud, half his face hidden beneath a bloody wad of bandages and duct tape.

"Uh . . ." said Blake into the phone, utterly perplexed. "I'll call you back . . . Yeah, smooches." Blake ended the call. "Can I—"

Lugg clamped an ungentle hand on the neck of Blake's salmon polo shirt and yanked him outside.

The red SUV continued down the road.

"It can't be him," said Cassy. "There's just no way."

"It's gotta be," replied Nell.

"How? I killed him. You all apparently killed him. Science tells us you only need to kill a person once to make them dead. Are you calling science a liar?"

"I'm saying he's not . . . normal."

"I'll say," said Josie. "I put him down with an ax to his head."

"And I electrocuted him," said Cassy. "Fried his ass good."

Nell nodded, not doubting their stories. "I smushed him with a van."

Cassy looked at Ana in the rearview. "How 'bout you, Eyepatch?"

Ana turned a glowering eye on her. "It's Ana."

"Okay, *Ana*, how did you kill him?"

Ana turned away. "Trapped him in a burning cabin. Watched the whole thing come down on him. No way he could've gotten out . . ."

The four of them sat in silence, each replaying the memory of the moment they thought they'd slain the monster known as Silas Crowe.

"What is he?" asked Josie. "Is he even human?"

Cassy scoffed. "What the hell're we talking about now? Literal monsters? Of course he's human! Some maniac fucked up on bath salts, or something."

Nell raised an eyebrow. "Bath salts?"

Cassy explained, "I once saw a guy, naked as all hell, his dick in a pumpkin, take two tasings from a couple cops, and not even flinch. Just kept right on fucking that winter squash. Bath salts, ladies."

"He's for sure not normal," said Josie.

"Oh, come on," said Cassy dismissively.

"I wish he was." Ana ruminated on the matter as she stared out the window. "Wish he was perfectly normal in every outward way. Just a regular guy with friends, family, loved ones I could go after to get to him." The others all looked concerned by such a statement. "That's the only real way to hurt someone like that, not by attacking them directly, but by taking away the things, the people they love. That's how I'd get to him."

Cassy leaned toward Nell as she not-too-discreetly whispered, "Should we be worried about her?"

Nell couldn't honestly say.

"Couldn't this just be another copycat?" Josie posited with weak hope. "That would make more sense, right?"

Nell shook her head. "So they were all copycats after the first? That's too many psychos for one place to have."

"Ever been to Florida?" Cassy quipped.

"But it's been so long," said Josie. "Thirty years. If it was really him, why'd it take him so long to appear again?"

"I dunno," said Nell. "The camp's been closed all this time, that could be it."

"There were a couple disappearances in the nineties," said Ana.

"Yeah, but since then Haven Cove's pretty much been a no-go zone. Bad things can only happen so many times in the same place before people get spooked enough to stay well-the-fuck away."

"And here we are making a beeline for it," said Cassy.

"So he just never leaves the forest?" asked Josie. "Just waits for people to come to him?"

"I . . ." Nell shrugged "I dunno."

"It's a copycat!" said Cassy. "Some sicko angry at the world 'cause no one wants to touch his pee-pee."

"Doesn't matter," said Ana. "Copycat or not, he dies."

"How?" Josie borderline demanded. "If it is him, really him, and he survived all the things we did, how do we kill him for good?"

"First we trap him," Ana explained. "Cut out his heart."

Josie winced at the thought.

"Then chop off his head and stick it on a pike for all to see."

Cassy's expression again questioned Ana's mental stability.

"We burn the rest of him."

Nell nodded in agreement.

"Then scatter his ashes to the wind. I'd like to see that sonuva bitch come back from that."

"The head, the tail, the whole damn thing, huh?" said Cassy.

"Whadda we do with the heart?" asked Josie.

"Cut it into four," Ana replied. "Each of us taking a piece."

"Eww!" bleated Cassy. "What for?"

"Burn it, bury it, cast it in resin as a keepsake, whatever."

"Same question, with greater emphasis on the *eww!*"

"To remind us that he's dead, that he can't hurt us, and that he's not coming back. Ever again."

The weight of Ana's words fell heavily upon them all. To think of a world where Silas Crowe did not exist as a constant and pervasive threat was, to them, akin to imagining a world without cancer, a thought almost too impossible to entertain.

Nell's stomach growled loudly in the silence. "Sorry, couldn't bring myself to eat anything this morning."

"All I had for breakfast was coffee and half a pack of cigarettes," said Josie.

"We should eat," said Ana. "We'll need the energy." She consulted her phone. "Gotta be a diner or something along the way."

"I brought sandwiches, remember?" said Cassy.

"What's in them?" asked Josie.

"Cucumber."

Josie turned to Ana. "You find anything?"

"Yeah," said Ana. "Should be a place coming up in a couple miles."

Cassy looked over at Nell in the hope she'd join team cucumber.

Nell gave her a shrug and halfhearted smile. "Something a little more . . . substantial would be nice."

Cassy frowned and grumbled as she set her eyes firmly on the road.

9

Fran's Diner was the stop, a mom-and-pop joint that seemed divorced from time, with its black-and-white tiled floor, mahogany paneling, and wizened lone waitress who looked like she'd been there since the 1930s. The air was thick with the smell of onions frying on a flattop grill, of bacon grease and burnt coffee.

Patsy Cline crooned "I Fall to Pieces" from a scratchy select-o-matic as Nell and the others waited for their order within one of the sun-warmed booths.

A disgruntled Cassy shifted around on the tattered seafoam-green vinyl. "Sitting on broken glass'd be more comfortable than this travesty of a seat."

Nell took in the place. The dining car looked to accommodate no more than twenty, but out here in the backwoods, she doubted if it ever reached half capacity. Besides the waitress, the only other visible staff was the short order cook, a pro multitasker apparently as he unabashedly ogled the four of them while mechanically rustling up their orders. Nell rolled her eyes away and took in more of the vintage decor. "Any of you ever come here before?"

Ana shook a no as she sighed, impatiently looking between the kitchen and her watch. She'd insisted on a seat facing the door and not by the window.

"No," said a distant Josie, sitting beside Ana, the main of her attention given to her phone as she turned it on.

Cassy responded with a dismissive wave. "Um, nah." Changing the subject, she asked Nell, "So, you're a writer, huh? That sounds . . . uh . . . h-how is that?"

Nell smirked wryly. "How's having homework for the rest of your life sound?"

"Like the worst kind of hell."

Nell gave a chuckling nod.

"I never was really much for school," said Cassy. She turned to the diner at large. "Worked in a place like this for a spell, though."

"Really?" asked Ana. "Wouldn't that involve getting your hands dirty?"

"Honey, you'd be surprised how dirty these hands have gotten."

"I am *not* your honey."

"Not with that attitude you're not." Cassy leaned closer to Ana. "Seriously, you got a problem with me?"

Ana leaned closer to Cassy. "Maybe I do."

Nell and Josie flicked eyes between the mean-mugging pair.

"Well maybe I do too."

Confusion blunted Ana's hostility. "Maybe you have a problem with yourself too?"

"No, maybe I . . . Shut up!"

Nell figured a tension breaker was needed, so turned to Cassy. "I saw you had kids."

Cassy's face lit up as she retrieved her phone, quick to forget the argument. "Yeah, Dale and Dakota." She brought up a picture and showed it to Nell. "Twins."

"Sweet."

As Cassy flicked through a few more pictures, Nell noted they all seemed to show her kids as teenagers.

"High schoolers?"

"Uh, no." Cassy slowed her slideshow. "No, they're actually both in their late twenties. I just um . . ." Her expression showed the briefest sting. "I don't have any recent pictures."

"Oh." Nell thought it best not to probe. "Had them pretty young, huh?"

"Too young!" The next picture Cassy flicked to looked old and not so sharp: a snapshot of an old Polaroid showing three youths posing on a beat-up car. Nell only caught a brief glimpse before Cassy pulled her phone away.

"What was—"

"Nothing, just some old . . . thing." And with that, Cassy shut the door to further conversation.

Seeking engagement elsewhere, Nell looked to Josie, who was still preoccupied with her phone, moving it around to find a signal. Ana remained disinterested, too concerned with how much time they were burning. She was put at ease by the sight of their food arriving in the hands of the waitress, whose name tag read Joy, though her demeanor conveyed anything but.

"Egg white omelet," she said, face slack and sour at the same time.

"Here," said Ana.

"Pecan pie."

Josie frustratedly gave up on her phone. "Yeah."

"Grilled veggies."

Nell unenthusiastically took her plate of charred mushrooms, potatoes, and corn on the cob, especially, and she suspected begrudgingly, made to accommodate her veganism. "Thanks?"

"Club sandwich."

"Right here," said Cassy, Botoxed forehead attempting to furl as she eyed her depressed-looking order. "I'm sorry, did the chef sit on this?"

"No," was Joy's lackadaisical response. "S'that all?"

Cassy pushed the plate back. "This is unacceptable." Joy's expression remained unchanged as she stared back. "That means I want a replacement," Cassy rudely clarified.

Joy took the plate, and as she did, Nell noted a small tattoo on her wrist of an eye with a dagger through it, the design style bringing to mind Egyptian hieroglyphs.

"Hm," was the waitress's response.

"Hm? That's all you have to say is hm? How about you 'hm' yourself back to the kitchen and make this right?"

The waitress cocked her head. "You look familiar . . ."

Cassy underwent an abrupt change of attitude, turning away slightly as she pulled the plate back to herself. "This'll do just fine, thank you thanks."

Joy scrutinized Cassy a moment longer, then left them to their meals.

Josie's phone buzzed with a rapid series of message-received tones. Startled, she turned the phone off in a flustered rush without reading any of those messages. She didn't need to. Lugg would be pissed, going absolutely crazy trying to find her. It wasn't because he cared, she knew, but because someone had gotten one over him in the worst way, and when you got one over on Lugg, Lugg got even, no matter what. The thought brought a sick feeling to Josie's stomach. She knew what he was capable of, what his definition of 'even' looked like.

Nell looked concernedly at Josie. "Everything okay?"

Josie nodded without eye contact. "Fine."

Nell and Ana shared a look, both guessing who the sender was. Some faint part of Ana worried that she'd gone too far with those guys back at Josie's, potentially creating a real problem for her when all this was done.

It was a tendency she had when it came to anger and violence. Excessiveness. A tendency she welcomed, nurtured even, firm in the belief that aggression could only be beaten with greater aggression. Hit first, hit hard, so hard the other person can't hit back. That's what it took to survive in this world; and if only the strong survive, then she was determined to be the strongest. Now, though, sitting next to the person who would have to deal with the possibly dangerous aftermath of her excessiveness, she felt a modicum of responsibility. *If it comes to it, I'll help her bury that bastard*, she swore, assuaging her concerns.

In a subconscious act of motherliness, Cassy took and thoroughly scrubbed everyone's cutlery with a serviette before handing them back. "You'd better believe this place'll be getting a one-star review on Yelp. Two in fact! Reviews that is, not stars." Then to Josie: "I've got a second account 'cause, y'know, sometimes you've gotta slap them with that second fuck you."

Josie smiled. She couldn't help but like Cassy, despite their initial introduction. Her light-heartedness did much to help put her at ease.

She liked Nell too, whose sincerity made Josie feel like she could trust her; that and the glimpses of vulnerability. She'd noticed Nell's little tics and habits, subtle and no doubt restrained, but recognizable. It was a thing that made Josie feel less bad about her own anxiety, because if Nell was struggling but striving through, then maybe she could too.

Ana, however, made her feel inferior. She saw the way she'd looked at her back at her place, with disdain. But she'd been kind too, letting her and Nell stay the night at her home, feeding them well, lending them clothes and anything else they'd needed, even letting them take her bed while she slept on the couch. It all left Josie feeling an odd mix of admiration and intimidation toward her.

Feeling Nell and Ana's thoughts on her and wanting to divert attention, Josie took a bite of her pie, squirming instantly at the taste. "This is . . . bad."

"I hear the secret ingredient is botulism," said Cassy, using a knife and fork to separate the filling of her sandwich from the squished bread.

Josie smiled despite the bad pie. Something in the way the sun hit their booth, in the way the dust motes ambled lazily through the light, drew forth a memory—faded but with the glow of bright summers in her grandma's kitchen. "My grandma used to make pecan pie whenever I visited. It's been so long since I've had any. I guess I was just hoping to . . . I dunno . . ." She shrugged, slightly embarrassed. "I dunno."

"Capture something good?" asked Nell.

Josie gave an abashed nod. "So dumb."

"Not even a little. I can get you something else if you like?"

Josie shook her head. "I'm good, thanks." It was nice to be asked, but Nell was already buying for everyone, and Josie didn't want to come across like some charity case.

"You want me to complain?" asked Cassy. "'Cause I'll bring a shit-storm of inconvenience down on this place. Trust me, I can be a nightmare."

"I don't doubt," said Ana.

"Oh, doubt all you want. No skin off my clit."

Josie smiled. "It's fine. I'm fine, really."

Cassy gave a conceding twist of her head. "If you change your mind, just say the word."

Casting disapproving glances at everyone else's food choices, Ana was especially critical of Nell's plate. "Want some of my eggs? Not a whole lotta protein in what you've got there. Not a whole lotta anything."

Nell raised her brow in agreement. "I packed a shake and some snack bars. I'll just have them when we get back to the car." Then, off Cassy's disapproving look, she amended, "Before I get in the car." Cassy gave a nod of approval.

As the four ate, or at least tried to, Cassy glanced between the others. Strangers really, but oddly not. It was a sensation she couldn't exactly explain. If yesterday morning you'd have told her that she'd be sitting in a shitty diner with three other women, the four of them intending to hunt and kill someone who may or may not be the person who'd almost killed each of them thirty years or so ago . . . She huffed with amusement at the weirdness of life. "Well, would you look at us. Just four gals, out on the road, making our way to murder a psycho like it's the most normal thing in the world."

"It's retribution," Ana corrected. "Not murder."

"Tomayto, tomahto."

"Having second thoughts?" asked Nell.

"I'm questioning my sanity just a little, yeah."

"We can make the rest of the way on our own if you wanna go back," said Ana.

The fearful and undeniably larger part of Josie perked up, wanting Cassy to say yes, in which case she'd join her. She just needed someone else to want to leave too, to say it was okay to not want to go any further.

"I'm sure you'd just love that," said Cassy.

Ana shrugged. "I wouldn't not love it."

Cassy shook her head. "I'm in it now. May as well see how it plays out."

"Glad to hear it," said Nell with relief that was immediately weighed down by the responsibility of having instigated this dangerous venture, thoughts of failure and death ever clouding any positivity.

Josie sank a little.

"But tell me," said Cassy. "Disturbing revenge fantasies aside, what's our plan exactly? All those heavy, dirty bags ruining my upholstery must mean you've got something pretty elaborate in mind."

Ana swallowed a mouthful of omelet. "Traps."

"Traps?"

"We're gonna turn the camp into one big trap," Nell explained. "Then lure him into it."

"With what?"

"Us."

"Sooo, what you're saying is we're gonna Home Alone this fucker?"

Nell nodded. "I guess so, yeah."

"Uh-huh. Whatever Plan B is, I vote for that."

"But what if he's there right away?" asked Josie. "Like as soon as we arrive, there he is, waiting."

"Not his MO," said Ana. "I checked the records. Every single incident, every murder, disappearance, and sighting as far back as I could find, all occurred at night."

"It was the same with this recent group of counselors," said Nell. "And the four from yesterday."

Cassy shrugged. "Guess our killer's a late riser."

"At our current rate of progress, we should make it there by around midday," said Ana. She nodded at Cassy's food. "Depending on how quick you eat that shitty sandwich. That'll give us a little less than nine hours to prepare, what with sunset scheduled for eight fifty-three."

"Let's hope the sun sticks to this strict schedule of yours."

"But won't the camp be a crime scene?" asked Josie.

Ana shook a skeptical no. "Given the law around here's less-than-stellar history of handling things, I doubt it'll still be active. A cop or two at most, but they shouldn't be too difficult to take care of."

Cassy jerked her head, incredulous. "I'm sorry, 'take care of?' The hell does that mean?"

"It means you can distract them with an Uhura fan dance while the rest of us sneak up and knock them out."

"That's just—I don't even—A what dance?"

The small bell above the diner door chimed to announce the arrival of two young men, locals and friends of the chef it seemed, given the familiar nods exchanged. Joy presented the pair with a couple of cold ones as they took seats at the counter. Sipping their beers, the twosome threw glances at Nell and the others, breaking their looks to whisper and chuckle with one another.

Finishing her last morsel of omelet, Ana rose. "Gonna use the restroom."

"Nice knowing you," said Cassy.

Nell looked on as the young men made silent but crude innuendos at Ana's back as she passed them. She shook her head. "Pricks."

Cassy looked up from her dissected sandwich. "Huh?"

Nell jutted her chin in the direction of the aforementioned pricks, who were staring back, the nearest swiveling on his stool, knees splayed to showcase his crotch.

Cassy chuckled. "Oh brother."

"Great," said Nell.

"What?" asked Josie, her back to the men.

"They're coming over."

Cassy rolled her eyes. "Ugh, here we go."

The lead of the two grinned widely as he stood over their table, while his friend seemed content to leer and grin over his shoulder. "Now, what's a fine-ass group of mature ladies like yourselves doing way out here unchaperoned?"

Cassy leaned over the table to eye the pair lecherously. "Hoping to find some of that pimple-dicked, inbred, lost-my-virginity-to-a-squealing-pig young meat these parts are so famous for, and lo and behold, here you are." She finished with a bite of her lower lip and a "Mmm."

Josie and Nell smirked while the men looked confused as to whether they'd just been dealt an insult or a come-on.

"What?" the mouthpiece of the pair asked.

"Look," Nell said. "We're just trying to enjoy our sub-par meals in peace. So why don't you two go do . . . whatever it is you do."

"Watch *a lot* of porn together, I imagine," said Cassy.

The men turned red-faced. "W-we don't—"

Cassy smiled mischievously. "You jerk each other off while you do it?"

The men's faces turned a deeper red. "You've got a filthy mouth on you," said the leader.

"Hey, it's cool, bro, no judgments here. You do you, or each other, whatever."

Josie couldn't help but laugh out loud.

The lead prick turned on her. "You think that's funny, skank?"

Josie shrank and turned away, feeling trapped and in danger, a reflex to confrontation instilled through her time with Lugg.

Nell was immediately out of her seat and in the guy's face. "Hey, don't you talk to her like that!"

"Or what?" He pressed her back with his larger frame and atrocious breath.

Nell called out to the staff, "Excuse me, we're being harassed over here!" The waitress and chef only stared, the latter visibly enjoying every minute of the drama.

"It must warm your mothers' hearts to know they raised such a fine pair of sex pests," said Cassy.

"Pests? Bitch, you'd be damn lucky to get a piece of this." He grabbed at his dick.

"Sweetheart, please, I've seen shower heads with more sex appeal than either of you lame pups. Now run along before I shove a fork up your ass."

The lead prick leaned closer to Cassy. "How 'bout I shove something else up your—"

"Hey."

The bothersome pair turned at that innocuous yet somehow most ominous of heys.

Ana stood a few feet away, drying her hands on a paper napkin.

Shit. Nell saw the warning signs: the subtle twist in Ana's shoulders, the slight drawing back of one foot behind the other, the light in her wolfish eye.

Nell spoke quickly. "Look, we're done here." She looked over to address the staff. "The food sucks, by the way." Then to the pests: "So fun's over, okay?"

The lead guy put a hand on Nell's shoulder, forcing her down onto her seat. "Not okay. You might be—"

A scream and "Fuck!" rang out.

The young man spun to his friend, and would have seen him wiping at an eyeful of stinging sugar granules had the dispenser not blinded him too, clocking him across the face and crushing his nose with a bloody burst.

Nell, Cassy, and Josie sprang up in their seats.

The short order cook came from the kitchen with a meat cleaver in one hand and grease-dripping pan in the other. Ana pelted the sugar dispenser at his face, snapping his head back and dropping him with the impact.

"Fucking bitch!" said the prick with the sugared eyes, grabbing Ana by the shoulder to face him. Ana dipped as she turned, buckling the man with an elbow to the knee, then seized his grabbing arm as she rose and—with a wet snap of bone that was felt in the arms of all present—forced his elbow ninety degrees counter to the joint.

The man wailed loud as hell, then felt his feet sweep backward before his face met the tiled floor teeth-first with a crack.

Cassy winced with an "Oooooh shiiiiit!"

His friend with the flattened nose snatched a beer from the counter, spilling the liquid as he held it by the neck and drew it back to club Ana.

Ana's feet squeaked as she spun to meet his attack, swerving around a pair of clobbering swipes before interrupting the third with a boot to the man's balls that folded him over with a high-pitched wheeze. A lunging knee to the side of his head laid him out.

Dazed, the man endeavored to rise, but Ana discouraged the notion with a sharp stamp that bounced his head off the now bloody floor.

Nell winced at the accompanying crack, unsure if it came from the tiles or the young man's skull.

Cassy voiced a "Daaaamn!"

Ana squatted with a knee upon the man's chest. "Apologize for ruining my meal, and I'll let you up."

Struggling to draw breath, the young man turned desperate eyes to the other women.

Ana forced his face back to hers. "The fuck you looking at them for? I said apologize." She knew full well he couldn't, gasping as he was. "Such a big mouth and now you don't wanna say anything? Okay." She took the discarded beer bottle and rammed the butt of it roughly between his grating teeth. "Let's see how much you can say after this." She shot upright, foot lifted for a stamp to the top of the bottle. The man screamed around it as the foot came down.

"He's done!" yelled Nell.

Caught by Nell's alarm, Ana stopped her stamp just short of contact. She lowered her foot and turned instead to the gawking waitress while taking and unscrewing a salt shaker from the counter. "There's too much salt in your food." She poured the salt directly onto the downed man's shattered nose. He shrieked from the biting burn, turning his head away, though yelped again when the empty shaker binked painfully off his head.

Rousing from unconsciousness, the broken-toothed man caught sight of his limply quivering arm, becoming so distressed he vomited over himself.

Ana turned to Nell and the others and wasn't sure if she was projecting or actually seeing fearful, shocked, and appalled expressions on their faces. "Time to go," she said, wanting to not care.

"I'd certainly say so!" said Cassy.

Ana calmly stepped over the whimpering man before her and exited the diner.

The others followed, Nell dropping some cash onto the table before bringing up the rear with a stern look at the waitress. "No tip!"

10

A souped-up Dodge Charger blared the distorted guitars and vicious vocals of a metal track as it tore down an empty country road.

Lugg's knuckles whitened on the steering wheel as he stewed on what he planned to do just as soon as he caught up with Josie and her little gang, especially that one-eyed bitch.

The rich prick's note said they'd all gone to that murder camp. Lugg knew about Josie's history there, but couldn't figure why she'd be going back, and without telling him. He wouldn't have let her go, of course. It was damn near three hours away and he didn't have the time to waste on dumb road trips, not when he had product to sling. But the fact she went with those other women without a word, without a note, leaving him to deal with The Druid, to fucking grovel, and after they'd . . . Fuck, it pissed him off.

Blake sat in the back beside Scud, who hadn't averted his eyes from the tech mogul since they'd left his fancy home. Blood from the scruffy thug's face wound was seeping through the haphazardly applied bandages, and the area nearest his mouth was sodden with pinkish drool.

Blake cleared his throat as a precursor to attempt conversation, though the sound was lost to the clamor of the migraine-inducing music. He dared a forward lean to better address Lugg.

Scud's hands leaped to his pant-holstered pistol. "Don moob, athole!" came his dribbling and distorted threat.

"Ah!" Blake thrust his hands out in front of him to signal he was no threat. Scud eased off his weapon. Blake took a breath to calm his jangled nerves, then, speaking as loudly as he dared, said, "Um . . . So . . . So why—"

Boiling bitterly on his own questions and looking for an outlet, Lugg turned the music down. "Were you fucking her?" There was danger in his voice.

Blake paled. "What? No! I-I don't even—"

"Then why was she at your home?"

"Yuh, whyaya humb?" echoed Scud, slurping back excess spittle as he touched lightly at his pained cheek.

A sheen of fear-induced sweat broke out on Blake's forehead. "I-I never even met her! I guess she must've been one of the people Cassy went with to this hippy camp."

Lugg grumbled something inaudible under his breath.

"How did you even figure your wife—"

"Girlfriend!" Lugg snapped. "Sorta."

Blake gulped, afraid that anything might set off this frightful crook's murder impulse. "Okay . . . Okay but, but h-how do you even know she was at my house?"

Lugg held up his cell phone, showing the tracking app open on the cracked screen. "I keep tabs on her. Lost the signal when she turned off her phone, but guess where one of her last-known locations was?"

"Yuh humb," answered Scud needlessly, again with an accompanying slurp and wince of pain.

Blake scrunched and turned his eyes away from Lugg, kicking himself for striking up this conversation. "I see . . ." Too afraid to move his hands, he used his lower lip to clear his upper lip of sweat as he considered how best to continue. "And what're you planning to do when you find her?"

"Bring her back."

"Uh-huh, sure, okay, but why d'you need me for that?"

"Don't you want your wife back?"

Blake thought on that for a second, which was far too long.

"Well?" Lugg demanded, jolting Blake from his thoughts.

"Yessir! Yeah, o-of course I do, but—"

"Then shut up."

Scud poked the barrel of his pistol into Blake's ribs.

"Y-Yep—Nope! Not a word from me! No sir!" Blake swore. Then, with a look to Scud, added, "Sirs."

11

Ana kept her gaze out her window, watching but not really seeing the scenery blur by. Her mind was preoccupied, striving to push down the feeling she'd once again gone too far. The looks the others gave her at the diner bothered her greatly, like *she* had been the villain in that situation, not those two assholes. Their silence since leaving the diner only compounded such feelings. What was she supposed to have done back there? Just taken those creeps' bullshit? Fuck. That. Take it once and you're taking it your whole life.

Cassy glanced at Ana through the rearview. "So, um . . . You know some shit, huh?"

"Some," Ana answered.

"You solve all your problems like that?"

"Like what?"

"China O'Brien."

"You saying those scumfucks weren't asking for it?"

Sitting beside her, Josie shifted uncomfortably, sensing the agitation in Ana's voice.

"No. No, they most definitely were," said Cassy. "And it was a blast to see 'em get it, but—"

"Sometimes you just gotta emasculate a motherfucker."

"I mean, sure, I'd buy that T-shirt. But you don't think you went just a little, y'know, OTT?"

"Good, then maybe they'll think twice before trying that shit on the next woman."

"Ever heard the saying that violence never solves anything?"

Despite Cassy echoing the nagging concerns of her inner voice, the larger part of Ana dug its heels in. "Solves a whole lot, in my experience."

"Oh, I don't doubt that."

She didn't need this, Ana thought. This was fucking stupid. A complete waste of thought and energy. She should have come alone. The others clearly didn't have what it was going to take to do this. "Have you forgotten where we're going? What we're gonna do there? If you can't stand the sight of blood, you're on the wrong ride. Harsh words and stern warnings weren't gonna work against those dickholes, and they sure as shit aren't gonna work against Silas Crowe. You have to attack. Go at them with a force so swift, so brutal, so un-fucking-expected, it absolutely shatters their sense of power."

Nell felt she should say something, but she had no idea what. Although the emotionless brutality she'd witnessed from Ana on two occasions now alarmed her, she also couldn't deny Ana's point. This literal and figurative road they were on was going to lead to more blood and violence, and they each had to acknowledge and prepare themselves for that. They didn't need Ana to turn it down. If anything, the rest of them needed to turn it up.

"I thought what you did was badass," said Josie, getting an appreciative grin from Ana in response.

A patrol car closed in on the SUV from the opposite lane. Sheriff Pewson sat behind the wheel, listening intently to a CD playing from the stereo.

"I have a powerful masculine presence."

"I have a powerful masculine presence," Pewson firmly repeated.

"I have a deep, masculine voice."

"I have a deep, masculine voice," he echoed in a pretense of such.

"I am proud of my physique and appearance."

"I—Well." He patted his gut, unconvinced. The sight of the approaching SUV perked him up. He stopped the CD .

"Wait . . ." Nell perked up in response to Pewson's perking.

Squinting and leaning forward, Pewson once again spoke in his natural timbre. "Ain't that . . ."

"Shit!" said Nell, recognizing the lawman, the two rubbernecking at each other as the vehicles passed by.

"Did he see us?" asked an alarmed Cassy.

"Were his eyes open?" asked Ana with obvious sarcasm.

"Yeah!" replied Cassy, missing the sarcasm.

"Then I'd say he saw us."

"Shit!"

Pewson turned his car around on the otherwise empty road, turning on his red and blues as he pursued the SUV.

Josie peered out the back, sinking low in her seat. "He's pulling us over."

"Shitty-shit-shit!" said Cassy.

"Whadda we do?"

Ana looked flummoxed by the nervousness of her companions. "How about we don't act suspicious?"

"You don't think the local sheriff is gonna find the only survivors of Silas Crowe driving toward Haven Cove with a trunk full of traps and weapons suspicious?" Cassy countered.

Nell held up a hand. "Everybody just be cool, all right? Cassy, pull over."

The patrol car came to a stop behind the SUV as it pulled over.

Cassy watched in her side mirror as Pewson exited, tucked in his tan shirt, hiked up his pants, and strolled on over with his thumbs hooked in his belt like some Old West hero. She put away her driving glasses and pulled the zipper on her tracksuit partway down, plumping up her cleavage. "I've been in situations like this before."

Nell jerked her head. "Uh, what're you doing?"

"Show a little tiddy, act cute–dumb. Worst thing he hands you is his phone number." She gave Nell a wink. "Trust me."

"I got a plan." Ana cracked her door open. "Keep his eyes on your tits."

Cassy gave her breasts another push. "Time to make momma proud, girls."

Nell rolled her eyes.

"Oh shit, hide this." Cassy hastily handed Nell a silver hip flask.

"Uh—"

"Glove box."

"Right." Nell popped the glove box, finding a suspect number of gum and mint packs. She added the flask to the contents, no questions asked. The hiding of one explained the need for the other.

"I have a powerful masculine presence," Pewson reminded himself. "I have a powerful masculine presence."

A nervous Josie watched Ana slip ninja-like out of the vehicle as Pewson stepped up alongside Cassy's window.

Cassy lowered it as he knocked. "What seems to be the pwobwem, owfficer?" she asked with a not-too-subtle pout.

Nell cringed at Cassy's exaggerated performance.

Perplexed but not wanting to appear so, Pewson narrowed his eyes and reached for that deep, masculine voice as he spoke. "Ma'am, have you been drinking? Your manner of speech is . . . dubious."

Cassy frowned.

Nell leaned over. "It's been a long time, Deputy—Sorry, sheriff now, right?"

Pewson bent down and poked back his Stetson to get a better look at the others. "Nell James!" His natural intonation was back. "Thought I recognized you." He studied Cassy and Josie in turn. "Cassandra Phong and Josie Jedford. Never thought I'd see any of you round these parts again."

"It's Rafferty, actually," Cassy grumped, zipping up her top.

"What in the heck're you ladies doing way out here?"

"We thought it'd be a good idea to come back and see the camp after all this time," Nell explained. "Kinda like exposure therapy. Face our fears and all that."

Pewson's face skewed with skepticism. "Together?"

Cassy took and stroked Nell's hand. "Yeah, we've formed like a . . . a sisterhood! Yeah, bonded by trauma, y'know? It's a very common thing." She turned to Nell. "What's it called?"

Nell took back her hand and shook her head.

"Trauma . . . syn . . . thesis," Cassy ventured with wobbly conviction.

If ever a man looked doubtful. "Trauma synthesis, huh?"

"Um-hm." Cassy nodded, adding a smile as an afterthought.

Keeping low, Ana moved stealthily up alongside Pewson's car.

"Well, you picked a helluva time to face your fears." Pewson tilted his head to regard Nell. "Y'know, I read your book, Miss James."

"Oh?" said Nell, knowing what was coming next.

"Can't say you were all that kind to me or the good folks round here. In fact, you kinda made us all out to be a buncha useless, backwater stump-jumpers who can't tell their poop hole from their pie hole."

"Was I supposed to lie?" asked Nell matter-of-factly.

"Is it true?" Josie butted in before a frowning Pewson could reply. "Is he back?"

"Who?"

Nell saw Josie struggling to voice the name, and so said it for her. "Silas Crowe."

Pewson balked. "Uh, no . . . No o-of course not. Silas Crowe? Lord, no!"

Ana pulled a tactical knife from a sheath on her boot and jabbed it into the car's front tire.

"Then what happened to those counselors?" asked Josie.

"Uh, w-we don't—"

Ana likewise killed the rear tire on the same side.

"And those kids last night?" Josie pressed.

"I-I don't, we don't know, in truth," came Pewson's flustered response.

Ana eased Pewson's passenger side door open, then leaned in and cut the wire on his radio. She took a moment to consider the racked shotgun but thought better of taking it.

"What do you know, Sheriff?" asked Nell with all the authority Pewson lacked.

Cassy frowned at Pewson as she lowered the zipper on her top again.

Overwhelmed by the grilling and confused by Cassy's cleavage, Pewson chewed air as his mind searched for a response, until at last he shook his head, remembering his role here. "Look, you shouldn't have come back. And heading to the camp is out of the . . ." He noticed the rear passenger door was slightly ajar. "Question?" Moving around to the back of the SUV, Pewson caught sight of Ana moving away from his vehicle. "Hey—" He pawed at the holstered pistol on his belt, freeing it after a botched first and second attempt and pointing it at Ana. "S-stop— Stop right there right now stop!"

Ana stepped to the side of the patrol car's hood, hands raised. She thrust her chin at Pewson's gun. "Safety's still on."

Pewson smirked. "You think I'm dumb enough to fall for that?" Despite his words, Pewson's confidence was quick to crumble under Ana's steely look. He checked his weapon—a window Ana seized, sliding across the hood of the car and swinging her legs around for a two-footed kick to Pewson's chest.

Josie watched slack-jawed as Pewson hit the asphalt. "She hit him! She hit a cop!"

"Shit!" was Nell and Cassy's joint reaction.

Ana left Pewson to curl up in pain on the road as she rushed into the SUV. "Punch it!" she urged, slamming her door shut.

"Shiiit!" yelped Cassy as she hurriedly keyed the ignition.

Pewson turned over and watched as the SUV peeled away at speed, throwing up a cloud of dust and fumes that left him spluttering as he salvaged his fallen hat and climbed unsteadily to his feet.

Still coughing as he fell into his car, Pewson started the engine. He plucked up the receiver on his radio, found it came away all too easily, saw the cut wire. "Gosh darn crap!" Pursuit his only recourse, Pewson urged his vehicle to the task, making it all of two feet before the car dragged heavily to one side.

"Sonuva—" Pewson stopped the car and jumped out, circling around to the passenger side to confirm his suspicions. "Mother"—he kicked the car, his foot the only victim—"ffff-fudger!"

Leaning against his lamed vehicle, Pewson watched uselessly as the SUV shrank in the distance.

12

Lugg stopped the car outside of Fran's Diner with a *psssht!* of discharged pressure from its turbo.

An ambulance was already on the scene.

Blake gawked as the paramedics wheeled out a whimpering young man with an elbow gruesomely opposed to its joint and fewer teeth than he'd started out the day with. "Oh my—What happened to him?"

Lugg frowned, having a good idea what, or more precisely, who. "Stay in the car," he instructed while exiting.

"Geh muh a sluthsy," said Scud.

Blake raised a hand. "Uh—B-but—"

Scud lifted his shirt to flash his pant-holstered pistol. "'ey."

Blake curled a defensive leg up between himself and Scud as he pressed himself against the door. "Yep."

Lugg approached the other young man, sitting on the ground with most of his head wrapped in bandages. He looked up as Lugg's heavy shadow fell over him. "Listen, man," he said with a croaky voice. "I ain't in the—"

"Who did this?" asked Lugg with the scorn of a disgruntled father.

The young man felt the weight of that fatherly gaze. "Some . . . fucking punks, man." He cleared his raw throat. "Bikers, I think. Real mean—" Lugg flicked at the young man's bandaged nose, eliciting a pained yowl. "What the fuck—"

"Who?"

"Some . . ." Bruised pride made him hesitate. "Some bitches, man. Coldcocked me while I was walking in." He gestured to the ambulance. "Fucked my buddy up too when he tried to help me out. You see what a mess he is?" He shook his head, the shame clear upon his face. "God damn."

"Describe 'em. What'd they look like?"

"I dunno, man, they were like, MILF-aged. A Black chick, Asian chick, white chick. Worst was the bitch with the eyepatch. Mexican, or something." He winced at some fresh pain in his face, then with petty bitterness added, "Probably an illegal."

Lugg exhaled an agitated breath through his teeth. "Shaved head?"

"Yeah, jacked too—f-for a chick I mean. Looking like she ain't never missed a fucking Pilates class in her life."

Lugg's blood boiled to see his defeat shared with this kid. This pathetic, bitch-ass excuse for a man.

"I swear, man, these chicks were psychos. Out for blood. All we did was pay 'em a little fucking compliment!" He huffed and shook his head. "Man, if I'd have seen them coming, shit'd be a whole 'nother story. But then I'd be the bad guy, know what I mean? 'Cause yain't supposed to . . ."

Lugg stopped listening to the young man's excuses, which he knew them to be, because he'd been spinning similar lies to himself all morning: *She caught me off guard. She must've had a weapon. The sun was in my eyes. I tripped and fell into her elbow at just the right angle.*

Those thoughts all rushed into a single lane of impotent frustration as he turned his bruise-blackened eyes down the road ahead. Oh, how he was looking forward to catching up with them.

13

Cassy's SUV pulled into a hovel of a gas station that looked so old and rickety a mouse might bring it down with a muzzled fart. A true relic from a bygone era, what with its pair of rusted antique pumps; a vintage Pepsi machine that didn't seem to be plugged in, and whose logo was so sun-faded it was virtually opaque; and the poorly taxidermied roadkill crowding the windows—two-for-one on squirrels, a sign exclaimed.

On the porch, rot-softened boards creaked a regular rhythm to the back-and-forth motions of a rocking chair, upon which sat Clem, sporting oil-stained overalls and a distressed trucker cap adorned with fishing lures. Every blue vein seemed visible beneath his near-translucent skin.

His jaundiced eyes squinted, and a grumble rose from his throat as the women exited their vehicle and approached.

Cassy took a disbelieving moment to take in the man before her. "Damn, you went from old as fuck to old as fuuuuck."

His face set in a perpetual snarl, Clem eyed each of them in turn. "I remember you. All a you."

"Like if Wikipedia had a page for crusty old fart, *you'd* be the image."

"Warned you not t'go to that camp. Didn't I warn you?"

"Seriously, how're you even alive?"

"You did," said Nell. "Now we're going back."

Clem looked suddenly stricken with some difficulty, palming his chest as if experiencing the first notes of a heart attack.

A concerned Nell stepped forward. "Hey, are you—"

A robust belch resolved the issue. "Back?" said Clem somewhere amid that burp. "What in the hell for?"

Ana matched Clem's glare. "To hit that bastard so hard he doesn't get back up."

Clem cackled phlegmily, then hocked a loogie and spat it off to the side, causing Nell to squirm, Ana to look away, and Cassy to gag and almost throw up in her mouth.

"It is him, isn't it?" asked Josie, accustomed to such gross displays.

Clem ran a bony, age-spotted forearm across his wet mouth. "Always and still."

"What is he?"

"Rage. Wrath. A reckoning."

"The hell's he got to be so pissed about?" asked an exasperated Cassy.

"And how do we kill him?" asked Nell.

Clem leaned forward, scowling right at her. "You can't kill a storm, girl."

"Challenge accepted," said Ana. "And we ain't girls."

Clem scowled as he sat back to resume his rocking.

"If you know something," said Nell. "Anything that can help us . . ."

"What more's there to say, other'n you're headed to your deaths," said Clem.

Nell shrugged. "Then I guess we'll need gas for the journey."

"And condoms," Ana added, drawing bewildered looks from the others.

14

Pewson plodded glumly down the road, shotgun yoked across his shoulders as the sun beat down on him. "Demotion, here I come. Way to go, Pewson. Way to fudgin' go."

The rapidly growing commotion of metal music turned him about in time to see Lugg's Dodge Charger round a wide bend.

Pewson stuck out a thumb. "At last."

"Cop," said Lugg.

Blake sprang up. "Help! Uh—That is, he might be able to help. M-maybe he saw my wife and your, uh, t-the others."

Lugg thought it over, then to Scud said, "Put it away."

"Flucking clops," said Scud, covering up his pistol.

The rumbling car pulled up beside Pewson with a sharp hiss.

The lawman gave the roof a grateful pat as he leaned into the open passenger window. "Hey there, friend." He looked first at Lugg, meeting a banged-up face of cold indifference. He looked next between Scud and Blake, the former also unfriendly and looking like he'd seen far better days, the latter looking terrified despite the wide, subtly twitching smile on his face. "You, uh . . . You fellas lost?"

"Are you?" countered Lugg.

"Would you believe a one-eyed woman wrecked my ride?"

The curling of Lugg's upper lip indicated he did indeed believe. "Shaved head?"

Pewson nodded. "Yeah. How do you—"

"Was there an Asian woman with her?" asked Blake.

"Cassandra Phong?"

"Rafferty, my wife."

Pewson narrowed his eyes. "So you fellas are—"

"Concerned partners," said Lugg. "Tryna find 'em before they do something stupid."

Pewson nodded, buying the story without hesitation. "Then we're headed the same way. They've gone to the camp."

Lugg gestured with his head. "Get in."

Blake caught eyes with the sheriff in the rearview mirror as he seated himself, and though he could not voice his distress, he gave his best *Help me I've been taken against my will to rescue a wife I give zero shits about* look. The lawman responded with frowny confusion, not receiving the message.

Lugg adjusted the mirror so Blake shared eyelines with him instead of the sheriff, and the message in Lugg's dark eyes was clear as crystal to decipher. Blake drew his lips into his mouth and shrank down in his seat as the car tore off.

15

The SUV came to a gravel-crunching stop before the overhanging sign for Camp Haven Cove. Despite being recently painted in cheery letters, it was unable to hide its portent of malevolence.

A collective shiver passed through the group. All were silent, pensive, for they knew that to pass beneath it, between its supporting trees, was to enter *his* domain. A place separate from the world and its precepts.

None of them had ventured within a mile of any woodland since their trauma. The mere thought of stepping forth into nature, albeit idyllic, was too much, and this dark and sprawling forest—in stark contrast to the verdant scenery they'd passed on the drive here—was far from idyllic.

Nell took a slow breath, her mouth suddenly so dry, chest tight, hands clammy. "Well . . . Here we are."

Though she remained doubtful of the real Silas's return, Cassy couldn't help but feel a growing unease at being back here, her stomach knotting as long-buried memories unearthed themselves like the decayed arms of the restless dead from moldering graves. *Alcohol.* She hastily removed her hip flask from the glove box and took a fortifying gulp of its biting contents, her tension easing with the spread of its heat. Booze, her poisonous savior. "What if he's not even here?" she asked. "What if we came all the way out here, and he—or *whoever*, doesn't even show?"

No one had an answer.

Nell looked back at Josie, shrunk in on herself and trembling as she took a pill. "You good?"

Josie gave a dishonest nod, then clenched her teary eyes and admitted the head-shaking truth. She felt vulnerable, exposed. Dread had latched taloned hands around her skull and squeezed to the point of nausea.

The way he'd stalked her around the camp that night, forcing her to sneak from cabin to cabin, terrified to a degree she couldn't have imagined possible . . . it was as if she were back there right now. "I- I can't do this. I shouldn't be here."

"Jesus," said an unsympathetic Ana, catching a disapproving look from Nell as she rolled her head away from Josie. "We shouldn't have brought her."

"Damn, you're one cold bitch," said Cassy.

"A realist is what I am," Ana countered. "She's a liability."

"Ana!" Nell chastised.

"What? Somebody's gotta say it. People like her get themselves and those around them killed."

"She's just scared—"

"We can't afford a weak link in this chain! Not here! Not against him!" She refrained from expressing her doubts about the others' dependability.

"You're tough, Ana," said Cassy. "No doubt there. But here's a little wisdom for you: Being an asshole doesn't make you any tougher."

Ana's impulse was to say something back, but her mind tripped on what. She turned her anger out of the window. She knew her people skills weren't exactly great. She could be rude, short-tempered, callous; living each day like you're downrange will do that to a person. Silas Crowe's reemergence amplified all that, making her feel especially antsy, which in turn made her fuse shorter than usual; her body like a stick of dynamite desperate to go off. Evidently, it was something she was finding difficult to control.

Josie dropped her head and began to weep. God, how she wished she were strong like Ana, brave like Nell, even skeptical like Cassy, anything but so uselessly terrified. "I just . . . I-I just—"

Nell placed a soothing hand on her knee. "Josie, hey. It's okay."

Josie labored to speak between shudders of stifled sobs. "Ana's right . . . I'm not cut out for this."

"Shit," said Cassy, "you think I am? Sitting here with my manicured nails, Valentino sneaks, eight-thousand-dollar tits, and this weird third nipple thing growing on my underarm . . . The other day, I sneezed, and some pee came out." She raised her hands to emphasize the absurdity. "People who piss themselves when they sneeze should not be doing battle with possibly immortal serial killers."

Nell found herself unable to deny her point. She was knocking on the door of fifty, expecting a tap on the shoulder from menopause any day now, taking trimonthly shots of B12, and losing ground to cellulite and pudge—though she didn't doubt Ana had abs like knotted rope. According to her spam folder, women their age were supposed to be taking it easy and building up a wardrobe of neutral colors—fading away, in other words.

Cassy dropped her hands. "Look, I still don't know if I even believe he's out there, or that we'll find anything at all. That's why I brought s'mores, y'know, so it wouldn't be a total bust."

"Then why'd you come?" Ana asked.

"Because . . ." Cassy looked out her window, sighing heavily, her facade lowering with the exhale. "Because maybe despite all the time that's passed, and all that's happened since, I still can't escape that night. And no amount of denial, or distance, or money, or luxury, or drinking myself to sleep night after night can get me out of this fucking camp.

"Maybe . . . Maybe the only way out is to go back in . . . or some deep and insightful shit like that." She looked at Ana in the rearview. "So yeah, maybe Josie's not cut out for this. Neither am I. But we need to be here all the same."

The car went silent with the profundity of Cassy's words.

Nell felt like she should say something; she'd brought them all here, after all. She understood their viewpoints, the manner in which each had ultimately chosen to deal with what happened to them. She could've easily become like Ana, heart so hardened it didn't allow for any degree of empathy, camaraderie, or love. She'd come frightfully close to the fear-exhausted shell Josie resembled, hiding so far away from life she may as well be dead. She'd certainly tried to be like Cassy, employing every trick she could think of to convince her mind there was nothing to fear anymore, that Silas Crowe was dead and that was that and life goes on and drink after drink to silence any counterarguments. But despite their differences, they'd all come here, needed to be here, just like Cassy said. "We're all here for the same reason," said Nell at last. "Because we wanna put an end to this. If any of us could've done it alone, we would've done it already, but we didn't. The only reason any of us are here now is because we're *all* here now. That's what it's gonna take to stop him. All of us. Together. All for one, one for all, all of that." Ana's hardness softened as she looked away. Josie wiped away her tears and calmed herself. Cassy nodded her accord. Nell turned frontward. "There's no turning back now."

"I mean, there is," said Cassy. Then with a look between the others: "I could totally turn us around. We could all go home, forget about this whole thing and carry on with our lives."

"How's that been working out for us so far?"

The four spent a long moment in silence, each of them staring down that dirt road; the knowledge of who and where it led to and all that had happened there weighing on their minds, pressing on their courage.

"Let's do it," said Nell.

"Fuckin' A," said Ana.

The others turned to Josie who, with a sniff, gave an unconfident nod.

"I guess that settles it," said Cassy, starting the engine. "No backsies."

The threshold was crossed.

16

The barren, wounded-looking trees on either side—each in disharmony with their neighbors—seemed to become more oppressive the deeper the vehicle went, as if traveling down the constricting gullet of a giant, the entwining boughs creating a liminal, ever-darkening passage from the everyday world to some wretched other; a world of anguish and violence, suffering and heartbreak. A world of death.

His world.

Overhead, a murder of crows swept past in the opposing direction.

"Well that's ominous," Cassy commented. The others gave no reply, nor seemed to even hear her, struggling in the mire of their own thoughts, a thing Cassy found disquieting. It seemed the closer they got to the camp, the more the notion that Silas Crowe was really back became a distinct possibility in her mind, and the longer that thought lingered, the more her scalp tightened.

A copycat. That's what she was expecting to find, if anything at all. Just some sick fuck, a Silas superfan they'd have to get medieval on. Or at least watch and cheer as Ana got medieval.

Earlier, she'd disputed the idea that it could actually be Silas Crowe, but now she posited the opposing idea to herself: What if it was? What would she do then? What could any of them do?

Cassy shook the thought from her mind and began toying with the AC. *Nah, definitely just some weirdo. I'll be home in time for mimosas and RuPaul.*

Nell kept her eyes forward and alert; the old wound in her shoulder gnawing at her. Her roving gaze fixed on one tree in particular, and something in its shape and size made her wonder if it was the same tree she'd crushed Silas against all those years ago. Crushed, but not killed.

If only she'd made sure. Lit the fuel that leaked from the van's busted gas tank, sending it and him up in annihilating flames. Stayed and watched as his flesh charred and flaked to ash. Maybe that would've been the end of it. Maybe nine more people wouldn't have lost their lives. The back of her neck ached with the weight of those lives.

Would success here do anything to alleviate the guilt she felt over them, or her friends? The sickly feeling in her gut told her no. Never.

Josie took a shivering breath to try to calm her thundering heart, loud in her ears. She felt hot, so very hot, her underarms damp. Her vision had gone fuzzy about the edges, and her lungs felt like they were being compressed.

She considered taking another Xan, but doubted its effectiveness in the present situation, or that she'd even be able to deliver the pill to her mouth, what with her unsteady hands. She endeavored instead to take deep breaths.

This was too much.

I shouldn't have come. What the fuck was I thinking?

It felt so wrong to be here, like they were all moving toward the churning teeth of a wood chipper.

She felt a near-desperate urge to tear at her wrists, to close crushing hands on her throat, to wrest Ana's gun away, press it under her chin, and blow her own brains out, to end herself on her terms while she yet had the chance, rather than risk Silas getting his hands on her again.

Perhaps that was the best she could hope for, the only real way she might hurt Silas, by denying him the pleasure of killing her himself.

She started at the sound of Ana racking the slide of her gun.

Ana gripped her pistol with both hands, finding reassurance in its firmness and weight. She'd been waiting for this opportunity for years, decades. Night after night lost in hate-sick meditation, indulging in thoughts so violent and disturbing she couldn't possibly divulge them to another for fear of being thought a psycho.

Things weren't going to play out the same as last time. She was a kid then, her life up to that point sheltered by a devout and overbearing mother, who warned often of dangers and devils, but never how to defend against them. That much, she'd taught herself. Then there was religion, which taught her that salvation was to be found with God, but had God saved her when Silas held her suspended by her hair and dug a sharp thumb into her face, clawing her ruptured eye from its socket? No. She'd saved herself.

Trauma counseling, anger management, cognitive behavioral therapy. These too had done nothing for her. Muay Thai, Kali, Jiu-Jitsu, extensive firearms training, donning a balaclava and hand wraps on select nights to stress-test her skills on local degenerates—these were the things that honed her fury to a keen edge, turning it into something she could use, something she could unleash when the world next came at her with a naked blade, which she expected would be any minute now. She wiped clammy hands on her pant legs.

Nell saw him.

Half-hidden behind a tree, watching as the vehicle passed by, looking just the way she remembered: unfathomable, monstrous, cut from the cloth of an alternate and nightmarish reality.

There he was again behind the next tree, and the tree after that, and the next, and all those beyond, and same was the view on the other side of the road behind every tree. He was everywhere.

"He knows we're here . . ."

None of the others spoke to question Nell, nor seemed alarmed by her barely audible words, for they too were rapt on the trees, seeing and thinking precisely the same thing.

17

Cassy stopped the car and cut the engine at the camp's perimeter, the log cabins ahead of them and the liquid-crystal lake to their rear.

The engine continued to tick, punctuating each protracted second as the four of them silently took in the scene: a summer camp like any other, surrounding forest notwithstanding. A place betoken of innocence, fun, and self-discovery. A place that gave no intimations of evil doings, no hint of the necrotic slime a mere scratch beneath the refurbished veneer.

Ana exited first with marked eagerness. Cassy removed her driving glasses and took a long pull on her flask before following with much less eagerness.

Nell took a deep breath to quell her surging anxiety, but knew the only way she was getting out of this car was to appease that unease, to exit with a *clean mind*, placing her first foot outside with no thoughts of dying or failure, then doing likewise with the other. If one of those steps should be accompanied by even the flicker of a bad thought, she would have to pull her feet back in, close the door, and start again, repeating until done correctly.

The company of others and fear of their judgment at such an odd habit usually overrode her need to perform these mental rituals, but today was different. She needed to do this, even if the whole world was staring with pointed fingers.

Safe thoughts. That's how she usually managed it. Reciting song lyrics, recalling a happy memory, naming state capitals in alphabetical order, thinking of puppies, of lunch, of the last movie she saw, anything to distract her mind from its morbid musings long enough for her to get out of a car, or pass through a doorway, or flick off a light switch, or slide hastily into bed, often with tears of frustration and self-loathing in her eyes. To do any of these with a bad thought in her head would assure disaster. Her rational mind knew it was absurd to believe her thoughts could affect reality in such a way, but her physical body was not so rational, responding to her defiance of these rituals with swift panic. It was so utterly exhausting.

Her OCD had manifested in the years after her ordeal, starting as innocuous habits such as rechecking locks and double-checking the stove was off. But the more she engaged with her anxieties, the stronger and more numerous they became. Now they were akin to a pernicious heckler constantly at her ear, hell-bent on her mental and physical self-destruction as it whispered an unending litany of fears, doubts, and untruths, telling her she would fail, would die, that the others would die, that it would all be her fault, just like it had been before.

Maybe those intrusive thoughts were right. Maybe they would fail, perhaps even most likely would, and it *would* be her fault because she'd persuaded the others to come. More lives added to the weight of those she already felt encumbered by.

Nell watched Ana and Cassy, the former scanning the environment, pistol clutched close to her chest and angled down, the latter thumbing a smudge off the hood of her flash SUV.

Nell's eyes shifted focus to the rearview mirror. Josie was still in the back, looking out of her window with waterlogged eyes. "Josie?"

"We can't beat him, Nell," she took a quick breath in a bid to hold back her tears. They fell anyway. She turned those wet eyes on Nell. "We can't."

"I . . ." Nell struggled to counter Josie's fears. What could she say when a large part of her thought the same?

Josie wiped at her eyes. "Aren't you scared?"

"I'm . . ." Nell didn't know how to articulate just how afraid she was. "Absolutely terrified . . . but we're not alone here. You're not alone here. Me, Ana"—she said the next with less certainty—"Cassy. We've all got your back."

Josie nodded, wanting to believe that, positive that she did. Even during their short time together, among these other women she'd started to once again feel like a person, a human being and not just some faded, barely there shadow. For the first time in a long time, she felt seen, heard, understood. It was enough to dare believing in life after this. She wanted to believe her next words too. "And me yours."

Nell smiled. "All right. Let's go."

They exited together, and Nell ignored the ritualistic demands of her anxiety for Josie's sake, despite the terrible thoughts that flooded her mind as she stepped out of the vehicle.

The four of them formed a line in front of the SUV, surveying what was to be their battleground.

The cabins were painted in differing, cheery hues, no doubt to offset the morbidly glum surroundings. The obstacle course had been remade, looking more like the kind of apparatus intended to test the mettle of prospective SEAL team members rather than kids hopped-up on bug juice and jelly nougats.

Despite the impressive facelift, it was the same camp in each of their minds.

"Fuck . . ." said Cassy. "Did thirty years even happen? Feels like I was here just yesterday."

"Feels like I never left," said Ana.

"We never did," said Nell. "We're right where we've always been."

"It's like I can still smell the blood in the air," said Josie. And not only the scent, but the sight, and worse. Here a severed leg, there a hollowed torso, her dismantled friends scattered across the campgrounds, soaking the earth, soaking her. Memories that had become mercifully hazed with time, brought now into over-saturated sharpness.

Ana was preoccupied with one cabin in particular, not seeing the new construction, but the burning deathtrap that once stood in its place. Her scars itched in response.

Cassy too seemed focused on a specific area of the camp—a span of ground between two large trees. She broke the trance with a shake of her head.

Nell's eyes lingered on the rec hall.

A memory of Stan's smiling face under disco lights.

Blood dripping from a sneaker.

She turned away, focusing instead on the circle of stones where she and her friends had sat around a fire, listening to Stan's scary story about vengeful witches and depraved sacrifices, all of them blissfully unaware of the true horror that would soon befall them.

Had he been watching them as they sat there? Closing the distance as they basked in the warm glow of the fire, too inebriated and carefree to detect an encroaching predator, or even imagine a world in which one such as Silas Crowe could exist.

Was he watching them now? Or was he truly dormant in the day, like Ana theorized?

Nell looked around at the forest. Still as ever.

It seemed so intrinsically linked to Silas—like something out of a dark fairy tale, a place whose very essence and physical character had been shaped by the history and emotions played out upon its soil, where each forlorn tree represented a victim lost to the monster who called this place home.

The research she'd done for her books had enlightened Nell on the various myths surrounding Silas and his inception; these themselves had been altered and added to over the years to a degree that the truth was anyone's guess. Maybe he was just some freakish lunatic who'd somehow survived apparent death on numerous occasions. Or maybe he was something else. Something dreadfully more.

Nell's roving gaze caught the peaking sun. "We should get a hustle on."

"Wait," Ana insisted, going to the trunk of the SUV and returning with a backpack. "From here on out, everybody carries a weapon." Reaching inside the bag, she handed them each a holstered Glock fitted with an aftermarket trigger with a built-in manual safety.

Nell's body tensed. She looked away as she took hers, intrusive thoughts flashing through her mind of turning the gun on the others and then herself.

"You couldn't have brought bigger guns?" asked Cassy.

"Wasn't sure if we'd run into cops, so needed something easy to conceal. Besides, they're loaded with hollow points."

"Meaning?"

"That fucker's gonna know he's been shot."

Josie accepted hers with unsure hands, while Cassy held hers between thumb and forefinger as if it were a soiled diaper. "Will putting my prints on this indict me in something?"

Ana ignored her. "Any of you fired one before?"

Nell nodded as she fastened the holster to her belt. "I go to the range a couple times a year." Respectively on Stan's birthday and the anniversary of that night is what she didn't say.

"I've cracked off a few shots in the yard," said Josie.

Cassy shook a no. "Guns aren't my thing."

Ana gave a quick demonstration, starting with the safety. "On, won't shoot. Off, something's gonna die. One hand firm around the grip, the other cupping that hand tight. Point it center mass of what you want dead, squeeze the trigger until it drops, then squeeze it some more to be sure—*always* be sure." She opened up the backpack and held it before the others. "Take a close-quarters weapon too."

"I don't wanna get close," said Josie.

"You might not get a choice."

Assenting, Josie reached in and found a buck knife.

Cassy rummaged through the bag with the pickiness of an old lady at a melon stand, settling at last on a couple of butterfly knives. "Oh, yas! Now this, this is my thing!"

"Don't cut yourself with those," said Ana.

With a cocksure smirk, Cassy flipped the knives open, spinning them in her hands like she made a comfortable living doing such tricks, until one flew from her grip. "Shit." She chased after it.

Nell's thoughts again turned sinister as she took a Bowie knife, her mind urging her to jab herself in the throat with it. Such thoughts always plagued her whenever she handled any potentially dangerous object. She couldn't drive her car without envisioning plowing into people on the sidewalk or deliberately steering into oncoming traffic. After a quick shake of her head to throw those thoughts aside, and to deflect any awkward questions from Ana who was looking right at her, Nell asked, "What about you?"

Ana returned to the trunk, placed the bag back and, from another, pulled forth a leather-sheathed blade whose shape and design tipped its classification from machete to short sword. She drew it into sunlight that gleamed upon a bronze crossguard, slid across a gently curving edge, and winked off a piercing point. This was no mere tool for cutting brush. This was a weapon, made for one hand, one purpose.

"Daaamn, Xena!" said Cassy.

Ana gave the sword a slow turn. "Nineteen-inch, ten-sixty carbon steel blade, with a bronze-finished hilt." She lifted it to showcase the handle. "Full tang, and leather-wrapped grip."

"You sure it's big enough?" joked Nell.

Ana ran a prideful eye over the polished, wicked sharp weapon that looked like Red Sonja's backup piece. Her very own Excalibur. "Forged it myself."

Cassy smirked. "You've named it, haven't you?"

"I—" Ana flushed with embarrassment. "No." She resheathed Grimthorn without another word.

"Y'know," Cassy began, "a bazooka would've been better than all these guns and knives. Just saying."

"Next time you can do the shopping."

The conversation drifted over Josie, whose full attention was directed at the forest, ears straining for the smallest of sounds, eyes scrutinizing every shadow. "You think he's watching us right now?" she asked, echoing Nell's earlier thought.

The others ceased their gibings and joined her in scouring their surroundings.

"I hope he is," said Ana. "Let him get a good look."

"No cops in sight," noted Nell. "I guess that's good."

"I dunno," said Cassy. "A few dozen more armed individuals sure would help to put me at ease."

Josie steadied her rattling nerves with a deep breath.

Standing beside her, Nell took her hand. Josie responded with a shaky smile and appreciative squeeze.

Nell turned back to the camp at large. "Well . . . Let's get busy with it."

"Wait, hold up." Cassy stepped in front of the others and thrust forth her downturned hand in a 'Go team!' gesture. "Shall we do one of these?"

Ana rolled her eyes and carried on past, tired of Cassy's light-hearted attitude. Nell followed with a "C'mon." Josie at least offered a conciliatory shrug as she limped ahead, leaving Cassy with her hand outheld.

Cassy put her own hand atop the other, completing the gesture herself with a deflated, "Yay. Go us. We're awesome. Hope we don't die."

18

Ana cleared the counselors' cabin like a seasoned SWAT officer, breaching the door and leading with her firearm as she checked the corners and swept the room until satisfied it was "Clear."

The others entered, assured by her proven competence.

Nell hesitated on the threshold, one foot in, the other out; the crushing urge to acquiesce to her anxiety-induced coping compulsions conflicting with her will and desire to not be so damn weak, especially in front of the others. The result left her unable to move, temples tightening, heartbeat racing, the world unsteady in her vision.

Having entered right before her, Josie looked back and saw Nell in her predicament.

Shame baked Nell's face. She was supposed to be the one who rallied and encouraged the others, yet here she was, unable to take a simple step, her fragility revealed under the spotlight of Josie's gaze. "I . . ."

Josie offered a hand and sympathetic smile. "Come on."

Nell's symptoms melted, and with their easing came the realization that she didn't have to hide from these women. There was no shame to be had in fear, nor was there shame in needing a helping hand to navigate through it. So, with a thankful smile, Nell took that hand and entered the cabin.

The interior showed the yet-to-be-cleaned-up signs of a party. Crumpled plastic cups, half-full take-out boxes, Nerf darts, and discarded items of clothing littered the floor.

Josie lit a cigarette as she hobbled over to inspect a series of framed pictures on the wall, arranged beneath an "In Loving Memory" banner. Each was of a different group of counselors from a particular year, dating back to the camp's opening in '84. She found the group from '85. Her group. A happy if mischievous-looking gang of teenagers having the time of their lives.

Sadness misted Josie's eyes. She hugged herself as she took in those faces, not seen in so long. These were her friends. She still knew their hopes and aspirations and individual quirks, remembered sneaking sips of booze with them at neighborhood barbecues and crying on their shoulders in restroom stalls.

Each of them, each beaming, bright-faced one of them, would not live to see the day after that picture was taken. Except for her. And why was that? She wondered. She hadn't been smart like Paula, who urged them all to barricade the doors and windows and find weapons. She hadn't been brave like Mike, her boyfriend, who tried to fight the monster off when he broke through their defenses. She hadn't been selfless like Edith, who ran interference when they saw the killer going for the younger kids' cabin, giving them time to escape to the road.

No.

She'd been the one who ran, who hid, who did nothing as Silas Crowe butchered her friends one by one. She'd been the one who fought back only because she was trapped, and who struck a lucky hit only because Sarah, her earliest and best friend, her virtual sister, threw her mortally wounded body at the monster's back, distracting him long enough for Josie to land that critical ax blow.

As far as Josie was concerned, cowardice and the sacrifices of others had saved her—a realization that made her feel unworthy of life, and that she, least of all, should have survived.

Such thoughts harried her frequently since.

Many had been the time she'd touched a razor to her wrist, unable to make the final motion, except for one occasion; though, in her hesitance, she'd failed even that, managing only to inconvenience her boyfriend at the time—for the last time—and the EMTs who'd helped her.

To Josie's mind, she'd been living like a coward ever since that night, hiding within a drug-induced fog instead of facing what needed to be faced, until now.

"I'm sorry," she said softly to the faces smiling back at her.

Nell stepped up beside her. "This your year?"

Josie nodded, pulling herself from melancholy with a draw on her cigarette. She pointed to a broadly smiling blonde in a pink sweater, the kind of girl who looked like she was the envy of all the other girls and lusted after by all the boys, which that girl was. "That was me. Captain of the cheerleading squad." *Was* felt entirely appropriate, for the giggly girl in the picture looked so different from the Josie of now as to beggar belief; so much so that it pained her almost to tears to look upon her younger self. Gone was the lustrous hair, the flawless skin, the athletic physique. Most notably, gone was the light that made her eyes stand out from all that.

Seeking to redirect her thoughts, Josie indicated the person next to her, an aesthetically fitting mate for the captain of the cheerleading team: a tall, handsome, broad-shouldered, square-jawed jock. "Mike, my boyfriend. We were king and queen of prom. Crazy in love." She shook her head at the thought of what her younger self would have made of her current choice of partner. The words 'horrified' and 'barf' came to mind.

Nell placed a hand on Josie's shoulder. "I'm sorry." She remembered attending Stan's funeral, and the cold reception she received there, to this day feeling all those accusatory eyes. She didn't attend the funerals of her other friends.

"I was a real bitch back then," Josie confessed. "All I cared about was being popular, having the right clothes, the right hair, the right guy . . ." She huffed in ironic amusement of her life now. "You weren't a counselor, right?"

"No." Nell turned again to the pictures. "No, just a dumb kid with her dumb friends, looking for a place to party."

Nell thought to a time when she, much like Josie, was overly concerned with fashion, makeup, and boys. Her youth ended that night, her former self gone with it. She never wore showy makeup again, nor strove to express herself with what she wore. Frivolous things to some, but to her the right makeup and clothes had been transformative, making her feel strong, confident, powerful. Armor and war paint. But in the years since, to stand out was the last thing she'd wanted.

"You couldn't have known," said Josie, bringing Nell back to the moment.

Nell didn't answer, diverting attention instead to the other pictures. "Where are Ana and Cassy?"

"Ana was the eighty-four group, so . . ."

The two of them searched the previous year's picture, studying each cheerful face in turn, though none jumped out as obviously being Ana.

"Um . . ." Nell struggled. "Hard to say."

"Hey, Ana," Josie called.

Ana returned from the adjacent room, stowing her weapon as she approached the pair.

Josie pointed to the picture. "Where are you on this?"

Ana seemed to hesitate and wrestle with embarrassment for a moment before pointing without looking at a mousy, gangly girl, self-consciously hunched in on herself. Her appearance was like the very caricature of an '80s nerd, complete with thick coke-bottle glasses, full-on headgear braces, bad acne, awkward smile—the works.

Nell and Josie leaned in as one, sharing a look of utter disbelief.

"*That's* you?" said Nell, incredulous and inwardly thinking the change with Josie seemed minor compared to Ana's then and now.

Ana frowned. "Why d'you have to say it like that?"

"I-I mean, I'm just . . . It . . . Wow!"

"I'm speechless!" said Josie.

Cassy came up behind and pushed her face between the others to get a look. "Shut up and get out! You look sooo cuuute!" Nell and Josie burst into laughter. "Aww, look at your little piggy tails!"

Ana's unmistakable irritation did little to calm the cackling trio. "Yeah, yeah. And I'm sure you were the picture of cool back then."

Cassy stepped away from the others, no longer as amused.

Nell and Josie's laughter petered out as they too became curious. "Yeah, Cassy," said Josie. "Show us."

"I'm, uh, I'm not in any of these pictures."

"Why not?"

Now it was Cassy's turn to hesitate with embarrassment. "I wasn't a counselor."

"Right," said Nell. "You were in eighty-six too. So then, what?"

With a sigh indicating she knew fighting to be futile, Cassy pulled a picture up on her phone, offering it to Nell though it was snatched by Ana. Nell and Josie gathered around.

It was the same picture Nell had briefly glimpsed at the diner. It showed Cassy and two guys posing on a hooptie of a car between a pair of large trees, dressed like punks straight out of an '80s B-Movie. Cassy herself wore fingerless gloves, a biker jacket, a red bandanna—the same she wore now as a neckerchief, and held a butterfly knife.

Nell seemed unclear about the picture. "So what, you were like, in a punk band or something?"

Cassy jerked her head in confusion. "Punk band? No! I was in a gang."

"A gang?" Nell blurted, the surprise of each of the others' backgrounds doing a real number on her.

"Seriously?" asked Josie.

"We weren't like the mafia or anything, just, I dunno. Thugs, delinquents."

"What did you do in this gang?"

Cassy shrugged. "I dunno. Boost cars, get high, get drunk, get into fights, rob liquor stores, bodegas, maybe Fran's Diner once or five times, try not to get arrested, get arrested. Y'know, gang shit."

Ana turned to Nell and Josie. "And you all thought my change was drastic."

"So I was a little wild in my youth. Who wasn't?"

"Me."

Josie looked again at the picture, then back to Cassy. "You really turned it all around, huh?"

"I was a messed-up kid," Cassy explained. "Bad home, a runaway, that whole story." She pointed to the larger of the two guys in the picture. "I met Cobra and—"

"Hold up!" Nell interjected. "Cobra?"

Josie snorted.

"Wait, what were you called?" asked Ana, the anticipatory smile that melted her usual sternness not going unnoticed by Nell, who found her own smile growing in turn.

Cassy rolled her eyes. "If you must know—"

"Oh, we absolutely must!" Nell stressed.

Cassy looked away as she mumbled something.

"I'm sorry, what?" asked Ana. "I couldn't hear you over your crippling embarrassment."

Cassy let out a frustrated sigh and threw out her arms. "Scorpio."

She was met with silence and three bewildered faces. Then those three faces crumbled with laughter.

Cassy crossed her arms and nodded to Ana. "Can't we go back to laughing at Little Miss Nerdlinger?"

Nell fought through her laughter. "W-wh-why Scorpio?"

At this, Cassy smiled, flicking out one of her butterfly knives. "'Cause I got a—" The knife flew from her hand. She chased after it with a "Shit." Returning, she pocketed the knife rather than risk further embarrassment. "A sting in my tail."

The others calmed themselves. Nell wiped a tear from her eye. "Oh shit. Oh . . . What were you doing here?"

"We were on the run from the cops and needed someplace to hide out. Thought this empty camp would do. Couple hours later . . . Well, we found out it wasn't so empty."

The mood took a steep downturn.

"Bastard came out of nowhere," she continued. "Took out Cobra before me and Diesel even knew what we were looking at." She reclaimed her phone and regarded the picture.

Nell was taken aback as Cassy's face softened, taking on an aspect of melancholy.

"We never even made the news, because who gives a shit about some no good punks, right?" Cassy sighed. "They were more than that to me. They were . . . my family, y'know?"

Two more lives, thought Nell. Two more lives that might have been spared had she ensured Silas's death when she had the chance. Two more lives on top of the nine she already felt the weight of, a weight that crushed her heart.

Josie nodded and looked to her year's picture. "I saw him kill Mike. Ripped his head right off his shoulders with his bare hands."

"My boyfriend, Stan . . ." said Nell. "He was killed here too."

They turned to Ana, who immediately felt the heat of their expectant eyes upon her face.

Truth was, she wasn't close to any of her fellow counselors. Didn't have any real friends back then at all. Definitely no boyfriend. Or girlfriend.

'Lesbi-Ana' is how she was known at high school. She'd been caught staring at one of the other girls in the changing rooms after a Phys. Ed. class, and that was all the kindling the bullies needed.

Perhaps the only reason she'd survived her encounter with Silas was because the others had locked her in a closet as a cruel prank, leaving her there while they played spin the bottle without her on account of not wanting 'dyke AIDS,' taunting her with repeated renditions of *Ana Ana bo bana, she hates the banana, 'cause she's a raging lesbi-Ana!*

When Silas appeared, she could do nothing other than watch in abject terror through the keyhole as he slaughtered the others in a tempest of violence that seemed so personal she questioned whether the monster was a manifestation of her venomous rage, a result of her mistreatment, a thought dashed aside when he smashed open the closet and came at her.

"Yeah, well, that's why we're here. To avenge them and all the others he butchered," Ana said snappishly. "So how about we quit all this memory lane bullshit and act like we have a purpose." She turned and left the cabin, knowing full well she wasn't here to avenge anyone other than herself. She gave no shits for those bullies and felt no guilt over that. She was here *because* of bullies, for what was Silas Crowe if not the ultimate expression of one, he whose reign of torment and terror had weighed on her every thought and action for over three decades? *No more*, she thought as she slammed the cabin door shut behind herself. *No fucking more.*

The others exchanged feel-bad glances, guessing well her past despite her not voicing it.

"She's right," said Nell. She checked her watch: twelve-thirty. Eight hours until sundown. "It's time to put our game faces on."

19

Clem's rocking chair squeaked back and forth on pliant floorboards. "Fuck you, cocksnot!" he said to an unknown other on his cell phone. Lugg's souped-up Charger pulled into his ramshackle place of business with an obnoxious, growling racket. "And drive safe." He ended the call, then slid his phone into a sock as the occupants of the car exited and made toward him, one of whom he recognized.

"Clem!" said Pewson with a misjudged smile, given the disposition of who he was addressing.

"The hell d'you pissants want?"

"Relax, Clem. These, uh, fine gentlemen and I just need fillin' up." His expectant look did nothing to move Clem. "Uh, if you wouldn't mind."

"Something wrong with your hands?"

Despite being the figure of authority here, Pewson shrank from Clem's bare-faced disrespect.

"Scud," said Lugg with a hard eye on Clem. His slushie-slurping lackey did the honor of refueling the car, the blue of his icy drink seeping through the bandages and duct tape over his cheek. Lugg stepped closer to Clem. "You see a group of women pass through here, old man?"

Standing furthermost of the group, Blake signed silent pleas at Clem, mouthing 'Help' and 'Call nine-one-one' while miming a phone call.

Clem scowled confusedly at the man. "Yeah, I seen 'em."

"When?" Lugg demanded.

Clem smirked as he took in Lugg's bruised face. "One of 'em give you those shiners?"

"Flucking shlot me flew vla flace tloo," said Scud in his warped speech. An unhappy look from Lugg silenced additional details.

Lugg took a well-practiced step toward Clem. "I only ask the once, old man."

Clem leaned forward, his unappreciation of Lugg's tone clear from his crotchety countenance. He churned his mouth a moment, then spat a murky wad of saliva, little of which cleared his chin, though the old-timer seemed not to care, maintaining his bold glare as the drool stretched and thinned before breaking off and spattering the leg of his overalls.

Pewson turned away. "Good lord."

"Couple hours ago, maybe," Clem answered. "What's it to you?"

"One's mine," said Lugg.

Clem scoffed. "You oughta keep her on a tighter leash."

"Clem, did they say anything else to you?" asked Pewson.

"I warned 'em. Warned 'em all."

Pewson rolled his eyes. "I know, I know, you warn everybody. Now, did they say anything or not?"

"Them fools've got it in their heads that they're gonna kill him, but you can't kill what won't die."

Lugg looked to be losing the single grain of patience he possessed. "The hell're you talking about?"

Blake tried again to signal Clem, desperation on his face as he exaggerated his previous motions. He ceased instantly and pretended to stretch when he caught Scud looking at him.

"Crowe, you dumb fuck!" answered Clem. "Silas. Crowe."

Blake searched his brain. "That killer on the news?"

Pewson huffed amusedly. "Now c'mon, Clem, we all know that's nothing but a—a big ol' buncha bullpucky."

"Ain't no bullpucky, ya damn fool! I tell ya they never shoulda reopened that hell hole."

Blake stepped forward. "Wait, why would my wife go there?"

"I guess what happened to Josie happened to your woman too," said Lugg.

The answer did nothing to abate Blake's apparent confusion. "What happened?"

The others all turned bewildered expressions on Blake. "She was almost killed by him," said Pewson.

"What? When?"

Lugg shook his head and turned his attention back to Clem. "You seem to know a lot about what's going on, old man."

"I know it all. Just can't get nobody to listen."

"Well, I'm listening, and I say you're coming with us."

"What?" asked Pewson, not sure if he heard right but fearing he had.

"The hell for?" asked Clem.

"'Cause I don't know if all this shit's true or not, but if it is, I want someone who knows about it beside me."

"Ta hell with that!" Clem asserted. "I ain't going no—"

Lugg reached around his back and pulled out a chrome Desert Eagle handgun—as polished and gleaming as his car—and pointed it at Clem.

Pewson started, hands thrust out in an attempt to pacify the situation. "Whoa, now! Wait just a—"

Scud pulled a gun too, waving it between Pewson and Blake, who dropped into a defensive squat with his hands atop his head as he pleaded, "Don't shoot! For the love of God don't shoot me, don't shoo-oot!"

Lugg stepped over to Pewson. "Officer, if you wouldn't mind kindly relinquishing your weapon." A nudge to the lawman's forehead with the barrel of the Eagle hurried the handover of the piece, which Lugg tucked straight into his belt. "Now, what say we all go to camp?"

20

Ana dropped one of the heavy duffle bags beside two others on the floor of the counselors' cabin. Nell, Josie, and Cassy gathered around as she unzipped them. Each held three bear traps, totaling nine.

"You sure you brought enough traps?" Cassy snarked.

"I bought up all they had at the hunting goods store," replied Ana, in all seriousness.

Cassy rolled her eyes. "I was being—"

"A bitch. I know."

"So what's our plan?" asked Josie.

Ana swept a mishmash of party trash off a table, making space for Nell to unfurl a map of the camp that had already been drawn upon with markers indicating where traps would be set, hiding spots, defensive positions, and weapon stashes.

"Okay," said Nell. "Here's how we're gonna do this . . ."

Ana and Josie entered the camp's equipment shed, wherein an array of implements and odds were kept: tools, sporting goods, fishing and diving gear, moldering boxes of miscellanea.

We don't know what direction he's gonna come from, but we do know we can lure him to a specific spot if we make enough noise.

Ana grabbed a sledgehammer and pickax while Josie took a pitchfork and claw hammer. She paused to regard a chainsaw. "This?" she asked Ana.

"Fuck. Yes."

Setting the items in hand aside, Josie hefted the chainsaw. Sunlight reflected off the tool's guide bar and across her eyes as she admired it.

So we'll bait him to the rec hall.

Nell rigged the sledgehammer above the rec hall's entrance to swing down and smash into the face of whoever opened the door.

Hit him as hard as we can from the get-go with either the door trap—

Cassy likewise rigged a trap at the same door with the pickax, this one intended to swing sidelong into the body. Ana watched impatiently as Cassy struggled to set the trap. Annoyance winning out, Ana shooed Cassy away and took over, using Nell, who stood in the doorway, as a measure of how high to position the pickax—crotch-level being Ana's thinking, though Nell proposed the abdomen.

—or the spike pit.

Ana, Josie, and Nell toiled from within the deep, wide hole they dug outside of the rec hall's fire exit, propped enticingly open. Cassy meanwhile stood outside the hole, making showy swipes at the air with her butterfly knives—a child excited to play with her new toys. Peeved, Ana shoveled some dirt over Cassy's Valentinos, much to her shock and outrage.

Nell planted the last of the javelins before the others secured a taut tarp over the hole, then spread loose dirt on top to camouflage the pit.

The Final Women

And if we can't get him at the rec hall . . .

Ana primed the last of nine bear traps in a wide, three-by-three square at the foot of the obstacle course. As with the others, she concealed this one with a covering of dirt.

. . . we'll lure him to the bear trap patch.

Josie placed colored pegs into the ground, marking the corners of the patch.

Still playing with her new knives, Cassy almost stepped right into the patch, until a panicked Josie sprang up and grabbed her a footfall from disaster. Hand on chest, Cassy chuckled at her absent-mindedness.

We'll use the surroundings to our advantage.

Ana squatted atop one of the elevated platforms of the obstacle course, filling condoms with lighter fluid and placing them gently within a washing basket they'd found.

Within the forest, Nell strung a simple perimeter alarm between the trees using hemp twine and some of the many discarded beer bottles littering the grounds.

Josie hid the chainsaw beneath the deck of a nearby cabin.

A miffed Cassy wiped dirt off her Valentinos.

Use whatever we can find.

In the counselors' cabin, the four of them each placed a weapon upon the table: Nell a flare gun and flares, Josie the pitchfork and claw hammer, Ana a bow and quiver of arrows, Cassy a Nerf gun. Ana immediately removed Cassy's contribution, replacing it with an aluminum Louisville Slugger.

The four of them tested their ability with bows at the archery range. Ana hit her target an inch left of center. Nell caught the edge of her target. Cassy bungled the shot altogether, her arrow tangling in her bowstring.

Most important, we need to get our heads straight.

Josie took a steadying breath, focused, lined up her shot, and loosed. Bullseye. She blushed as the others celebrated her skill in making such an impressive shot.

Tonight's been over thirty years in the making.

Inside the rec hall, Nell zipped her running top over the armored vest given to her by Ana.

Ana slid her armored vest over a black sports bra.

Tonight, we put it right.

Josie secured her vest over her pink hoodie.

Cassy slid her old biker jacket over her vest, pulling the sleeves up her forearms.

No more running.

Josie tied her hair back into a tight bun.

Nell applied her war paint, starting with electric blue eye shadow.

No more hiding.

Cassy pulled on fingerless gloves.

Nell applied thick black eyeliner.

We're here to hunt.

Ana holstered a pistol at her hip.

Nell applied pink blush.

To fight.

Ana slid her self-forged sword into the sheath strapped to her hip, then a tactical knife into her boot sheath.

Tonight, we put an end to this monster.

Nell applied candy red lipstick and pressed her lips together. Her old confidence returned.

Once and for all.

Josie slung a quiver of arrows across her back. Tested the tensile strength of her bowstring.

Whatever it takes.

Cassy tied her red kerchief around her head, no longer concerned with using the cloth to hide the horrid scar running across her throat.

Whatever the cost.

Nell double-knotted her shoelaces.

Ana tightened the hand wrap on one hand, then punched it into the wrapped other.

Silas Crowe dies tonight.

Finally, Cassy pulled a pair of leg warmers over the shins of her florid workout leggings. Then, off of the others' puzzled looks, asked, "What? It's nippy."

21

A void.

Grave-cold. Grave-dark.

The air thick with the cloying tang of decay. The rot-sodden earth aquiver with excitement. Ever the first inkling.

Then came the aroused throbs of entangling roots. Caressing, groping, urging, demanding.

The crescendoing lust of windborne coos confirmed that which the deathly forest whispered.

There would be blood.

Much blood.

When? asked Silas to the void.

And the void said, *Now* . . .

Silas sprang from the dark with grasping hands.

22

Lugg's Charger rumbled to a sissing stop, the eyes of all four occupants on the road ahead.

A logging truck had jackknifed, spilling its load across all lanes.

In the passenger seat, Pewson tutted and shook his head disapprovingly. "Stuff like this is always happening on these roads. People driving like bats outta heck just 'cause it's quiet."

"Aren't you gonna do something?" asked Lugg.

"Me? No, best to wait for the authorities to come sort all this out." He sank farther into his seat.

Lugg regarded Pewson like the idiot he did little to disprove himself of being. "You're the sheriff, dumbass."

"Oh," said Pewson. "Uh, yeah, right. I should, uh—"

"Hurry the fuck up!"

Pewson exited. "Right."

A bang came from the trunk. "Lemme outta here, you rotten sons a fucks!" came Clem's muffled voice.

Blake was the only one to acknowledge him. "Um, he's not gonna suffocate, is he?"

Neither Lugg nor Scud cared to answer.

23

Kindling popped and crackled with each lick of flame, the modest campfire—normally a soothing spectacle—doing little to dispel the mounting anxiety of the battle to come. The absolute stillness of the forest amplified the tension.

The women sat silently on encircling stumps, nervously scanning the deep dark of that surrounding woodland, hypervigilant and primed to act at the slightest suggestion of their foe's approach.

Their minds wrestled with the apprehension and absurdity of where they were and what they must do, simultaneously eager and afraid.

Was he out there? Was he watching them? Were they fools? Had they come here only to give themselves freely to the monster? To die by his hands, as their friends and so many others had?

Cassy took a shaky swig from her hip flask in the hope of tempering her nerves, but actually being here, waiting to face him—or whoever this was, as she was always quick to add—nullified the alcohol's normally remedying effect.

She couldn't stand the silence. Silence was an open door for thoughts and memories, the kind that brandish knives. Distraction, that's what she'd thrown herself into after the incident, but those wild days were long behind her. The combination of marriage, motherhood, and the pressure to maintain appearances had necessitated the abandoning of those old diversions.

Her affluent lifestyle afforded many alternatives, though, be it her outrageous spending sprees, the participation in and spectating of the trivial and sordid dramas of her neighbors, or just having the freedom to do whatever and go wherever she pleased without answering to anyone. Mostly, though, it was her kids she threw herself into. Too hard.

With them both gone, and absent of those other entertainments or the normally dulling influence of booze, her mind was forced to engage with the very thing she'd spent the last thirty years actively not engaging with.

She proffered the flask to the others, though none were inclined. "Yeah . . ." She put it away. "Guess we should stay sharp, huh?"

The tense silence returned, the atmosphere pregnant with their collective disquietude.

For Nell, the scene came with a potent sense of déjà vu. Of sitting around with her friends. Of those halcyon days before the world bared its fangs, taking a bite that had ripped away over half her life so far. All their lives.

Back then, Nell and her friends were eager and anxious for the possibilities laying ahead of them. Now she was here again, not looking forward with giddy nerves, but backward with pain, commingled with the weight of time gone, time wasted, time unlived. As for the future, she couldn't think of a single thing to look forward to, only more time spent looking back, living in worn out memories until she gradually faded from existence.

Desperate for a release of this crushing tension, Cassy spoke. "I can't believe we're really here. Really doing this." The statement got no reaction from Ana, unwavering in her vigil. Josie gave a nod, while Nell remained deep in gloom.

Pulling back, Nell said, "I wanna thank you all for coming. I'm not sure if I—No, I know for a fact I wouldn't have come here alone." It was Nell's turn to get a solemn response from the others.

"I wonder what it'll be like," said Josie. "After, I mean." Then, with a pessimistic bent, "If we get an after."

"Shit, I hope so," said Cassy. "I figure we're all long overdue one of those happy ever afters."

"It won't change what happened," said Nell. "Won't erase what was done. But maybe . . . maybe . . ." She struggled to reach the other side of that maybe.

"Maybe it'll bring back some of the light we lost," said Ana, maintaining her attentive surveillance. "Just enough to get us out of the dark. Maybe find the people we're supposed to be without all this."

Josie nodded, allowing a smidgen of hope for a better tomorrow to creep in, one in which Silas Crowe, Lugg, and all the other bullshit that seemed to hold her fixed in this dismal and unending period of time and space were no longer there. That's why she'd come, she reminded herself. Not to face death, but to face life. To reclaim it. By any means necessary.

Nell's thoughts lingered on that last part of Ana's words too. Who was she besides a survivor of Silas Crowe? Her identity, her career even, felt so entangled with the label that she honestly couldn't say anymore. Perhaps finding the answer was one thing to actually look ahead to; one more reason to see this through.

She then found her thoughts taking a decidedly bleaker track, asking herself the questions: *What if none of this makes a difference? Even if we do kill him, what if nothing changes for us at all?* She decided not to voice such thoughts, responsible as she felt for maintaining morale.

Cassy thought about the path her life had taken. It was a cushy one, no doubt there, though deep down she knew the rich life wasn't really her. Being away from all that, on the road with what felt an awful lot like a gang, had caused some of the false veneer to flake away, allowing more of her old, true self to surface. She'd broken two nails during all the trap setting and was mostly fine with that. She stank too, having forgotten to pack deodorant—this she was a little less fine with. Overall, though, she liked the change and hoped it stuck around once this was done.

The thought was spoiled by the realization of what she'd be returning to: a near thirty-year loveless marriage, and kids who . . .

She shook the thought off. Searching for some lighter avenue, Cassy remembered the brown paper bag beside her. "Sandwiches!" She lifted and shook the bag. "Anybody?"

Nos all around.

Cassy shrugged. "Suit yourselves. Making all those death traps has given me an appetite." She removed and unwrapped a crustless triangle, taking an eager bite of the cucumber and mayo sandwich. Hunger meant she took the first mouthful down without much fare. She raised her sandwich and smiled at the others. "It's—" She interrupted herself with a second greedy bite, and it was on this slower-worked morsel that her expression soured with each successive chew. She spat aside the masticated mush. "Ugh . . ." A swig and a swirl from her hip flask were employed to burn off the taste. "Bleurgh! I've eaten ass that tasted better than this."

Josie burst out with laughter, while Nell practically gasped at the disclosure. Even Ana failed to stifle a bark of amusement.

"What?" chuckled Cassy, succumbing to the group's mounting hysterics.

The four laughed, full and unrestrained. Knees were slapped, bellies were held, tears were wiped. And perhaps they all laughed a little too hard.

The tension in Nell's body slackened at this cheery turn, foolish though it seemed in light of what was coming; still, she felt a degree of warmth and comfort at this moment that she hadn't known in forever.

In the company of these other women, whom she'd unknowingly been living in parallel to in many ways, Nell felt a sense of security, of belonging, of newfound strength and courage.

A sisterhood.

The laughter wound down, leaving the group with smiling faces and buoyed spirits.

Not wanting the oppressive silence to return, Cassy asked, "So, any of you married?"

Josie widened amused eyes and shook a definite no.

"Nah," said Nell.

Ana raised an eyebrow. "You really need to ask?"

"Really?" asked Cassy. "None of you? Wow. Partners? Dating?"

Josie shook another wry no.

"I gave the whole internet thing a try a little while back," said Nell, "but it didn't lead to anything. And just recent—get this shit—I started getting emails to join Silver and Single. Fucking silver! That's what we are now, apparently!"

Cassy touched up her hair. "Not so long as L'Oréal keeps selling their Liquorice Black Casting Crème Gloss."

The others chuckled.

"No, but, uh, I guess . . ." Nell began. "I guess I've been too afraid to get close to anyone. Straight-up avoid it, in fact. Then when I try, it's just . . . It's hard, y'know?"

Josie nodded, knowing all too well what she meant. "I was too afraid to be alone. That's how I wound up with Lugg, and all the Luggs before him." Saying those words aloud brought home just how much she'd let fear shape her life.

She'd only had one decent relationship in all these years—Clayton, a fellow patient at the psych ward where she'd been committed soon after the incident on account of her frequent self-harming and severe panic attacks. He was a gentle, sensitive soul who listened rather than advised, and who introduced her to new music and experiences, drugs chief among them. He died from an overdose five months into their relationship, and Josie, dejected and lost, found herself shacked up with their scumbag dealer. Such was the cut of the men thereafter, leading to her present situation with Lugg.

Josie instinctively sought for Lugg's positive traits, but quickly came up empty, realizing that reflex was her mind's way of tricking her into seeing light when in truth there was only the complete absence of it.

Lugg never hit her—though the threat had been ever-present—but he was shitty, constantly wearing down her sense of self-worth. He knew he could get away with it too, because who else would take her? No one, he'd repeatedly tell her, until his words became hard facts to Josie's mind. And she couldn't be alone. She just couldn't. If nothing else, the bastard's possessive nature kept her safe, insomuch as a caged bird is safe. She hated him. And she hated that she needed him. Until now. Though, having come to that realization, Josie knew Lugg wouldn't make leaving him easy, would make it a nightmare in fact, one she might never escape. One more on top of the nightmare she was already living.

Putting aside such worries for now, Josie joined the others in turning to Ana, who shifted with the unease of the coming admission, of the lowering of her stout defenses; but given the very real prospect of not surviving the night, she felt the near-desperate need to reveal something of herself to someone, to simply be known.

Ana looked up at the others, each of them looking back patiently. "I was . . ." She turned her eye down to the fire, struggling against her nature to remain locked up. "I was afraid of . . . well, everything." She kept her eye on those writhing flames. "That's why all the self-defense and weapons training, security fences, barred windows, *mean*-ass dogs, all of it . . ." She dared a glance up, certain she'd overshared. She was relieved to find sympathetic nods and smiles rather than the ridicule she'd always convinced herself would be there.

Nell put a comforting hand on her shoulder.

Ana smiled, relishing the moment. It felt nice to be touched by a tender and well-meaning hand. More so, it felt nice to belong, even under these circumstances.

For Ana—and she didn't doubt for the others too—life since that night had seemed unendingly cold, perpetually unsafe, and unbearably lonely, some days to a debilitating degree, like she was locked inside herself and clawing to escape. She figured that was why she let Nell into her home that day. Why she agreed to join forces in this endeavor, despite part of her chastising herself for needing anyone but herself.

The terrifyingly abrupt way her life had gone from being one thing to something completely other—day to endless night in a blink—left her convinced that the world was a wholly dark and dangerous place that was constantly trying to trick her with sunshine and smiles; deceptions not to be trusted.

She'd always thought this justified paranoia, this necessary state of being on constant red alert, this self-imposed exile, kept her alive. Here, now, she realized it had in truth only kept her from living.

She felt a sudden flush of emotion behind her eye and a burgeoning lump in her throat, though quickly swallowed it down as she adjusted her seating.

Sensing Ana's discomfort, Cassy moved on to a different subject. "Any of you got kids?"

Nell shook her head. "Nope."

"I hate kids," said Ana, thankful for the distracting question.

"Oh, you hate everything," said Cassy, getting a laugh from the others, Ana included.

Attention went to Josie, who looked hesitant to answer. After a moment's consideration, she stood, lowering the top of her pants enough to show her lower abdomen and the deep, vicious scar it bore.

Cassy sucked air through her teeth at the sight.

Ana shook her head.

"Silas," Nell knew.

Josie nodded. "Cut right into my uterus. Gave me this limp. Doctors said I was lucky to survive, but yeah, he took at least one other life that night, though I'd always had my heart set on having two."

Ana paid Nell's earlier kindness forward, placing a comforting hand on Josie's shoulder. Josie smiled softly and touched back.

The somberness deepened.

Cassy thought of her kids, the two of them settled and about to start their own families with committed long-term partners—a turn of events Cassy found weird given what they'd had as an example growing up. But maybe it was because of her and Blake's poor relationship that their kids were so determined to get it right.

Cassy sighed over the empty, lonely years since they'd left home. "I haven't seen my kids in a few years," she admitted. "Haven't spoken to them in two, though not for lack of trying."

The others gave their full attention.

"I know I like to project like I've been doing just fine. Like what happened at this camp didn't affect me and I'm not afraid and all that. And I'm not . . . Or"—she shook her head—"I didn't used to be . . . Never cared enough about myself to be afraid of anything, but . . ." That "but" hung for a long moment amid the crackling camp.

"When I was way younger and *waaay* dumber, I used to think that if I ever had kids that I'd be this badass mom, y'know, like Cher in that movie. What's it called? The one where Sam Elliott gives mustache rides or whatever . . . Anyway, I pictured myself taking them to biker bars and riding Harleys with them in a baby carrier. But that's not how it was at all . . .

"When my kids were born—" Cassy straightened as she flapped her hands at her eyes. "Damn, you're gonna make me ugly cry!" The others chuckled, a momentary lightening of gravity. Cassy shook herself and continued. "When my kids were born, and the nurses took them away for examinations, I freaked the fuck out. Like, they had to sedate me, because who the hell was this person taking my babies away? They could be some baby-napping, baby-eating psycho for all I knew . . . Scariest moment of my entire life." Her gaze drifted forward a few years. "I remember their first day of kindergarten, I dropped them off, then stayed in the car out front. Just sat there and kept watch the entire time. And I kept on keeping watch, even when they were in elementary and into high school. Did it until the teachers and other parents started to notice and called the cops on me, at which point I just got a new car and parked a little farther away.

"I wouldn't let them go to slumber parties. The other kids always had to come to our place." She shook her head. "They hated me for that. But that's who I was, all through their childhood and teen years. Not the badass mom. The scared mom. Still am, even though they're both grown-ass adults.

"They left home as soon as they could, and they ignore my calls now because they know I'm contagious—don't want me infecting their kids' minds like I did theirs." Her gaze was lost in the campfire's flames, glistening tears threatening to fall. "I spend whole days sometimes in their old rooms—looking the same as the day they left. Just sitting there, alone, drowning in a river of tears and Long Island iced teas, thinking about how bad I screwed up."

She pulled her watery eyes away from the fire. "I shouldn't have been a mom, y'know? I was never that person. I couldn't care for a goldfish, and now all of a sudden I've got a baby in each arm, and what the fuck am I supposed to do? I didn't grow up with love and affection and kisses goodnight and packed lunches and 'Mom, can you help me with this math problem,' 'Mom, I scraped my knee,' 'Mom, I love you,' 'Mom, I hate you, 'Mom, I'm scared and need you to chase away the monsters.'" Cassy wiped at her eyes with a frustrated sigh. The others too looked affected by her story. "But when I first held those cute little shits, I knew . . . knew I was gonna have to break and remake myself into the kind of person who would and could do those things. Who would and could chase away the monsters, no matter how big or scary . . . but I fucked up." Her shoulders dropped in acceptance of an unspoken truth. "They needed a strong mother, and I wasn't that, and it kills me that I wasn't. I wanna be . . . But I can't chase away monsters while still running from this one." She took in and blew out a breath to regain composure. "Any of that make a lick of sense, or am I just a shitty mom?"

Nell and Josie comforted Cassy. "Makes perfect sense," Nell assured.

Silence hung.

Ana broke it. "Cher, huh?"

Cassy smiled and wiped again at her eyes. "I mean, I have the leathers."

"What is she, like a hundred now?" asked Nell.

"And still with a better ass than any of us," said Josie.

"Speak for yourself," said Ana.

"Same!" said Cassy. "I paid a lot of my husband's money for this ass."

The group chuckled.

Josie nodded to the scar across Cassy's throat. "You never thought about doing something with that?"

"Oh . . ." Cassy ran her fingers across it. "I guess not."

"It's a damn miracle you survived a wound like that," said Ana.

Cassy pulled her hand away. "A ball hair deeper and I'd have been a goner for sure."

"Hard to beat that, but . . ." Nell unzipped her running top and uncovered her shoulder to show the old stab wound there.

"Please," said Ana. "That's a hickey compared to this." Ana lifted off her armored vest, showing the others the extent of the burn scarring on her back—a landscape of uneven tissue, raised and thicker here, indented and taut there. "Happened when I fought that fucker in a burning cabin."

"Fuck," said Cassy.

"Then this . . ." Ana lifted her eyepatch, giving them all a look at the sunken flesh beneath. "Gouged right out of my head."

Nell squirmed. "Oh, nasty."

"Girl, if you want nasty, I'll drop my pants and show you my hemorrhoids," said Cassy.

The others laughed.

"Looks like I got away pretty unscathed compared to you guys," said Nell.

"He still got you, though," said Josie somberly. "Got all of us."

The mood darkened again. The mournful truth of Josie's words were undeniable to all, that the entire course of their lives had been so drastically altered—dictated by the trauma Silas Crowe had inflicted, denying them of the people they might have otherwise been, of the lives they might have otherwise led.

It was a truth that struck Ana in particular. So consumed had she been with her own vengeance quest, she hadn't considered till now just how much the others needed this too.

Nell stood up with a "Fuck that!" jerking the others from their melancholic musings. "Our minds, our bodies, our lives, this bastard doesn't get to own those! Those are ours!" The others nodded in silent agreement. "Those are fucking ours!" she repeated, this time with a force that inspired more assured agreement from the others.

"That's right!" Ana rose beside Nell. "This shit stain's eclipsed our lives for too fucking long! No more! I'm done with it! Straight-up won't allow it!"

"We're not broken!" said Josie, also standing. "We're not prey! We're not meat for him and every other wannabe big bad wolf to chew up and spit out!"

Cassy jumped up, giddy with excitement. "Right!"

"We coulda stayed behind our locked doors," said Nell, "spent the rest of our lives worrying, waiting, but we didn't!"

A unified "No!" from the others.

"We tooled the fuck up! Came back with knives of our own! Came back to rip and tear and chop and smash this motherfucker to pieces!"

"Yeah!" said Josie, feeling more certain and more confident in their purpose here since she'd left her home.

Cassy gave a double clap of her hands. "I feel so pumped right now!"

"Together we're strong!" said Nell.

The others cheered.

"Together we're fierce!" said Ana.

The others cheered.

"Together we're un-fucking-breakable!" said Josie.

The others cheered.

"Together there's nothing we can't—" A cawing crow swooped low, almost hitting a screaming Cassy in the face. "Save me, bitches!" With a panicked flourish of her arms, Cassy tripped over the stump at her feet, falling hard on her ass. "Ow, fuck!"

The crow cawed again as it disappeared into the darksome forest.

The others burst into unrestrained laughter.

Cassy looked far less amused as Nell helped her up. "Oh, ha ha."

The distant clinking of glass iced through the burgeoning mirth and swelling courage, disarming the four with severe immediacy.

Fear took a firm hold of Josie as she recognized the sound of the perimeter alarm. "He's here!"

Cassy moved closer to the others. "Oh God!"

Ana tore out her pistol and moved toward the sound, though an outstretched hand from Nell caught her short. "Ana, no."

Ana threw her off and continued undeterred.

"We have to stick to the plan!" Nell pleaded. "Please."

Ana stopped, staring for an unyielding moment into the dark forest, then turning on Nell with anger so profound she seemed close to tears; but the sincere gravity of Nell's words checked the impulse to attack head-on.

Relieved but quick to refocus, Nell looked between Ana and Cassy. "Positions."

"Oh God, okay, oh shit!" Cassy ran for the rec hall while Ana headed for the obstacle course.

Josie backed away from Nell, trembling and afraid despite the bolstering pep talk mere moments ago. "We've gotta run. W-we've gotta—"

Nell grabbed her. "Josie."

"H-he's coming and he's gonna ki—"

"Josie!" Nell reclaimed her attention. "We can't do this without you. Are you with us?"

Josie fixed Nell with wide, fearful eyes and squeezed back at her arms with a terror-stricken grip, but found herself nodding despite it all, because she did want to be with them—needed to be.

"Okay." Nell gave Josie's shoulders a reassuring squeeze, though her next words were as much for her own benefit. "Now, let's do what we came here to do."

24

Silas's breaths came in gurgled wheezes as he stalked heavy-footed toward the camp, roused by the activity of interlopers into his domain, guided by teases of orange between night-blackened boughs, spurred by restless crows greedy for the carrion he would provide, and compelled further by urges and voices that were not his own. A malformed marionette at the whim of a veiled puppeteer.

What little mind Silas possessed struggled through tallow-thick fog for some measure of meaning and understanding of this uncertain existence, asking those same questions he always asked. *Where?*

Back came the answers, like sinister secrets from a seashell. *Here.*

When?
Now.
Who?
All.
Why?

There was no answer.

Silas hastened his step.

25

Cassy turned on the rec hall's audio system. broadcasting Public Image Ltd's "The Order of Death", John Lydon repeating the album title *This Is What You Want . . . This Is What You Get* as a sneering mantra. Nell flicked on the disco lights—the multicolored beams striking off the same mirror ball from thirty years ago. As those lights played once again across her face, Nell felt an aching echo of the past, of watching Stan dancing like a fool in the middle of this very hall.

Silas saw the colorful lights emanating from the rec hall windows—the rainbow rays tracing brazenly across the campground and up to the nighted firmament as the exterior speakers aired the song's doomy sonics.

Ana moved low along an elevated walkway of the obstacle course to take up her position. Josie crouched upon a platform nearby, bow and arrow in white-knuckled hands, eyes wide and bright, scared to the brink of stupefaction as the shadow belonging to the scourge from her nightmares—ominously elongated by the full moon above—preceded his appearance from the stygian forest.

The darkness unleashed its monster, head aslant against his humped shoulder, a length of razor-edged moonlight in hand, the purpose in his rapid approach explicit.

Josie clenched her eyes tight, too afraid to look, to see the truth. Fighting against her shaking body, she forced her eyes open, and the truth stole her breath.

There he was. There the son of a bitch was. Entirely unchanged from the image in Ana's mind. Her body trembled. She convinced herself it was from anger, that her every muscle was screaming for her to leap down atop him, to stab and stab and stab until she'd bled every drop of life from his body. Her fists hurt from over-clenching her pistol—from anger, she once more asserted.

Watching through a slatted rec hall window under the kaleidoscopic colors of the disco lights, Nell felt her stomach drop and heart falter at Silas's appearance. The sight sent her back in time, to when he appeared from the side of the rec hall after having killed Stan. The shock and awe she felt now were the same. The intrusive thoughts were a ceaseless klaxon in her mind: *You're going to die! You're all going to die! Silas Crowe is going to kill you! You're all going to die!*

Cassy stepped up beside Nell, aluminum bat gripped tight. "Oh my God . . ." Her mind still endeavored to reject the sight, a final burst of desperate denial; but as the killer drew closer, all doubt and skepticism fled, along with the color from her face. It was him. Not a copycat. Not a prank. "It's him . . . It's really, really him." She felt a phantom chill across her throat, caused by the mere visual of that hideous, glinting weapon he held—scarred and stained by the taking of countless lives.

Silas closed the distance on the rec hall, climbing the stairs to the deck one pounding footfall at a time.

A single crow alighted before the entrance, blocking Silas's path. The swollen-headed juggernaut stopped before the crow as it pecked at the deck, and before the crow he remained, still as a statue.

The moment stretched. The tension unbearable.

None of the women could take their unblinking eyes off the frightful figure, desperate for him to take that remaining step through the booby-trapped entrance, which would land them a devastating opening hit.

"What's he doing?" Cassy whispered.

Nell shook her head.

Silas backed away from the entrance.

"Shit!" said Josie, observing from her elevated position as Silas retreated down the steps.

"Shit!" said Ana as Silas moved instead around the right side of the rec hall.

"Shit!" said Nell as Silas disappeared from her view.

"Shit?" asked an alarmed Cassy. "Why shit? Bad shit? No—No shit!"

"He must know something's up," answered Nell.

"Only other way in's through the fire exit."

"Right. So the spike pit'll get—"

Silas entered with the sound of a TNT blast, turning a boarded window into a door, and without a halt in his step, came stomping toward the pair with single-minded purpose.

"Shit!" bleated Cassy.

"Go!"

Cassy scrambled out of the nearest window, though Nell did not have time to do likewise, for Silas was on her. She ducked an air-shearing swing that would have torn her head from her shoulders and ran for the hall's rear windows.

Silas turned and launched his knife at her back, missing his target but hitting the frame of the window Nell was aiming for. The sudden shock sent Nell through the nearby kitchen doors instead.

She shut and locked the doors behind herself.

Silas threw the nailed fist of his longer arm at the audio equipment as he made to pursue, silencing the '80s.

Ana watched as Cassy came racing from the rec hall. "What happened?"

"Where's Nell?" asked Josie.

Cassy spun to the rec hall, thinking Nell had followed her out. She groaned in frustration at the realization that she'd have to go back in to help her.

Silas ripped his weapon from the window frame with a blast of splinters.

Moving in a stealthy crouch, Nell hid behind a long, stainless steel countertop littered with various pots and utensils.

The kitchen doors gave all the resistance of cardboard as Silas pounded them open. He stood a moment in the doorway like a specter of grim tidings, head resting on his humped shoulder as he reached out with some sixth sense.

Nell eased her pistol free from its holster, her actions slow and quiet as her breaths.

Silas bent himself to enter, his footsteps heavy on the red-tiled floor. Jerking his heavy head upright, he scored the countertop with the point of his barbaric murder tool as he went, the screech eroding Nell's bravery as it pierced through her skull.

Silas rounded the side of the counter, fully expecting to find his prey cowering and pleading, as they always did when he discovered them.

She wasn't there.

Nell sprang up from the other side of the counter, snapping her pistol at Silas's head for a point-blank shot.

Reacting with a swiftness that belied his hulking appearance, Silas knocked the pistol out of Nell's hand as it fired wide. She brought her knife to bear, but that too was swatted away. With the monstrous strength of a single arm, he seized her by the throat and slammed her onto the counter before dragging her across it, utensils clattering in the flailing struggle.

Fuck, he's got me! He's fucking got me! Nell's hands groped and slapped at the counter in a panicked bid to grasp a weapon. Her windpipe strained under his crushing grip, temples throbbing and eyes bugging with asphyxiation. Darkness closed on her vision. Fear rushed in. She'd failed. Now she was going to die. Vengeance had been dashed aside like a foolishly absurd notion; vengeance for her, and all those other stolen lives she shouldered the burden of. She was stupid to think this night would go any other way, and now she was going to die.

The shadow of Silas's blade passed over her choked face as it ascended, primed to slam down through her skull.

Nell's raking fingers scratched across metal. *I'm going to die!* Her hand found a carving fork. She shanked it through Silas's forearm. The monster made a terse yet horrid squeal as he dropped his weapon and released her.

Freed, Nell scrambled away.

A rough hand caught her two steps into her flight, followed quick by something cold biting into her lower back.

He got me . . .

The others arrived in the kitchen doorway to the harrowing sight of Silas lifting Nell off the floor by the impaling fork, moonlight through the windows behind them backlighting the shocking tableau.

"Nell!" Cassy yelled.

Silas turned, giving the others a clear view of their expiring sister-in-arms as blood poured from the fork to the floor, searing the image of her murder forever in their minds.

Josie put her hands to her mouth.

Ana bared her teeth in rage.

Cassy stared slack-jawed.

With a step and a turn, Silas smashed Nell through a closed window, her body crashing outside in a shower of glass and splintered wood, atop which she sprawled motionless, the fork protruding from her back.

Reality seemed to slow as Josie watched Silas turn toward them. Toward her.

She noted Ana moving in her periphery, running at Silas, screaming fury, though she sounded distant, an echo from another plane. The most distinct sounds to Josie were those of her tremulous breaths and the rush of blood in her ears.

She blinked, and in that instant, Silas had torn the pot rack suspended above the counter from its holdings. She blinked again, and Ana was sprawled beneath the flung rack, the clamorous crash of those pots and pans little more than a succession of softly tinkling bells to Josie's benumbed senses.

She felt a gust at her side, and without averting her gaze, knew that Cassy had deserted.

A small voice inside begged her to do likewise, but her feet were heavy, scraping backward with no sense of urgency despite the big-headed boogeyman closing on her with earthquaking steps.

A firm touch from the rear wall denied any further retreat. She slid down until the floor halted her in kind.

Silas's shadow chilled her to the bone as it crept over her. Drowned her. He loomed large, taking up the whole of her vision as if he were existence absolute.

Gone was the valor and grit fostered at the campfire with her fearless allies. Josie was no longer a determined slayer of an undying killer. Having seen who she considered to be their leader and the most capable member both taken out in a matter of seconds, she was little better than a child—trembling and tearful, incapable of action, flayed by fear, and helpless before this bringer of death.

Helpless, and alone.

26

This. This was the moment Josie had been living in constant dread of for the past thirty years; to once again be at the mercy of this nightmare man. And though the tears fell unbidden down her cheeks, she did not sob, nor plead or beg or even attempt escape. Instead, it was an odd calmness that took hold, an acceptance of fate and futility. The delayed kill stroke that had been chasing her since that night, gaining ground year-by-year, had finally caught up, and there was nothing to be done about it, so why fight? Why run? Why weep?

There. Silas lifted his crudely forged knife, and in a moment it would fall, bringing what Josie hoped would be but an instant of jarring pain, and then peace—from fear, from guilt, from the train wreck of a life she'd led.

Let it land, she thought. Let the final darkness fall.

Josie shut her eyes.

Reality made an abrupt return with two barking flashes from behind her eyelids. She reopened them.

Silas was down with a corresponding number of smoking holes in the side of his head, where Josie approximated his cheek might be beneath that thorny covering.

Ana hurried painfully over, gun in hand, pulling Josie to her feet. "Come on!" It took a second jolt to tear Josie from her stupor. "Josie!"

Josie resisted. "But Nell—"

"She's gone!" Ana pushed Josie out of the kitchen ahead of her.

Stirred by the chill of their swift passing, Silas's fingers began to move, tapping filthy, broken fingernails on the red-tiled floor.

Cassy ran for a nearby cabin and turned around one of its sides, falling back against the logs to catch her hasty breaths and steady her racing thoughts.

Nell and Ana.

Were they dead? She didn't doubt it in Nell's case, but Ana might have survived. *Might have . . . Josie . . . Oh fuck, Josie!* She'd abandoned her without a second's hesitation, fear and panic dashing any assumption of camaraderie built between the two. The moment she'd stood facing Silas, her mind and body focused solely upon survival; her own.

Josie was likely dead, or in the gruesome process of dying. Could she have saved her? She could have dragged her along at least, maybe fired at Silas to give them a chance.

A sound.

Cassy peered around the cabin to see Ana and Josie both limping from the rec hall. *They're alive!*

The two of them headed straight for one of the other cabins, mounting its stairs and shutting the door behind themselves.

Cassy thought to signal them, but quickly shrank back when Silas appeared from out of the rec hall a moment later, stopping between it and the other cabins as if contemplating which to pillage.

Ana and Josie crouched beneath windows on either side of the cabin door. "Oh my God," said Josie, eyes panicked. "He k-killed Nell . . . He—"

Ana shushed her, then chanced a tentative look over the window frame.

Silas stood like a hideous statue, every swell, striation, and depression of his sinewy physique etched by pale moonlight.

"He killed Nell and now he's gonna—"

"Josie!" Ana whispered harshly, but effectively, for Josie turned to her, looking chastened and afraid. "He's gonna die for what he did. I swear he will. But right now I need you to focus." And focus did not come without difficulty for Ana herself, for her body screamed in several pained places. But pain would have to wait.

Nell, the glue that had kept their group together, was dead. And the moment she died, the rest of them had fallen apart. Cassy had split, and Josie was now the burden Ana feared she would become.

Josie shook her disbelieving head. "A-and Cassy—"

"Is gone," said Ana as she verified the remaining rounds in her mag before slapping it home and performing a chamber check. "Fucking left us. Coward."

For a second Josie thought she was addressing her, the sound of that word delivered with Ana's caustic inflection stinging her deep. She looked away.

It wasn't supposed to be like this. They had a plan. They had a right. After decades of misery, they were owed justice. It wasn't supposed to be like this.

"No one's coming to save us, Josie." Ana racked the slide on her pistol. "You and me, that's all there is."

Cassy watched as a trio of corvids circled and cawed above the cabin Ana and Josie were in. Silas headed straight for that cabin. "No-no-no! Shit!"

Ana took another peek over the lip of the window, immediately dropping down and readying her pistol in response to the sight she beheld. "He's coming."

A shaky Josie took her pistol out too.

Silas stomped up the steps to the cabin door, each footfall a deathly countdown.

Josie felt her airway tighten as if Silas's hand was already at her throat. She gulped the feeling down and pressed the barrel of the gun to the underside of her chin.

The shadows of Silas's feet cut the strip of light beneath the door.

"I'm not gonna let him get me." Josie's finger pressed on the trigger.

Ana turned to Josie, alarm gaping her eye. She reached across. "Jo—"

BANG!

"Hey!" sounded Cassy's voice from outside, followed by a second attention-grabbing shot.

Silas turned to see Cassy standing out in the open, aluminum bat in one hand, pistol pointed skyward in the other, looking like a deer in the headlights of his attention.

She expelled a "Shit" before mustering herself again. "Come get me, you peckerless fuck!"

Silas all too eagerly obliged.

Cassy turned and ran with a second hasty "Shit!"

Ana held out a hand. "Josie."

Josie kept the gun to her chin.

"Josie, snap out of it."

Josie shut her eyes tight, releasing the tears held within them.

Ana exhaled in frustration. On top of everything else, the last thing she needed to be feeling right now was awkward. Part of her hated herself for feeling so, but truth was she wasn't good at these kinds of moments, these emotions—either expressing her own or dealing with those of others. The walls she'd built around herself didn't allow for them. She knew she had to say something, though. Cassy needed them.

"Josie, I'm not Nell. I'm not good at speeches and pep talks, and even if I was, we don't have time. Cassy doesn't have time. She needs our help. And I need your help to help her."

The gun slumped to Josie's lap.

A weight fell from Ana's shoulders. "We've still got a shot here," she stressed. "We have to take it. For Nell."

Josie took a quivering breath to calm herself.

Ana stood. "I . . ." The coming words resisted her, because seeing now what the return of Silas really meant, what he'd done to Nell, then herself in a matter of moments, made them true. "I can't do it alone . . . So please"—she held out her hand—"stand the fuck up with me, and let's go kill this son of a bitch."

Josie wiped her eyes, turned them up to Ana, took her hand firmly in her own.

And stood the fuck up.

27

"Fuck, I'm dead!" said Cassy as she ran from Silas. "I'm so fucking dead!" She skidded to a halt, looking between the spike pit on one side and the bear trap patch on the other. "Gotta trap him!" Spotting Ana and Josie dashing for the obstacle course beside the bear traps made the decision for her. "Over here, you scrote!" she yelled to her pursuer, then ran toward her allies.

Josie got to her perch and took up her bow, readying a cloth-headed arrow. She watched as Cassy crossed the markers for the bear traps, carefully picking her path between them to stop in the center of the patch.

Cassy turned to check Silas's heated approach. "That's right, fuckhead. Come get it."

On a platform above, Ana was crouched and poised with one of the lighter fluid-filled rubbers. "Couple more steps."

A cawing crow swept across Silas's path, causing him to pause right before one of the camouflaged traps.

"C'mon!" Cassy yelled. "You and me, fucko, let's go!"

The killer seemed to scan the ground. Shrugging his head off his bulging shoulder, he advanced, stepping between the traps as he did.

Cassy's face dropped. "Uh . . . You guys?"

"Hey, Silas!"

Silas turned his attention up to Ana and was greeted by a hurled condom, which he instinctively tried to catch, only for it to explode upon contact with his hand. A second splashed across his chest, with a swift third soaking his head.

Josie flicked her lighter and ignited the head of her arrow.

Ana turned to her. "Now!"

Trembling under the pressure, Josie took aim and quickly released. The arrow went wide. "Fuck!"

Silas menaced toward Cassy; his shorter, blade-wielding arm rising.

Cassy fearfully aimed her gun. "Help!"

"Josie!" Ana urged.

Josie hurried to light and nock another arrow. "Shit!"

Cassy pulled the trigger. Nothing. "Fuck—Help, please!" Cassy implored, struggling with the unresponsive gun, not realizing the safety was on.

Josie aimed and swiftly shot. Another miss. "Goddammit!"

Cassy voiced her terror as she dropped the pistol and swung her bat at Silas before he could strike. The killer caught and beat the bat back into her face, dropping her onto one of the traps with a jumbled nose and split lip, the blood from both smearing across her cheek. Her body missed the trigger plate but landed on the teeth, which stabbed into her shoulder, evoking a sharp cry.

Ana sprinted across one of the obstacle course's rope bridges.

Cassy rolled off the bear trap and gripped at her injured shoulder, her pain-racked form darkened by Silas's shadow. She turned and looked up.

Silas's knife was primed for the killing blow—a glint of moonlight traveling from its wide base to tapered point.

Something behind him caught Cassy's attention: Ana, flying down the zip line toward her, toward Silas.

Ana extended her legs and rammed both feet into Silas's back, stumbling him away from Cassy and onto a bear trap, which snapped with a penetrating crunch on the shin and calf of his right leg.

Silas made a horrid sound somewhere between a squealing pig and bawling infant at the trap's hard chomp. Dropping his weapon, his hands made light work of prying the trap apart. The damage was evident, his freed leg oozing dark liquid. He turned to face the one responsible.

With a blazing eye on Silas, Ana slid Grimthorn from its sheath, throwing the leather covering aside as she shifted into a combat stance. "This has been a long time coming."

Silas seized his weapon and charged, showing no bug in his step from the trap's bite.

Ana rushed him with a berserker's roar.

The earth drummed at the impending collision.

Ana ducked past a decapitating swing, coming up behind Silas. The two spun simultaneously, blades clashing with a resounding spark.

Their exchange was a storm of moon-flashing steel, set to the furious clangs and air-shredding whooshes of each desperately checked hit and barely dodged miss.

Silas's rough-hewn blade was a whistling menace, his larger arm coming with skull-shattering haymakers and barbed backfists.

Ana weaved and arched from those deadly gestures, every evasion accompanied by a blood-slinging slice to Silas's bare flesh, every block and deflection paired with vicious kicks to his trap-wounded shin. No opportunity to inflict damage was wasted.

Both kept half a mind on avoiding the perilous traps at their feet, which offered either favor or devastation depending on who fell afoul.

Ana tornadoed her body to power a roaring chop. Silas deflected the first, but a hasty second lifted a thick flap of brawn off his shoulder, the cascading blood black as pitch. He voiced a shrill squeal at the sword's deep kiss.

The smack of his unclean blood in her nostrils combined with that horrid outcry was nitrous for the kick Ana blasted into Silas's side.

"Yas!" cheered Cassy, returning to wobbly feet.

Ana slung the blood off her blackly dripping sword, then flourished it high for a double-handed chop.

Silas whirled about before it could land, driving Ana back with a sweep of his mace-like fist, then catching her with his scything blade.

Her armored vest took the lethality out of the blow, but not the inhuman might that powered it, which spun her off her feet, hurtling toward a trap's trigger plate. Her nose came within an inch of the mechanism, halted thanks to her bracing arms on either side.

Above the brutal melee, Josie fought a battle all her own. Fear had once again seized her mind and body, maiming her already shaky courage. Her clenched eyes and clasped ears could not block out the tumult below, but somewhere, unbidden through all that inner and outer noise, were the words spoken to her by Nell, words about them all having her back. And as Josie remembered her reply to that promise, she became aware of a burgeoning heat within.

Ana rolled aside before an angry stomp could cave her torso, regaining her feet in the nick of time to parry Silas's follow-up stab with a back-peddling wheel of Grimthorn.

The two came again to flashing blade-strokes, each voracious in their desire to smite the other dead. Steel ground against steel, rang apart, and danced again in shimmering whirls.

Barely avoiding a hissing lash at her face, Ana ripped her wetted blade across Silas's attacking forearm, splitting tissue and giving a blink of scored bone beneath, his pain made vocal.

Ana gave a wild shout as she pressed the advantage.

Slapping her blade aside with his own, Silas swung his larger arm around like a stegosaurus's spiked tail.

Twisting to avoid that blow, Ana caught a piercing lick of Silas's knife across her thigh, pain icing through her body.

With not an instant to recover, she smote his next attack.

Blue sparks erupted along the lengths of their scraping blades, the violent union unbalancing Ana. Focus momentarily diverted to avoid an imminent trap, she was caught by a silver arc of Silas's weapon, which tore her face from cheekbone to brow, cutting away her eyepatch with a burst of crimson.

Silas snatched Ana by the throat before she could fall, lifting her off the ground by more than half her height with belittling ease.

"No!" cried Josie, leaning over her elevated position to see Ana kicking weakly against Silas.

Fast-encroaching darkness obscured the vision in Ana's eye. She could catch no air through his grip, nor muster the strength to break free.

"Fuckfuckfuck!" said Cassy, looking around for a weapon.

Silas lanced his blade into the earth, then reached a coarse hand to Ana's face, running his grimy thumb over her ruined eye as if fondly reminiscing about the evil he'd done to her at their last encounter.

Ana was there too. Surrounded by fire. Surrounded by death. Piercing pain through her skull. A terrified girl in the red claws of a monster. Under all the muscle—strong and ingrained with combat reflexes—she was once again the dorky, helpless teen. But she'd fought him off then, against all odds. Risen from flames to live. Risen from flames to fight. She could do it again. She'd gotten this far with the help of the others. The others . . .

Nell.

Josie.

Cassy.

Her friends.

Ana dug her fingers into Silas's forearm wound, tearing at the spaghetti-like ligaments that resembled fine tree roots in both appearance and texture.

Silas jerked his arm away with a horrid howl, dropping Ana to the ground in a fit of racking coughs.

"Fucker!" Cassy sprang up behind Silas, denting her aluminum bat across his oversized head. He turned before her second swing could land, throwing out his longer arm for a walloping blow.

Cassy crashed between two traps, dazed and heaving to recover the breath bashed from her lungs.

Ana darted in as Silas swung around, sheathing her sword in his abdomen. Blood frothing through clenched teeth, she brought the entirety of her hatred to bear as she crammed Grimthorn hilt-deep into his squelching meat; then, with a drooling snarl and wrathful twist, she tore it murderously upward, shearing bone, drenching her hands with his glutting fluid, and exposing reeking innards that cemented his inhuman biology, for what slopped at their feet was slimy pulp that may have been rotted plant matter or putridity of more bestial origin, or some repulsive blend.

Silas butted his huge head into Ana's, sprawling her to the ground as he faltered from the critical hit.

Cassy sluggishly distanced herself from the giant as he extracted the sword with a heavy splatter, tossing the weapon aside where it could cause no further harm.

Half her face painted bloody, Ana spat aside a tooth and ran the back of her hand across her mouth as she rose to her feet.

Seemingly recovered from that last blow, Silas turned his attention back to his primary foe. He reached for his rooted weapon, then stopped for a ponderous moment before stepping around it, preferring this irksome individual's death be dealt with bare hands.

Ana slid her hands into the pockets of her cargoes, and when they came back out, they did so wearing spiked brass knuckles. Her lips snarled back from blood-washed teeth as she presented those fists before herself, seething animosity in her eye as she roared a spittle-flinging, "Come on!"

Silas obliged with extreme prejudice, closing the gap with a gusting flail of his apish arm.

Ana ducked beneath the sweep of that attack, tearing away Silas's kneecap with a sharp fist to the joint, which sluiced black from its ragged opening.

His shrill squeal was music to Ana's ears.

Hard, fast, and feral-eyed came her assault—her full weight behind every spiked punch that crunched bone and tore wet furrows in the monster's bawling bulk.

Never before had Silas been the recipient of such a violent onslaught. Never before had the prey proven so formidable. This was more than a vicious mauling; this was an imposing of Ana's will upon him. He *would* be hit, *would* be hurt, *would* bleed and scream, and there was *nothing* he could do to stop it.

Josie's gleaming eyes widened in awe, the heat within her soaring as she witnessed the pure intent of Ana's savage mania. "Kill him, Ana!" she screamed, tears rolling down her face with the desperate plea. "Kill him!"

Ana was lost in the extremity of her anger. Her movements were lightning, her strikes world-smashing meteors, her roars the thunder of an incensed war goddess. She burned bright, burned fierce, a livid sun transcendent with rage.

And yet, Silas Crowe would not go down.

Ana swung a kick at his injured leg, but Silas was quick to draw it back. She spun full-circle nonetheless, bringing that same kick high against the side of his head on the return—or would have, had Silas not caught it, snatched the knife offered by that arrested boot, and stabbed it through her calf, throwing her screaming to the ground.

Ana gritted her teeth at the lodged blade, its point poking out the other side.

Casting off the gore-encumbered knuckles, she raged back onto her feet, using the pain to fuel a corkscrewing leap at the bastard that ended with a head-whipping fist, staggering him.

Silas recovered, shouldered Ana's next kick aside, then met her punch with a butt of his prickly head.

Stumbling away, Ana leaped back at him like an enraged panther. Silas punched her out of the air, leaving her dazed at his feet.

The hand of his elongated arm seized her throat. Gasping, Ana beat and pulled against that arm, but to no avail.

She drew up her knife-stuck leg and kicked out to the side of his head—the protruding blade slicing between the vines to open a gash that spat blackly upon her.

A wailing Silas released his hold, allowing Ana to regain her feet.

He struck back, and though Ana folded an arm beside her head to take the blow, the world turned hard on its side, her defending arm numbed.

A merciless kick landed her some feet away with an internal crack.

Curling from the agony, Ana felt Silas's advance through the earth. Urging herself to stand despite the protestations of her damaged body, she gave a defiant bellow and raised shaky fists in the growing shadow of Silas's unhurried tread.

A groggy punch was the best she could muster—a punch Silas caught in his crushing hand. Pain detonated up Ana's arm as he swung her screaming up and over himself, pelting her to the ground with a force that silenced her and almost tore that arm from her shoulder, but fortunately stopped at dislocation.

Still reeling from Silas's strike, Cassy looked over at a weakly writhing Ana as the monster reclaimed his killing implement. "Ana!"

Silas stalked toward his finally conquered adversary, calloused fingers flexing around his weapon's ridged hilt.

"Ana, get up!"

Blood spilling off her face, Ana made a feeble attempt to rise, but sank under the weight of her injuries.

All the years of training hadn't been enough. She was furious that her body was unable to complete the demands of her burning will: to rise, to fight, to face death with fists at the ready, because that's what a fighter does, because that's how a warrior ought to die, because fuck this world and its monsters.

Cassy lunged for her pistol.

Silas raised his blade.

Cassy's aim was too shaky. "Ana!"

Gunfire blasted from elsewhere before Cassy could fire a shot. She looked for the source.

Nell appeared determinedly from the rec hall, her wrathful face showing a myriad of cuts from the shattered window. Her sports top was gone and a Saran Wrap bandage poked out from beneath her armored vest, which had reduced the carving fork stab from fatal to flesh wound. Pistol in one hand, claw hammer in the other, her arms were cross-stacked for support as the gun barked fiery lead.

Silas was rocked by each bullet punching into and bursting out of him with a liquid eruption.

The sight of Nell was the final ingredient required to rally Josie's spirit.

Nell lowered her gun as she broke into a screaming run. Leaping over a trap, hammer drawn high, she landed with a skull-denting whack to Silas's thorny head.

She went for him again before he could recoup from that staggering blow, spinning the hammer in her hand and striking with the claw side, the twin prongs gouging ghastly grooves with each hit in a brutal barrage.

The baton had passed hands.

The violent intrusive thoughts that Nell was so accustomed to suppressing—thoughts born of the trauma this monster had inflicted—were wholly unleashed, compelling her hand with bold and utter hatred.

Silas strove to fight back, but Nell was too much, bringing her pistol into play between hammer blows to further stun and stifle his offensive attempts, smothering him with the unbridled totality of her elemental fury.

The frenetic ferocity of her assault and accompanying yells communicated a single, unmistakable sentiment: This abhorrent son of a fucking bitch must die.

28

Silas winged his arms at Nell in an attempted bear hug. She dropped beneath them, hammer claw chomping into his foot before being torn out through his toes, stripping off two of the crooked digits with the blood-spurting motion.

Silas's perturbed squeal was interrupted by two repelling blasts from Nell's gun.

She rose and struck him all over his considerable frame, denying him an instant to defend, let alone counter, undamming thirty years of impotent rage and toxic pain as she inflicted wounds that would otherwise maim and kill a normal person.

Her opponent, however, was not normal.

Despite his mortal blood loss, despite his torn and perforated flesh, his blackly ravaged, bullet-ridden body still stood in direct contempt of natural law.

Her ammo spent, Nell swung the hammer at the center of Silas's face.

The monster took the hammer's claw through his shielding palm, where it lodged and was pulled from Nell's grip, allowing him the opportunity to cut back at her with his blade.

Nell jerked away from its razor-edged arc, but could not avoid the follow-up kick, which propelled her backward and onto a bear trap.

The teeth clacked hard on her thigh, evoking a throat-shredding scream.

Silas went for his trapped prey, but his progress was buckled two steps in by a blow to the rear of his injured leg.

Cassy pummeled the killer with her aluminum bat—her entire body behind each hate-inflamed swing. "Kill you! Fucking kill you!"

Silas endured her unceasing attacks as he turned and drove his huge knife at her face.

Cassy smacked the weapon free from his grip then struck again at his head, continuing to clobber it left and right as he gave ground.

Silas absorbed a ferocious volley before deflecting, blocking, and countering with the hammer still transfixed through his hand.

Gaining the advantage, he at last snatched the bat away from Cassy, clocking her around the face with the hammer as he did.

Stars burst into Cassy's vision. Her ears shrilled. Face numbed. The taste of blood thick in her mouth. Her senses unsure of her physical position in the world.

A gruff twist turned her onto her back, letting her know she was both grounded and at the mercy of Silas, who loomed over her with the baseball bat lifted.

Cassy inhaled sharply, the image of her executioner reflected in her terror-widened eye—the other having swollen shut.

A flame-headed arrow whistled into Silas's forearm, igniting the lighter fluid still slicking his skin. Silas shrieked that hideous cry of his as he wiped at the spreading fire.

Josie nocked an unlit arrow, and with a steadying breath, shot again.

The arrow thrummed into Silas's upper chest.

Swiftly came another, and another, a third to the head, a fourth to the injured leg.

Josie loosed arrow after whizzing arrow in a frenzied, screaming succession, but despite the volley, Silas succeeded in snuffing out the flames that singed his arm.

Josie ran across a rope bridge to the platform where Ana had left the basket of lighter fluid-filled condoms. Taking a contraceptive in each hand, she pelted them down at an arrow-stuck Silas, who turned away from the falling bombs; flammable liquid splashing across his back and about his feet with each burst rubber.

Josie flicked her lighter and kindled the cloth head of her remaining arrow. She drew it back, knowing she would not miss, knowing this would put the monster down for good.

The eyes of her comrades were rapt on that arrow; the final blow remaining to them.

Josie took a sharp breath. Held it. Sighted along the shaft.

The arrow flew.

Silas spun with the bat, shattering the humming missile, then—with inhuman strength—threw his weapon end-over-end at Josie, striking her defensively raised arms and knocking her off the platform, bringing her earthward with a jolting thud that took both the wind and fight out of her, the broken bow at her side.

With a bloodied hand, Silas snuffed out the lingering flames that crisped his skin with a defiance that said there would be no heroic comeback here.

Ana lifted her bloodied face.

Nell abandoned her strained efforts against the bear trap.

Cassy spat a mouthful of blood.

Josie strained her dazed and sluggish body up on a wobbly arm.

The four were battered, beaten, spent. They'd fought fiercely, fought bravely, balled their fists, stared their foe in the eye, and given it their all.

Still, he stood.

They exchanged despairing final looks with one another—sharing in the unspoken acknowledgment of their failure, of being unequal to the task, of realizing that they were all about to die.

29

Nell glanced between each of her injured allies.
It can't end like this.
Her thigh throbbed between the trap's teeth.
Not after everything.
Silas Crowe stood despite his shocking injuries.
Not like this.
Stood and seemed to stare right at Nell.
Not like this.
Tauntingly.
Not like this!
Nell beat a fist against the earth and turned a look on the others that imparted some measure of her indignation, for they each underwent a change of attitude.

Ana nodded back resolutely as she felt her old scars burning, though not from any external fire—this heat came from within.

Thoughts of her son and daughter washed away the pain and defeat that held Cassy in their grip. *For them.*

Josie had been here before: At the mercy of some thing, someone, some man. This time, it would be she who showed no mercy.

The air became charged. The fire returned to their eyes, a second wind gusted at their souls, and with a shared nod of agreement, they remembered that they had not come here to merely try. They had come to fucking win.

Sensing the atmospheric shift as an animal does the impending storm, Silas ripped the hammer free from his hand and raised it, ready to pound, though his body looked notably sagged from the battering he'd taken.

Ana grabbed the wrist of her injured arm, teeth clenched as she pulled it out in front of her and jerked her body to pop the dislocated shoulder back in.

Josie turned to the cabin beneath which the chainsaw was stashed, her jaw set.

Cassy dragged herself up and swished her butterfly knives open, eyes locked on Silas like a tiger through tall grass.

Nell gripped the bear trap, putting the full force of her being into freeing her leg as she snarled, not in difficulty of the ensuing pain, but in relish of it as fuel for her cause.

Agony iced through Ana's nerves and exited out her mouth—her shoulder back in place.

Spurred by those notes of pain from her allies, Cassy rushed at her foe.

Silas made a swing at Cassy that would have burst her brainpan had she not spun beneath it, slashing his side with both knives in the rotation.

Josie limped with urgency toward the cabin, teeth grit against the sharp stabs in her side and back wrought by each painful step.

Silas's longer arm swooshed upward in an uppercut. Cassy juked around it, jabbing at his exposed side with both knives in turn.

Ana bit down on a growl as she tore the knife from her calf.

Silas swung the hammer at Cassy's face, but she dodged again, adding another laceration to the hump of his wide back.

Ana wound the wrap from her uninjured hand tight around her stabbed calf.

Silas dipped and swung his head at Cassy, ragdolling her through the air with the impact.

She hit the ground with a roll, her haywire senses unable to orient the world when she came to a stop. Fighting through, she shakily rose to hands and knees.

Ana closed in at a pain-be-damned sprint, launching herself off Cassy's back with a prodigious leap to soar through the air at Silas with knees extended.

Those doubled knees drove into Silas's chest, the blow staggering him onto the trigger plate of a trap, which slammed shut on his previously injured leg, audibly paining the giant.

As Ana rose, Cassy wobbled up beside her, their eyes locked on Silas.

"You good?" asked Ana.

"Fan-fucking-tabulous," said Cassy, sounding anything but.

Silas dropped the hammer and broke the trap apart, freeing his leg.

The duo split left and right as they charged, confusing their enemy.

Silas could not counter their coordinated assault. Each time he strived to clobber one, the other would interfere with an attack of their own. Maddened, he spun with a low sweep of his longer arm, taking Cassy's legs out from under her.

He turned as Ana made to intervene, seizing her by the throat with that same long arm and lifting her so high her feet were level with his face.

He sank to a bent knee as he brought her down to snap her spine across it.

Cassy thwarted that deadly action by stabbing her knife up into Silas's exposed perineum.

The resulting squeal he made was the worst yet.

Cassy growled through her teeth as she made several more hasty, squishing stabs into his taint before ramming and twisting the deeply plunged knife, black blood pouring from the insertion as if from a broken faucet. "How you like that, bitch!"

Silas dropped Ana and elbowed Cassy, freeing himself of the knife in the process.

Josie slid beneath the deck of the nearby cabin and dragged out the glinting chainsaw.

Looking to take advantage of his pained predicament, Ana hurled her uninjured leg at Silas's head. Silas caught the kick beside his head and backflipped her to the churned mud as he shot upright.

Grabbing her by the hem of her pants, he flung Ana into Cassy, who'd just gotten back on her feet, the pair crashing to the ground.

Nell strained as her leg struggled to pass between the bear trap's scraping teeth.

Cassy came at Silas with knives slashing.

Silas jerked away from her rapid cuts.

Trying for a kick to his non-existent balls, Cassy found the trajectory of her leg abruptly reversed and pulling her backward several feet when Silas punted her foot, dropping her prone and in a great deal of pain—not least in that struck foot, its toes broken.

Silas lifted his foot to pancake her head, but Ana made a desperate lunge for Cassy's legs, grabbing and

The Final Women

pulling her back an instant before that foot mushed earth.

As Cassy rolled aside, Ana heaved a nearby trap.

Silas closed the distance with a propulsive punch, bashing Ana away with all the force of a charging bull, the trap clanking uselessly to the mud.

Cassy leaped onto Silas's back and sank her teeth into the meat between his head and shoulder with a growling chomp. Her mouth filled with his acrid lifeblood, but her snarling ire was far more caustic.

Silas reached behind and pulled her over his shoulder.

Cassy kicked and struggled but could not break his hold, and in the next moment, she found the world spinning around her, the wind shrieking in her ears, her eyes catching a glimpse of the bear trap coming at her like an open-mouthed shark.

And then Ana was there.

Still reeling from Silas's punch, Ana threw herself onto the bear trap not a second before Cassy would have felt its bite, sandwiching herself between it and her ally. Her scream was sharp and sudden in Cassy's ears.

The pair were pinned, one atop the other, and at the mercy of Silas. He pressed down on Cassy, her body crushing Ana harder onto the penetrating teeth, which found those fleshy niches her armored vest did not protect.

Exerting herself with a mighty effort, Nell at last freed her leg from the trap, opening fresh cuts in the process.

With one hand firm and heavy on Cassy's throat, Silas recovered the nearby hammer and brought it down claw-first at her face.

The pinned women threw up four hands, halting the hammer's fatal crack.

The pair strained and pushed mightily against Silas, and though his strength was significantly diminished, the advantage remained his. The hammer made an assured descent until it broke the skin and scraped the bone above Cassy's brow.

The sharp whir of a chainsaw roared to life behind Silas, the fuming tool held aloft by Josie, who screamed a banshee's venom as she swung and shredded into his side, inky blood misting heavily from the trauma.

In the throes of distress, Silas released Cassy and Ana, throwing his arm back to whack Josie and her chainsaw away.

Cassy kicked her legs into Silas, shunting him onto his back.

Nell scooped up Grimthorn, ignoring the stabs in her leg as she hurried to aid the others.

Cassy peeled Ana painfully off the bear trap.

Silas rose unsteadily, unable to reach his full height, his grossly damaged body hemorrhaging what constituted its life fluids from a myriad of gaping wounds.

He was not accustomed to facing such adversity. His prey rarely fought back, and when they did it was as panicked individuals, making them easy to dispatch, but these four were a force unlike anything Silas had ever encountered.

Picking up his bladed weapon, he turned to take in each of the grim-faced women who surrounded him on all four sides.

Some hazy part of him remembered them.

He'd felt some recognition when he'd touched the empty socket of the one-eyed woman, when he'd

The Final Women

seized the one with the painted face, when he'd stood over the one with the defeated eyes, and when the one with the red bandanna yelled her taunts.

These were the ones who had sent him back to the void before his work was done. Now they were here, together, to do it again. For the first time in his vague existence, Silas Crowe felt alone, vulnerable, and at the mercy of a greater force.

Nell brought Grimthorn up at her side.

Ana raised her fists—bloody knife gripped in the unfractured lead.

Cassy whirled her butterfly knives.

Josie tore at the chainsaw's starter chord with her entire being, revving it to life with a guttural roar, a roar she contributed to with one of her own.

The others added to that surging fury, which carried them upon its tide as they charged as one.

Ana made a jumping slash at Silas's back, spinning him to Nell, who chopped him sidelong in the gut, bending him over, then ripped the sword out of his side as she continued past.

Cassy pounded one, then the second of her knives into Silas's bowed head.

Silas made weak swipes with his weapon to fend them off.

Josie brought the buzzing, hungry-toothed chainsaw down on that blade-wielding arm, chewing it angrily at the elbow before severing it entirely, leaving a pouring stump protruding with rigid roots.

The monster screamed as he fell to his knees.

Nell hoisted up a bear trap, snapping it shut on Silas's head, then pulling him rearward.

The monster screamed as he fell to his back.

Cassy clamped another bear trap on Silas's leg with a squelching *chud*.

The monster screamed.

Ana closed another trap on the other kicking leg.

The monster screamed.

Josie rammed the roaring chainsaw into Silas's deformed genitalia, putting her full weight behind the tool as she forced a ragged path up his spasming body, painting herself with his abundantly jetting blood.

The monster screamed.

The roar of the chainsaw died abruptly as the smoking tool locked up in Silas's midsection, having split him from groin to gut. Severed roots poked through the putrid offal that slopped from the opening.

Nell took Silas's own bladed weapon from the ground and brought it down with both hands to impale him.

Silas caught the stab inches from his chest with his remaining hand, blood oozing from his clasped fingers as he pushed the razor-sharp blade away.

Nell exerted her full force, pressing down with all she had left to deliver the killing blow she wished she'd made thirty years ago. The weight of eleven lives behind her. But it wasn't enough.

Josie's hands stacked atop Nell's, their combined weight slowing Silas's push.

Ana added her weight to the cause, the might of all three lowering the blade's point by slow degrees. Cassy's strength tipped the balance wholly in their favor.

The four roared as their heaped, bloody hands brought the blade down with inevitability, puncturing Silas's chest, pushing through flesh, and stabbing into the earth beneath.

The monster screamed.

He made frantic grabs at the women. Ana seized his apish appendage, wrapping her arms around the wrist while pressing her knee against the elbow joint. Cassy joined her, the two of them craning back against that joint until it broke with the sound of a mighty branch.

The monster screamed.

Still did Silas struggle with unending life, breath bubbling in his throat with each choked wheeze.

Those whispering voices came to Silas in a delirious and overlapping deluge that he could not comprehend, except for the emotion behind them, *that* he knew intimately. It was the same emotion he'd heard countless times in the panicked and frantic screams of his victims before he offered them to the unappeasable void.

The women encircled Silas's quivering, butchered body, the fetor of his spoiled guts thick in the air.

They drew their pistols, Ana and Nell reloading theirs.

The moonlight at once silhouetted and nimbused their dire forms as they stood over him like vengeant Valkyries; they killer, he prey.

"Do you even know our names, you son of a bitch?" asked Nell, seethingly. "Do you even know our *fucking* names?"

Silas Crowe did not.

Whereas he had changed every facet of these women's lives, they—as with all his victims—had been nothing more than convenient targets, forgotten the instant their purpose was served.

Nell pointed her gun at Silas's head and declared, "Nell James!" She fired.

Ana had the look of a stone-cold executioner as she aimed her gun one-handed. "Ana Gómez." She fired.

Cassy firmed up and stood tall as she raised her gun. "Cassy Phong!" She fired.

The gun in Josie's hands trembled, her expression a storm of anger. "Josie fucking Jedford!" She fired, kept firing, joined by the others, all of them unloading their guns into Silas's grossly swollen head, shooting to a lethal excess, his face erupting with rapid spurts of blood.

Muzzle flash etched the crazed countenance of each woman in nightmarish relief—eyes shining in the thunderous salvo.

The guns clicked.

Silas no longer moved. His head was a bloody, sunken mess that oozed black between the vines.

Click.

The women stared down at the slain monster.

Click.

Each of them had been through a war, splattered and dripping with blood that was both theirs and not.

Click.

Chewed up, spat out, broken.

Click.

But alive.

Click.

Wide-eyed at all they'd been through, of what they'd done, of who they'd beaten.

Click.

Ana spat vindictively at the unmoving Silas.

Click.

Nell placed a trembling hand over Josie's, which still sought to plug rounds into the fiend. She eased off the trigger and lowered the gun.

They'd won.

Ana's chest heaved, hastened, swelled, and—with face and fists thrust skyward—exploded with the most savage of roars: a primal, throat-searing exultation of a sort known only to those who've triumphed through the most hard-fought of battles. The roar of a conquering warrior queen when the war is ended.

The crows—once loyal to Silas—fled from their perches among the surrounding trees.

Josie began to cry. There was nothing else for her body to do, no other thought in her mind at that moment other than surrendering to the heavy, unrestrained wailing that threatened to drop her to the ground.

Nell pulled Josie to herself and hugged her tight before she could fall, her own tears beginning to flow. Was this another of her dreams? Had all that really just happened? The painful stabs and throbs of her various wounds spoke to the reality of events.

Cassy continued to stare at Silas's corpse, the truth of it all too difficult a thing to absorb. This morning she hadn't believed him real. Now she stood over the slain demon, soaked in his blood. *Holy mother fuck.*

Lowering her arms as the roar melted through the forest, Ana too began to cry, her body sagging as over thirty years' worth of caged emotions sloughed off her like an iron cloak. Her fortress of pain and anger crumbled to dust. She didn't want it anymore, the suffocating rage, the endless paranoia; she was so very fucking exhausted by all of it.

Nell pulled her into the hug with Josie, and then Cassy turned and joined the group embrace.

Nell grasped the others tighter and felt each of them respond in kind. *Alive*, she thought, pressing her head against theirs. *We're alive. And Silas Crowe is dead* . . .

He's dead.

No eye was dry in that circle of sob-racked bodies.

Silas Crowe had been a tornado through their lives, yet here they were, still standing, leaning on one another for support amid the wreckage, their bond sealed forevermore with the completion of this most arduous of deeds.

"We did it," said Nell, the salt of her tears upon her lips. "It's over."

30

Cassy finished tying off her bandanna over Ana's face wound. Nell cinched one of Cassy's leg warmers around her own injured leg. Josie flexed her hurt back.

The four turned to look again at their slain foe.

"What now?" asked Josie.

Ana wiped her eye. "We burn—"

The white of headlights washed over them, interrupting their moment of victory and turning them squinting to the source.

Lugg's Charger rumbled to a stop beside Cassy's SUV, the blow-off valve giving a sharp whistle.

The occupants exited and approached the women. Scud kept his gun on Blake, while Pewson moved under the barrel of his own shotgun, now in Lugg's possession.

Their steps petered to a stop once they saw, then smelled the rancid carnage painting the women in a mess of red and black—vivid eyes hauntingly agleam through the gore. The ground about their feet was also fouled with bloodshed, the nucleus being the thoroughly butchered corpse of Silas Crowe.

Pewson scanned the grisly scene, then each of the women in turn. "Well, jeez . . . You ladies sure look like you've been through it."

"The fuck?" asked Lugg, as taken aback as the rest.

"Blake? What the shit are you doing here?" asked Cassy with acerbic confusion.

Blake was too stunned to hear, his mind unable or unwilling to process what he was looking at, or that his wife had some involvement in it.

A dull banging came from the car's trunk.

Lugg gave a nod to Scud, who kept his gun on Blake as he popped the trunk and dragged out Clem, missing the cell phone that'd come free from the old man's sock as he did.

"Can't hardly breathe in there!" Clem groused.

"Sshlut up, olm man."

"Blake!" Cassy snapped.

Blake turned a nervous glance on Lugg. "Uh, this . . . this man, brought me here against my will."

Cassy crossed her arms and shifted her weight to one foot, her expression souring. "I see. So not out of heartfelt concern for your wife, huh? Bet you were on the phone to Krista the second you knew I was gone, weren't you?"

It took a moment for words to sound from Blake's flapping mouth. "I-I mean—"

Cassy pointed her gun at him. "Weren't you? You piece of fuck!"

Blake shut his eyes and clasped pleading hands. "It's true! Please don't shoot me! I love living!"

Cassy waved the argument off. "Relax, I'm just fucking with you. How is she?"

Lugg stepped forward. "What the fuck, Josie?"

There was a moment, a fleeting flicker, where despite everything just endured, the lifelong reckoning now surmounted, Josie almost reverted to the meek woman she always seemed to become around Lugg.

That impulse died within her the moment it attempted to take flight, and she instead fixed the man—looking smaller to her now—with an impassive stare.

"You know how much trouble you caused me?" he continued, irritated. "Making me come all the way out here?" Lugg turned away and pointed firmly to the Charger. "Get in the car."

Josie did not.

The lack of obedience turned him back. Unused to such a reaction from anyone, least of all Josie, Lugg dug deeper into his irritation. "Get in the goddamn car!"

"No!" said Josie, resolute and defiant.

Lugg looked bursting-at-the-neck angry. Who the fuck did she think she was, talking to him like that? And in front of all these people. "What did you—"

"Shut the fuck up!" she erupted, the sound of his voice repulsing her on an atomic level. To hear one more word, one more threat, command, or snide putdown on top of all those she'd endured over the past ten years felt so hair-tearingly unbearable at this moment. "Do you have any idea what we've done here tonight? What we've been through? Any idea who we killed?"

Clem took a cautious step toward the gruesome wreckage that was Silas. "You really killed 'im? You killed Silas Crowe?"

"Killed?" Cassy *pfft*. "This motherfucker got straight-up *murked*." She turned to the others with a self-satisfied grin. "That's what the kids say." Back to the men: "They say 'murked.'"

"And we're not quite done with him just yet," said Nell.

Pewson backed away from the mutilated killer. "Sure looks done to me."

"*This* is the big bad from your past?" asked Lugg.

"Was," Ana corrected. "Past tense."

"And after dealing with him, do you really think some insignificant, minor league, try-hard alpha like you's gonna intimidate us?" asked Josie.

"Fuck. That," added Nell.

Pieces of a puzzle were starting to connect for Blake, though he kept quiet.

Lugg bristled, face flushing with a cocktail of anger and embarrassment. "Josie, don't make me tell you again."

All four women aimed their guns at Lugg, aware the weapons were empty but also that he didn't know that.

"Oh, really? You gonna shoot me?" he asked with a nervous hint he couldn't fully mask.

"Fuck around and find out," said Josie.

More lights splintered through the trees. A small convoy it seemed, the frontmost leading with flashes of red and blue.

A baffled Cassy turned to the others. "What the—Was there like a group invite for this whole thing that I wasn't in on?"

As the half dozen other cars parked up at the forest's perimeter, the lead patrol car came to a halt beside Lugg's pride and joy.

Two officers leaped out, drawing weapons atop their doors while yelling overlapping orders of "Drop your weapons!" and "Hands in the air!"

Nell huffed sardonically. "Punctual, as usual." She and the others complied with both orders, as did Lugg and Scud.

"Pewson, ya damn putz!" Clem approached Lugg from behind. "This one's fixin' ta pull a fast one." Lugg frowned as Clem removed both the shiny Desert Eagle and Pewson's service weapon tucked into the rear of his pants. "Now go on and get back."

Pewson took his pistol from Clem, brandishing it at his former captors. "Yeah, back!" he said, putting on a tough guy tone in an obvious bid to reassert some authority. "I have a deep, masculine voice."

Clem scrunched his face. "What?"

"What?"

"Clem?" came a voice from somewhere behind the officers and glaring lights.

"That you, Leeman?" Clem called.

Mayor Leeman came around the side of the officers with his toupee askew, followed closely by his wife and a dozen other locals—an unassuming group of men and women of all ages. Nell recognized the waitress and cook from Fran's Diner among them, as well as the main of the two pricks who'd hassled her and the others, staring daggers at Ana between his bandages as he neared.

Pewson stood to attention. "Mister Mayor." He then reverted to your overly friendly neighborhood lawman. "Gloria, hi!"

The sweet-faced mayor's wife flapped a hand at Pewson. "Good to see you, sweetie! You well?"

"As can be."

Leeman regarded Nell and the others as they exchanged confused glances. "So, these are them, huh? The ones that got away."

"Took your time," said an irate Clem.

Gloria waved him off. "Blame me, Clem." She removed her earrings. "I held everybody up. Wanted to make sure I looked proper for the occasion." She undid her pearl necklace. "Nothing but the finest for tonight."

Leeman began to undo his tie. "We weren't expecting this night until the camp reopened. I've got accounts to settle, and—"

Clem set to unfastening his overalls. "The hell does any of that matter after tonight?"

"I don't like leaving loose ends," said Leeman, hands working on unbuttoning his shirt. And in fact, all the new arrivals were gradually undressing, and as they did, Nell noted they all carried the same tattoo on various parts of their bodies: the glyph-like image she'd seen on the waitress at the diner of an eye with a dagger through it.

The mayor took a few steps toward the women as he threw off his shirt. "Speaking of, you four couldn't have just died here all those years back? Had to make us wait all this time, only to come up here and not die again."

Clem gestured to Silas. "An' look at what they done to the Vessel."

"How barbarous," said Gloria. She cast contemptuous eyes at the four. "No way at all for women to behave, 'specially not at your age."

Cassy looked about herself. "Where my knives at? Imma cut this bitch."

Nell's confusion deepened. "Somebody wanna tell us what the hell's going on here?"

Leeman scoffed. "I s'pose it doesn't matter now. Past is past. Besides, all you did was postpone your deaths to tonight." He turned to Clem. "How many lambs we short?"

"Let's see now . . ." Clem scratched at the underside of his chin with the gun barrel as he did the math.

"What with that last flock of four, five 'fore that, that would make us short by . . . one?"

Leeman spread his hands at the gathered group of disparate parties. "Fish in a barrel."

"Right." Clem turned the heavy handgun on the confused men and women before him, eeny-meeny-ing the weapon between each bracing individual. Blake yelped into a low squat while defensively covering his head as the barrel turned on him.

Clem settled on Scud.

"Hah, waib a mi—" Scud was knocked off his retreating feet with a skull-hollowing blast.

Applause rang out from the assembled locals, now fully naked.

Cassy took a startled step back along with the others. "Whoa!"

Lugg made a threatening move toward Clem. "Mother fu—"

Clem arrested any further steps with the pointed gun and a "Nuh, uh, uh."

Scud's vital fluids soaked into the earth.

"What's your angle here, old man?" asked Ana, unperturbed by the execution.

"We are what you'd call witting thralls," answered Gloria, now down to her unmentionables.

Cassy couldn't have looked more baffled. "Whatting whats?"

"Votaries to the Three Rakes," explained Pewson, stripped to his tighty-whities and Stetson.

It turned out Cassy could look more baffled. "Three whos?"

A memory struck Nell. Of sitting around a campfire with her friends. Of a story about murder, witchcraft, and revenge—one of many local legends she'd delved into for her book and passed off as nonsense.

"Witches . . . the ones who were killed for trying to summon a demon?"

Clem gave her a respectful nod. "Nice to see someone round here knows their history. Though, witches is kinda a misperception. Sorcerers is what they are. Masters of blasphemous magics and forgotten necromancies that grant dominion over flesh."

Nell shook her head at the absurd notion. "But that's just some batshit folktale. You don't really—"

"Believe it?" beamed Leeman as he plucked off his remaining sock. "Hell, we live it!"

The naked locals took turns cautiously wrapping lengths of coiled thorns around their heads in a symbolic display of their devotion to Silas, though a chorus of air sucked through teeth indicated the pain of the prickly undertaking.

An eventual "Fuck this" from one was all the catalyst needed for the others to abandon the head-wrapping idea—the limits of their piety reached.

"There's a long lineage of their followers round these parts," said Gloria with an imperious air. "Long and pure."

"Sounds like someone's *real* close with their relatives," said Cassy.

"From the gray mists of prehistory came they," Clem began all too happily. "Disciples of the Once-Were. Chosen to—"

"This a long story?" Ana interrupted. "Some of us are bleeding out and could do with medical attention."

Clem's face crinkled in irritation.

"So, what, you're trying to resurrect them?" Nell searched her memory. "Six lives for each of theirs, right?"

"Six?" scoffed Leeman.

Gloria gave her a motherly smile. "Oh, sweetie, if all we needed were six for each, they'd have been resurrected centuries back."

Nell shook her head. "I don't—"

"That's right," said the prick from the diner with a hoarse voice. "You don't. And you won't, so why waste time explaining it? Let's just get this party started!" He wooed with nervous energy. "'Cause I-I'm starting to get a little antsy here."

The waitress put a comforting arm around the young man. "Oh, hush now, ain't no need to be scared."

"Scared?" Clem pointed at Nell and the others. "If anyone's got a reason to be scared, it's these good-for-nothings." He spread his arms to the locals. "We are the faithful! The Desired! Each and every one of us have toiled and suffered under the bullshit of the *Un*desired for generations. But now, the time of our eternal reward is at hand. Let us usher forth our unholy fathers, so that they might complete their ritual."

"What ritual?" asked Josie through the cheer that followed Clem's exaltation.

"To summon Xo'gaal," said Clem, worked up to a state of messianic zeal. "The All Consumer. He will come, and He will make the world anew!"

The women reacted with utter silence, until an incredulous Cassy responded with an "Uh . . . huh."

"You literally just referred to this god, or whatever, as the *All* Consumer," said Nell. "So, won't you be consumed too?"

Clem smiled in a most unhinged fashion. "Oh, don't worry 'bout me. For my part as the Shepherd, I"—he spread his hands again to the rest of the Desired—"along with my flock, am assured the fruits of the Scarlet Garden. So is it written in the Fœdissima Clāvis."

The women absorbed that revelation, their conclusion perfectly communicated via a giggle-snort from Cassy.

"But you warned us against coming here," said Josie. "You've been warning people for decades."

Clem tapped a finger to his temple. "Simple reverse psychology. Ya see, humans, they're dumb, teenagers especially. You tell 'em not to drink, do drugs, or the sex, and they're gonna organize a drunken orgy in a crack house. All I had to do was point in one direction, then watch all a'you rebellious little shits race off in the other."

"All those lives . . ." Nell's mind caught a glimpse behind the curtain of her lifelong grief, of monstrous cogs turning in the dark, grinding the life out of her friends and countless others, breaking families, their light forever extinguished—and to grasp any more of the machination was beyond her means or will. "You let all those people die."

"Sure did," said Leeman. "More deaths mean more infamy. More infamy means more provender for our gods."

"It didn't hurt the local economy either," added Gloria.

"Pewson?" asked Josie. "You too?"

The lawman shrugged as he hitched his thumbs into his briefs. "It was either join up or deal with all that paperwork, so . . ." He dropped his underpants to his ankles as his bright-eyed and naked deputies stepped to either side of him.

Clem looked at the bloody ground with wide eyes and timorous reverence, feeling himself in the eye of a world-shattering storm. "And so, here we stand, on that blood-soaked precipice of rebirth!"

Edging toward Clem on all fours in a beseeching but cautious manner, Blake raised a timid hand. "Um . . ." He cleared the nerves from his throat. "Can I please go, mister Clem, sir?"

Clem pointed the gun at Blake. "Call me high priest—No, archpriest." He turned to Leeman. "Which one's higher in rank?"

Leeman rolled his eyes. "Thought you were *the Shepherd?*"

A groveling Blake continued. "I promise I won't say a word about your little Satan club, sir high archpriest Clem, sir. Please. I just wa—Ow!" Blake jerked and flapped his other hand from the earth as if stung by a hot stove. Looking at the ground, he saw the reason why.

Steam rose in languid curls from the blood-sodden earth where Blake's hand was previously pressed—and not just there, but from two other patches, spaced in a wide triangular formation.

Blood began to bubble up from those areas, hastening, churning, mixing with earth to form a bloody, muddy, boiling soup.

Cassy once again voiced the collective sentiment, "Uhhhhh, what?"

"It begins!" Clem proclaimed, alive with the fervor of religious fanaticism. "Arise, unholy fathers! Arise!"

Those steaming patches grew wider and ever more turbulent, their heat driving the non-worshipping bystanders back in bewilderment.

Clem raised supplicating hands. "He of the Enchanting Eye!"

"Arise!" spoke the other adherents of this apocalyptic cult—all but the diner prick, who looked utterly horrified.

"He of the Gilded Tongue!"

"Arise!"

"He of the Alluring Grace!"

"Arise!"

From one of those steaming, bubbling puddles broke forth a pair of long, cadaverous arms, dripping with that mud and blood admixture as they pressed and clawed into the softened earth. The ridged, exaggerated curls of ram-like horns rose between them, thickening toward an emerging skeletal mien that, instead of two eye sockets, had a single inverted triangular cavity dominating the upper face. The Satyr.

Piercing from another puddle was a huge curve of gore-strewn beak, preceding a man-sized raptorial skull. The dripping beak opened with a sound like air rushing from a breached tomb, and all the women present felt a sickening dizziness at that exhalation. Its wasted body followed without the aid of arms, for it possessed none. The Siren.

Another pair of arms slapped down on either side of the last roiling quagmire, then a third arm, then a fourth, each emaciated limb adorned with muck-caked armlets and bracelets; gemmed rings banding many of the fingers. In their wake rose a withered head, the face of which was concealed by a begrimed mask of male beauty, though a section about one eye had broken away, revealing a pair of abutting blue-black orbs: the arachnid eyes of the final awakened horror. The Incubus.

Cassy was once again the first to speak, or at least attempt it. "H-ho . . . h-h-ho—"

"—lee fuck," Ana finished.

The trio of resurrected sorcerers screeched demonically from sticky mouths as they struggled up from the earth, causing those not a part of the cult to cover their ears at the piercing din.

The diner prick backed away from the spectacle. "Fucked . . . This shit's fucked!" Two others who'd drunk deeper of the occulted Kool-Aid took hold of him. "Hey wh—" They wrestled him to the ground. "Get the—" The diner waitress plunged her hand into the young man's open mouth, the shock of the insertion clear on his mumbling face. She forced her hand deeper down his throat, until the man's teeth were midway up her forearm, at which point his choked objections and desperate struggles ceased. The waitress removed her arm, now gloved in sleek claret.

With a resolute "Fuck this!" Lugg scooped up the shotgun and ran for the cabins, snatching Josie along as he did, followed by an incoherently whimpering Blake.

Nell backed up, her eyes struggling to process the hellish scene unraveling before her. "W-we should, uh—" Cassy ran as fast as her injured foot allowed, and Ana in turn urged Nell along, the three following Lugg's example in bidding a hasty retreat for the cabins.

"Where y'all going?" yelled Clem after the fleeing forms. He raised the large-caliber gun and started firing errant shots into the night sky, the bucking blasts pealing off the darkness of the enclosing forest. "Stick around and witness the beginning of the new beginning!"

31

Startled by the shots, the group split off into two. Ana followed after Josie and Lugg toward one of the dorm cabins, while Nell, Cassy, and Blake made for the rec hall.

Blake ran earnestly for the front door.

The trap-set tools glinted in anticipation.

Cassy yanked him around the right side of the building. "Not that door!"

The encircling cultists bowed down in all their flopping, or—in the case of Clem—shriveled glory before the sorcerers as they emerged fully from the earth. The eldritch forms stretched their worm-ravaged, red-glistening bodies to their full height, shrieking ghoulish cries to the night above.

Now arisen, the spideryness of the Incubus was on full display, for it had six arms, the legs bringing its limb count to eight. And whereas it and the hooved Satyr were naked in their horror, the Siren yet wore the tattered remnants of a once fine and ornate vestment that ran down to avian feet.

Lugg pulled Josie up the stairs of the counselors' cabin with Ana close on their heels. Last to enter, Ana immediately shut and locked the door. "We sh—" The world went black.

"Ana!" cried Josie.

Lugg stood over her unconscious friend, the butt of the shotgun angled down at her. He swung the weapon on Josie as she made to intervene.

Nell, Cassy, and Blake entered the rec hall through the hole Silas made earlier. Nell and Cassy went straight for the windows, while Blake paced like a panicked hummingbird at their rear. "What is happening? What do we do? What was that? What is happening?"

Cassy kept her disbelieving eyes on the spectacle outside. "Get ahold of yourself, Blake!"

Unaccustomed to motion, the bent and gnarled sorcerers toddled unsteadily toward Silas's body while the kneeling cultists chanted some low-toned and distinctly sinister plainsong.

Lugg kept the shotgun on Josie as she pulled her buck knife with a venomous "You son of a bitch!"

Lugg raised a calming hand. "Josie—Josie, listen! You and me, we're gettin' outta here."

The sorcerers took up positions around Silas, and with the monotone mantra of the cultists as an arcane underscore, began reciting a spell in some obscene tongue through desiccated vocal pipes.

The profane Sabbat had begun.

Cassy turned to Nell. "Tell me you've got a plan?" Afflicted with horrified awe, Nell said nothing, could say nothing, could only watch the unholy madness taking place outside.

Blake looked at his wife and was struck by how strange she appeared, and not just because of her confusing ensemble. Who was this woman who'd come to this camp to kill that monster-man outside? Who was this woman who was defying a group of nude devil cultists and *literal* demons? Who was this woman who was still here, asking about plans, instead of running far, far away?

Cassandra, apparently. His wife. And only now did Blake see her—the bigger picture that was her—beyond what he'd taken the little time and effort to see for all these years. Shame panged him despite all else.

He stepped to Cassy's side, his hand twitching with the notion of taking hers, but that notion fell away along with all other thought at the sight that his eyes beheld as he looked out and up, choking out a not-quite scream. Hearing his shrill exclamation, Nell and Cassy looked up too.

The sky was a roiling ocean, displacing the moon and stars in its violence such that their colors smeared and ghosted together like a ruined painting.

Cassy inched forward. "What the fuck is this fresh—"

There came a sound like the rending of reality's fabric as a cyclopean oculus yawned within the chaos of the sky, deafening the world as it opened to a blackness so absolute it tripped the mind. The rim of this awesome eyeful bloomed a searing redness that spread across the firmament like blood through water until all below was awash in crimson twilight.

Lugg and Josie clutched their ears against this aural assault.

Nell, Cassy and Blake did likewise, staggering under this nightmare imposing into their reality. Screams torn from their throats were stretched, deformed, riven to shreds that were snatched into the larger tumult.

The corrupted night uncovered a churning within the center of that aperture—a living mandala, grotesque in its writhing evolutions, paining and turning away all eyes that strove to look upon it.

The world was a phantasmagorical fever dream, all existence violated.

Nell's sanity might have surrendered right there had Cassy's voice not penetrated with an unsurprised "Sure, why not this as well, right?" Then, with annoyed outrage, added, "I mean why the *fuck* not!"

The sorcerers' intonations grew in power and volume, accompanied by the hastening chants and orgiastic writhings of the doomsday cultists, half of whom took up a second perverse chorus. An abrupt and forceful wind carried that direful symphony up to the bewitched sky and throughout the camp and surrounding forest, where it echoed off the attendant trees.

A finger on Silas's hand stiffened.

Ana stirred, Lugg's voice pushing through the fugue as her senses returned.

Lugg placed the shotgun on the floor nice and slow. "Baby," he began in a voice so falsely affectionate it was sickening. "Baby, look. Now, I-I know—I *know* I was—That I could—Shoulda been better—"

"Oh, fuck you!" said Josie with a disgusted grimace.

"Now's our chance to get away! While those freaks—"

"No!"

"I ain't asking!" said Lugg, the pretense of tenderness gone.

Their breathless hymn and lascivious gesticulations heightening, the cultists stood upright and opened their now entirely white eyes, the person they were departed, their blended voices continuing as the chorus of a chthonic choir in dark Mass.

Blake backed away from the window and ran trembling fingers through his thickly pomaded hair—his do holding solid its newly alarmed form. "Didn't you have guns?"

Cassy checked the holster on her hip. "Shit! I left mine out there."

Nell pulled the Bowie knife from her belt. "Same." She scanned about to see what other weapons they'd stowed for their fight against Silas. Immediately catching her attention were those on the table. "We'll have to make do with what we got."

"Wait, what?" asked Blake. "Make do with—" He turned to his wife, hoping to find someone with more sense. "Ca—Uh, honey, let's just run!"

Though a significant part of her agreed with Blake, Cassy found herself joining Nell at the table and picking up a pitchfork.

Blake exhaled his disbelief. "Did you not see the biblical-level crazy going on out there?"

"Yeah, I did," said Cassy. "And it *really* looks like something the rest of the world would be super grateful for us to stop."

Milk-white tears leaked heavily from the droning cultists' blank eyes, like shiny orbs of melting wax dripping down their faces.

Silas's body twitched and jerked with increasing restlessness as the sorcerers continued their wicked incantation.

Lugg shook his head. "I come out here to rescue you—"

"The fuck you did!"

"Drop the fucking knife!" he ordered.

From behind Lugg, Ana gave a discreet nod, and with this Josie lowered her knife.

Lugg held out his hand. "Good girl. Now, let's get outta here while we still got a chance."

Silas spasmed violently, sloshing black blood from his assorted wounds and splayed torso. Heads and—where applicable—arms rising as one, the sorcerers shrieked a devil's joy as their spell came to an end, the wind gone with it.

The red world was held in a profound stillness beneath the restless and unknowable black gaze above.

A Nerf dart bopped off the Satyr's head, bouncing harmlessly away. The resurrected horrors and their adoring cultists turned as one toward the offending culprit.

Nell stood outside the rec hall, Nerf gun in hand, looking like she'd just made the biggest mistake of her life. Even so, she endeavored to feign strength and authority. "Um . . . Knock that shit off!"

The hive-minded cultists—red wraiths beneath the ensorcelled vault—pointed accusatory fingers and released outraged wails at Nell, who with an emphatic "Shit!" ran back for the rec hall.

The Satyr and Incubus shambled after her. The Siren drifted at their side, levitating an inch from the ground, and like the dorsal fin of a shark there arose from the earth beside it the hilt of a huge sword, leading to a downturned blade that once unearthed was equal in height and near-equal in width to a man— seemingly formed from a single slab of igneous rock. The double-edged weapon floated obediently alongside its master.

The Incubus's legs bent against the knee joints, dropping it to its six hands, which worked in tandem with the feet to move it entirely in the ghastly manner of an arachnid.

Ana swept Lugg's legs out from under him, crashing him to the floor, his head bouncing off the planks.

Scrambling atop, she pounded elbow after elbow into his face, rage burning through her pains and fatigue. "Mother! Fucker!"

Nell hissed with pain as she clambered through the rec hall window, aided by Cassy, who asked, "Well?"

"Oh, yeah," said Nell, touching at the stab wound in her back. "That did it, all right!"

As the ghoulish triad closed on the rec hall with spasmodic steps, the Incubus halted to turn its head upon a creaking neck. The spiderish eyes laid bare by the broken mask fixed upon the counselors' cabin, from where it sensed an unfolding commotion.

Lugg struck Ana off himself, unintentionally landing her within arm's reach of the shotgun.

She went for it.

Her hand slipped from the stock as Lugg pulled her by the leg, pinning her beneath himself as he took the advantage—stifling her bucks and struggles with his greater weight as he flicked open a switchblade.

"You're dead, bitch."

Josie grabbed her knife off the floor and leaped upon Lugg. "No!" she cried, planting the blade deep into his back.

Gasping sharply from the blade's chill incision, Lugg threw Josie off.

Seizing the moment, Ana drove a knee into Lugg's groin, then shoved his recoiling mass off herself.

The cultists removed the bear traps, chainsaw, and huge pinning knife yet troubling their deity's vessel. Then, from within their discarded clothes, each produced an athame bladed with some manner of lambent crystal and hilted with twisted oak.

Encircling Silas, they raised an arm before themselves, drawing the softly luminous daggers along their wrists to open sizzling, blistering wounds that apparently caused no pain and from which poured white liquid of the kind that leaked from their eyes. They directed the flow of this pearly ichor over the gaping wounds of Silas's body.

The Satyr and Siren paused outside of the rec hall, a sibilance of dead breath escaping from their throats. The Siren drew in a grating lungful, releasing it as a ringing, protracted caw.

To Blake's assaulted ears, that's all the sound was, but to Nell and Cassy it was warmest ambrosia, a choral melody that dissolved all fear, all regret, all shame, and promised love—unrestrained, unconditional, unending love. A god's love.

The Bowie knife and pitchfork clanged to the floor. Lost to the Siren's Song, Nell and Cassy sauntered toward the rec hall's broken wall.

"What are you doing?" asked a baffled Blake, though he was resolutely ignored by the pair as they ambled past with dreamy eyes.

The ichor saturating Silas's sundered body became increasingly viscid, congealing as raw, pulsing flesh between the wreckage. The auditive accompaniment to the work of this sorcerous elixir was a sickening discord of sucking meat, muscle fibers threading and seeking like sinister roots over grim detritus, and bone creaking like warping wood.

Blake skidded around the front of Nell and Cassy, pushing them back by their shoulders. "Stop, goddammit!" They did not, continuing instead to calmly resist.

Galled by their delay, the Siren floated up to the front door, its attendant sword in tow, while the Satyr sank to a crouch before springing supernaturally upward.

THUMP!

Encumbered by the unceasing pair, Blake started at the sound of the sorcerer's landing upon the roof.

Ana took up the shotgun and sprang to her feet in front of Josie, who looked horrified and conflicted by what she'd just done to Lugg; this piece of shit she'd wasted the worst part of a decade with.

The large brute reached and, with painful difficulty, pulled the bloody knife from his back. He dropped it clattering to the floor and staggered away from the pair. "Baby . . . you fuck—fucking stabbed me . . ."

The Siren willed open the door to the rec hall and, as it entered, tripped the trap previously set by the women. The pickax swung sidelong, punching hard into the sorcerer's stomach with an outburst of black blood and maggots. The Siren's Song shattered into an anguished wail, which was in turn silenced by the down-swinging sledgehammer—its avian head exploding in a mess of skull shards, dark liquid, and assorted insects. The stone sword afloat at its rear dropped heavily, planting upright in the deck.

Blake was relieved to see Nell and Cassy snap out of their mesmerism, turning confused glances around themselves until they saw the Siren's headless form crumple to the deck.

"Oh," said Cassy with surprise.

THUMP!

The three looked up.

Ana and Josie remained on guard as Lugg teetered toward the door.

It opened at his arrival, and there to welcome him was the Incubus, upside down in the doorway, its masked face level with his.

As Lugg gaped at its profane face, the sorcerer clasped hands onto either side of his head. Lugg's scream was quickly muffled and even quicker ended as the Incubus plunged its thumbs so deep into his spurting eyes that the talon-like nails scratched the back of his skull from the inside.

THUMP!

Their weapons retrieved, Nell handed her Bowie knife to Cassy and took a felling ax from their table of armaments.

THUMP!

Cassy took the knife and thrust the pitchfork into Blake's blundering hands, much to his dismay.

The three of them spread out, eyes fixed on the ceiling in anticipation.

As the gooey remnants of his burst optics rusted with blood and stretched between his ruined sockets and the Incubus's extracted thumbs, Lugg slumped to his knees and thunked to his side.

Scurrying over his corpse, the Incubus took to the wall inside and paused on splayed limbs to consider Ana and Josie, meeting their horrified faces with the impassive countenance of its mask, looking all the more shocking in the hellish vermilion light, which cast its shadow like the many-fingered hand of a demon across the cabin interior.

CRASH!

The Satyr broke through the rec hall's roof, landing with a downpour of flinders and sawdust between Nell, Cassy, and Blake, the three of them falling back from the impact.

Ana pumped and fired, shredding one of the sorcerer's legs with an eruption of blood and insects: spiders, maggots, beetles, and centipedes splashed to the floor, writhing and drowning in inky foulness.

The air trembled with the fiend's abhorrent scream and strobed with an ephemeral light, revealing luminous threads that webbed the entirety of the room.

The Final Women

Ana and Josie recoiled as the sound screeched like feedback in their skulls.

Grimacing through the pain, Ana aimed to shoot again. The Incubus raised a hand and hissed a vile syllable that plowed through Ana's mind with a force that flung her backward in a crashing heap, the shotgun falling from her hands.

Josie dove for it but was struck by another of the sorcerer's spell words.

A raspy sigh passed through the thorny brambles wrapped around Silas's depressed head as they crackled to accommodate the swelling mass beneath.

Nell and Cassy got to their feet, weapons poised. "Fuck it up!" cried Nell, and the two charged.

The Satyr spat a hex as it lifted a hand at Nell, pulling her up to the rafters by the ax she gripped.

Turning sharply on Cassy, it circled its bloated gut with a thumbnail that drew blood as it grumbled another phlegmy utterance, the effect buckling her to the floor, sides clutched tight as she retched up an ungodly amount of yellow-green bile abundant with squiggling maggots and pieces of semi-digested cucumber.

A sniveling Blake rose on the spot as the sorcerer leveled its eye upon him, the immensity of its mesmeric gaze pinning him with mountainous oppression. In that moment of purest dominance, the fiend conveyed glee despite its lipless maw and hollowed, triangular socket—a lone worm dangling tear-like from the irregular cavity while others burrowed sluggishly from out of its mephitic face. And as Blake plummeted into the depths of that reversed triangle, his consciousness drowned in darkness and the discordant laughter of a thousand hyenas.

Recovered, Ana slid for and seized the buck knife, rounding and closing to stab at the Incubus's foul heart.

Another word from the sorcerer froze Ana at the height of her attack, leaving her with no control over her movements.

"Do something!" came Nell's strained cry from above, jerking Blake from his fear-induced inertia, but it was too late, for his mind was undone.

Dropping the pitchfork, Blake cried out in the manner of a lunatic as he ran with crazed arms at the Satyr, then passed it, laughing to himself as he climbed out of the window, leaving Nell and Cassy to their fates.

Cassy looked up between gut-rushing expulsions. "Useless f—" She retched again.

The Incubus unfurled a bejeweled finger to its throat, and Ana saw her confused face in its exposed eyes, each a black mirror in which she found herself mimicking the action, lifting the knife to her own throat as a sharp rush of whispered chatter spiked through her mind—*kill*, *obey*, and *whore* among them.

Nell released the ax handle, falling hard on her side as she hit the floor, crying out with the impact.

Pushing through the pain, she locked eyes on the pitchfork between herself and the Satyr, who instantly knew her mind, and so made a chop motion with its hand, bringing the ax down.

Nell rolled out from its whirring trajectory, the ax missing her and embedding into the floor.

Seizing the pitchfork as she came out of that roll, Nell hurled it trident-like, fixing it in the infernal thing's leg, the resulting inhuman howl leaving no doubt she'd hurt the fiend.

His mind a scrambled wreck, Blake showed no concern for the naked cultists—looking alarmingly depleted after their unnatural bloodletting—blocking his path with their demented, white-dripping faces and crystal-bladed daggers ready to kill.

Clem was the first to lunge at the gibbering Blake, who threw himself at the old man, landing a clumsy punch that grounded them both.

Shaking off the stunned aftereffect of the sorcerer's magic words, Josie got to her hands and knees.

"Close your eyes! Don't look at it!" Ana quickly warned.

Josie kept her head down and eyes closed as instructed. The Incubus chittered in amusement.

Ana strained against the spell that made her a slave to the demon's whim. The blade drew blood as it pressed into her neck. She spied the shotgun in the corner of her panicked eye. "The gun!" she called to Josie. "To your right!"

Josie turned and probed blindly in the indicated direction.

The Satyr continued its pained wailing as it pulled the pitchfork free from its leg, and as it did, Cassy found she was free from the spell that had her ejecting maggot and cucumber-strewn puke.

Josie's hands found the shotgun.

Eyes shut tight, she aimed the weapon in the general direction of the Incubus and fired. "I get it?"

She did not.

Hissing in vexation, the sorcerer turned on Josie, taking its hand away from its throat and pointing instead at her. Ana in kind removed the knife from her throat and found herself moving irresistibly toward Josie with forced, jerky steps. "No!"

The cultists closed in on Blake, blocking off all avenues of flight.

Still gabbering incoherently, Blake retained enough lizard-brain wherewithal to recognize and take up the nearby chainsaw. He seized and brought the tool to roaring life, waving it at the encroaching occult nudists in a cloud of its own exhaust fumes, his nonsense tirade communicating aggression.

Nell tore the ax from the floor and ran with a loaded swing at the Satyr.

The demonic creature froze Nell with a word, halting her swing mid-flight.

Eyes still shut, Josie aimed with uncertainty in the sorcerer's direction. "Where?"

A spellbound Ana moved ever closer to her oblivious friend, feet dragging but unswayable from their course.

The knife in her hand rose for the inevitable stab, as dictated by the Incubus's own gestures. She strained with every fiber against the unseen strings that compelled her, the rushing voices that commanded her, but she could do nothing to avert her actions. "Two o'clock!"

Josie adjusted her aim. Fired. Missed. The blast opened a red column of light through the cabin wall.

The Incubus crawled higher up to the sloped ceiling as murky, insect-ridden blood pattered from its wounded leg to the planks beneath.

A maniacal Blake kept the cultists at bay with back-and-forth swipes of the chainsaw, chewing up a line of flesh across Mayor Leeman's arm as he tried to snatch the tool, then making mincemeat of another local's hand when they attempted the same from the other side.

The cultists kept smiling despite their dreadful wounds.

Nell was powerless against the stasis, able only to watch as the Satyr gimped toward her with a drooling sneer of profane delight.

Ana stood right over Josie, and as the Incubus raised its hand, so did she raise the knife, aimed at the top of Josie's head.

Time was up. Ana couldn't let Josie die. "Nine o'clock!"

Josie did as instructed, then lowered the weapon when she sensed she was pointing the gun at Ana. "But—"

"Shoot!" Ana stressed.

The Satyr stopped before Nell, and from its triangular eye socket slithered a glittering, onyx-scaled snake, its tail curling and uncurling from the sorcerer's open mouth like a foul tongue.

The serpent fixed Nell with cold, reptilian eyes, its own tongue rattling as it coiled to deliver its deathly kiss.

Not yet fully recovered from her vomiting fit, Cassy looked up. "Nell—" she strained between heaving coughs.

The knife in Ana's hand reached its peak.

The Incubus cackled—a grotesque sound of unabashed blasphemy—as it mimed a stabbing motion.

"Shoot!" cried Ana, every ounce of will and strength that remained in her battered body taxed to hold back the knife's fall.

It was not enough.

Cassy reared the Bowie knife and threw it at the Satyr. The semi-dead thing shrieked as the blade speared into its lower back.

Josie threw herself onto her side, missing Ana's stab by a hair-brushing millimeter.

She turned the shotgun in the direction of the Incubus's hideous cackle and fired.

The scattershot ripped away two-thirds of the fiend's head, plastering the wall behind with a mess of rank gunk and bugs, its reluctant body thunking to the floor a moment after. And as its legs curled into a gnarled rigor, the gentle drooping of scintillant threads could be glimpsed across the rubescent room.

Free from the paralysis spell, Nell roared as she completed her ax swing, taking the Satyr's head clean off its shoulders, dark blood and frantic insects spewing from the neck stump.

Josie and Ana hugged in relief.

Nell pulled Cassy up into a firm embrace.

The cultists stopped their assault on Blake and stepped away, leaving their chainsaw-wielding target to express indecipherable frustration. A large shadow fell over him, bringing with it a disquieting chill that ran an icy finger up his spine. His nonsense petered to a subdued ramble, chainsaw idling to a low growl.

Blake turned, and there before him—towering over him—stood Silas, bloodied but mended, back to his terrifying self, with one notable exception: The thorny vines wrapping his tumescent head writhed and pulsed, and before Blake's vacuous eyes, those vines seemed to alter in texture, going from that of dead wood to supple, squirming flesh.

Blake smiled dumbly.

The vines unspooled and whipped forward to smother Blake's confused outcry.

32

Cassy started at the clipped sound of her husband's cry. "Blake!" She rushed outside with Nell a staggering step behind.

Ana and Josie exited at the same time as Cassy and Nell, and the sight that greeted the four left them bereft of words.

Blake was entangled in a mess of restless, thorny tendrils branching from the space between Silas's shoulders. The slim, curling, slime-webbed things that minutes ago appeared to be dead vines never concealed a head, but *were* the head of Silas all along. Now they restrained Blake—coiling around and constricting his limbs to bone-snapping angles as they drew him into Silas's pulpous torso with a sound like sucking mud, his screams choked by a trio of tendrils stuffed down his grossly expanded throat.

"Blake!" yelled Cassy.

Nell caught her as she made toward him. "Cassy, no!"

Sinking deeper into Silas's slurping bulk, Blake gaped watering eyes at his wife—his only means to communicate a desperate plea for help, until two more of the tendrils burrowed squelchingly into his sockets, robbing him of sight.

"No!" cried Cassy.

Blake disappeared entirely into Silas, his face submerging into the monster's squishy flesh as if into a wall of putty.

The score of ever-smiling cultists approached their reborn deity with open arms and gleaming eyes, willfully surrendering themselves to its tendrils, which snaked about and draped their bodies like macabre garlands, sensually savoring their taste before receiving their mortal oblation, yanking them one by one into the excitedly quivering main whereupon they deliquesced rapidly into steaming, pinkish sludge to enlarge their master's insatiable form.

The women watched stunned as the sickening feast played out.

Reality had reshaped for each of them. First the seemingly undying Silas, then the sorcerers, then the very sky, and now this . . . thing. What was the world now if such nightmares could take physical form within it?

Silas Crowe was no more. Now, there was only the sorcerers' ultimate maleficium: the All Consumer.

It was a monstrous thing of perpetually morphing flesh, nearly three times Silas's original size after its feasting. Huge, eyeless heads yawned out and over one another, gumming at, merging with, and falling back into each other's toothless maws, or else belching additional heads to continue the anarchic process.

Screaming, semi-digested forms strove to pull themselves from the thing's body, only for their oozing flesh and jellied bones to fuse back into the sludgy bulk. Stringy clots would slough away and be reabsorbed, as if its loathsome body struggled in a frantic state of escape and return. Giant insectoid limbs sprouted forth to rake the flesh with a fleeting wildness before plunging inward. Elephant-thick legs supporting the biological derangement cycled through the same nauseatingly hypnotic process.

Those undulating heads howled a polyphonic chorus of harrowing agony, all while slimy tendrils feverishly probed the immediate area for additional meat to add to their own.

Above, the patterns within that nullity of night intensified their revolutions.

For the women below, to stand before such a vision of chaos was to be told somehow that they didn't matter, that they were nothing—an unoriginal sentiment to each of them, instilled as it had been for decades by partners, family, so-called authority, and by the wider culture that considered them past their shelf life.

Ana turned at the sound of Josie cocking the shotgun.

"No," said Josie, firm in her determination as she defied the sky and limp-ran toward the demon.

"Josie!" called Ana.

Something in the sight of the nightmare had broken a dam in Josie.

They'd fought for their goddamn lives, spilled their fucking blood, overcome the greatest of their collective fears, all to end him. And they had. They had ended him. They had killed Silas Crowe. But as a final insult, a final fuck you from the cosmos, he'd come back. An amalgam of himself and all those who'd allowed him to be.

Were they supposed to just accept that? After all the suffering they'd endured, were they supposed to just let this motherfucker insist himself on their world once again?

A blast from the shotgun spoke a resounding, *No!*

Josie fired twice more at the monster as she fearlessly closed in, each shot ripping into its body, eliciting outraged cries from the mouths of its myriad heads.

The demon reformed itself, its body firming in response to being attacked. Its torso became a beautiful example of the ideal masculine. Its insectoid limbs fused and bulged into brawny humanoid arms. Its legs split into spiderish equivalents. Its undulating heads formed into a single head featured with the faces of all those consumed, each one distinctly recognizable and looking as if every second of existence in this new form was white-hot agony; their wide, crazed eyes swirling every which way, their mouths voicing such terrible cries. This, their eternal reward.

Josie would not become one of them, would not allow this abomination to consume any more of her life than it already had. It ended here, for an unspoken vow had been made this night, by herself, to herself, born of the facing and apparent slaying of Silas Crowe, bolstered by the plunging of a knife into the back of her scumbag ex, and cemented when she blew the head off one of the sorcerers responsible for this entire ungodly mess.

She'd vowed never again to be a victim.

Josie's bold and indignant example supercharged the air.

Nell felt it, her body tingling, her numerous pains receding, muscles twitching. She looked up to the platform where the combustible condoms were, and an idea arose. She left a stunned Cassy's side, disappearing briefly into the rec hall and returning with the flare gun in hand, snapping it shut on a loaded cartridge as she dashed for the ladder leading up to the platform.

Cassy voiced no objection or caution, her gaze set on the demon ahead. She turned to the Siren's oversized sword, still fixed in the deck. Stepping over the dead fiend, she gripped the hilt and pulled, pushed, yanked, strained, but it would not budge. Abandoning that notion, she zeroed in on the lustrous crystalline athames previously wielded by the cultists, scattered across the ground between her and the monster. Expression firming, she limped hurriedly for them.

Ana was already headed for the equipment shed, putting a quickly formed plan into action.

Its head flopping to its shoulder, the demon shrugged it upright then lashed out at Josie with thorny tendrils snaking from its gooey groin area. Josie narrowly dodged the first whipping appendage, but the second smacked her away.

Retracting its tendrils, the horrifying behemoth crawled toward its downed attacker with a fury.

A hurled dagger in the back halted it, the flesh around the wound sizzling.

"Let's go, you ugly fuck!" Cassy yelled, picking up the chainsaw as she came at it.

The faces of the consumed sank within the demon's body, reappearing on its lower back, where they caught sight of Cassy a moment before she rammed the chainsaw deep into Clem's hysterical face with a brazen cry of "Suck my dick!"

Cassy screamed through her teeth against the jetting blood that soaked her, which was no longer an inhuman black, but a natural red. The grisly ordeal was further compounded by the charnel miasma emanating from the thing.

The demon swatted at Cassy, sending her hurtling and the chainsaw buzzing wildly across the ground.

A tendril whipped sharply around her ankle before she came to a stop, dragging her back toward its fleshy whole. Cassy's fingers dug furrows in the blood-soaked mud, trying in vain to halt her progress.

Her foot was sucked into the doughy flesh of the fell fiend's body, the burning sensation instant. Cassy screamed.

Back on her feet, Josie levelled the shotgun and fired into the monstrosity's side. The pain caused it to release Cassy, who wasted no time in reclaiming her stinging foot—minus her expensive sneaker—then fleeing as Josie kept the demon's attention with another blast from the shotgun.

From the demon's numerous faces came the collective roar of an infernal horde as it turned on Josie, whose responding shot came out as a click. "Shit." Josie dropped the weapon and bid a tactical retreat for the parked cars.

The demon gave chase.

Ana kicked open the door of the equipment shed. Inside, she grabbed an oxygen canister and monkey wrench.

Nell got to the condoms.

Josie dove into the patrol car before the demon could seize her. Frustrated, it hammered the car with its huge hand, smashing it near in half. Ducked down as far as she could, Josie screamed as the car bounced and glass smashed around her.

Ana dropped the oxygen canister beside the door to the counselors' cabin, then, using the monkey wrench, began attacking the building's protruding stove pipe, breaking off a section.

As Josie struggled within the crumpled car, the monster raised its fist for another blow. A condom burst on its back, halting it. A huge, milky blue eye with an ink splotch of a pupil opened vertically on that struck area, looking like a giant bluish zit one poke from bursting. Scanning for threats, it made a sound like a sickly churning stomach with each movement.

"Up here!" Nell threw projectile after projectile at the abomination until all were spent. She took aim with the flare gun, ready to send this demon back to whatever fiery hell spawned it.

The zit-like eye turned up, followed by incensed tendrils that shot out at Nell, causing her to dive aside as they smashed apart the platform she was previously crouched upon. They didn't stop, coming at her with a flailing fury, tearing up the obstacle course in her retreating wake.

In her mad dash to live, the flare gun fell from Nell's hand to the ground below. Cassy saw the gun land and scrambled toward it while the demon was distracted.

With no other option, Nell leaped for a tree adjacent to the obstacle course, but the sum of her injuries brought that leap up short.

A tendril caught her mid-fall, helping her to the ground with an air-robbing thump.

Josie struggled out of the busted patrol car and scurried for Lugg's Dodge Charger.

Ana took the freed section of stove pipe and slid the oxygen canister inside.

Nell was dragged roughly across the ground by her feet.

Turning herself, she saw the demon's back split wide beneath that gross eye into a giant, slobbering mouth, from which reached eager tongues that brought to mind purple pythons, each with their own mouths. The mucus-flinging bellow from that newly formed orifice was an earth-shaking, prehistoric sound that would have sent the most fearsome predators of that age fleeing, its gusting breath the hot reek of an unventilated abattoir.

Nell's scream was lost in the abominable cacophony as she sped toward the monstrous cavity, powerless to stop herself.

"Hey, Silas or whatever!"

The demon turned its eye on Cassy, who stood with the flare gun pointed. "Consume this!" The flare rocketed at the demon with a fizz and a flash, hitting its mark right in that huge, pustulent eye, popping it with a heavy spew of opaque blue goo and igniting the lighter fluid that coated the vile thing.

The demon roared as the flames engulfed it.

Nell continued to be pulled toward the flaming monster, its barbed tendril biting harder into her ankle.

"Nell!" Cassy dove for her as she passed, their hands finding each other. "I gotchu!" And though she did, her added weight was not enough, both now being dragged across the mud toward the beast.

Their trajectory brought them right past Grimthorn, which Nell caught and swung at the tendril, severing its hold and sending it thrashing bloodily back to its body like an unchecked hose on full power.

Cassy helped Nell to her feet.

A colossal roar turned them both to the flame-cloaked demon, who ran at the pair in a last-ditch effort to end them.

White light bathed the burning monster, and in the next instant, Lugg's beloved Charger plowed into its side, rushing it away from Nell and Cassy.

Josie gave a roar of her own from behind the wheel.

The various faces of the consumed pressed against the windshield, screaming at her and vomiting corrosive bile that clouded and sizzled the glass.

Nell and Cassy watched as the car veered straight for the spike pit beside the mess hall.

Ana lifted her DIY bazooka, balancing it upon the cabin's deck railing.

Josie tried to open the door to jump out, but the demon's all-encompassing bulk had molded over the sides, holding the doors firmly shut, leaving her helpless as the car fell into the pit.

The spikes of the planted javelins punched through the demon and into the car. Josie screamed as one impaled the windshield, stabbing through her armored vest, her shoulder, and the seat, pinning her to it.

Though the demon was only partially stuck within the pit, it was nonetheless jammed on account of the javelins and the car. Its roar was an avalanche around Josie—the intermingled torment of countless unfortunates that she felt in her marrow.

The sulfuric heat coming off its burning flesh, combined with its malodorous breath and the thickening smoke, was a suffocating combination, racking Josie's body with coughs and creeping deeper down her throat with each snatch of scorching air.

"Josie!" Nell and Cassy rushed toward the wreck of flames, crumpled metal, and grotesque appendages in turmoil.

Josie reached down and pulled the seat release, pushing off the dash with her feet and a scream, sliding back inch by torturous inch until her shoulder was free of the javelin's point.

The demon's many faces persisted in their agonized peals and explosive pukings from the other side of the cracked windshield, mashing, biting, and slamming themselves against the glass while its copious spiked tendrils enveloped the car and wormed their way through breaks to breach the interior. A couple latched onto Josie, who fought them off as she suffocated on smoke and the acrid commixture of bile and the melting vinyl of the dash, her skin tightening from the intense heat.

This was it, Josie knew. Her time was up. But at least she'd go out with an act of bravery—a literal blaze of glory.

As her vision blurred and her energy evaporated, she hoped such an end would absolve her of what she felt was an otherwise worthless existence.

Hoped dearly.

Josie closed her eyes, falling willingly into darkness.

The rear window smashed apart, startling Josie awake with a downpour of shattered glass.

Nell reached for her. "C'mon!" She took Josie's hand, and Cassy caught her by the other, the two of them working through coughs and much pain to pull her out.

The demon's various heads sprouted above the inferno on giraffe-long necks, flailing hydra-like in their wailing death throes as it struggled and burned beneath the car.

As Josie climbed out with Nell and Cassy's aid, there came a shout. "Move!" The three turned and saw Ana pointing her improvised weapon in their direction.

Cassy pointed back. "What's she—"

"Just run!" Nell dragged Cassy and Josie along into a stumbling run away from the wreck.

With the sound of a tree being torn from the earth, a great, dragon-like wing burst from the demon's side.

The astounding sight gave Ana a moment's pause.

Another leathery sail tore free on the demon's other side.

Cassy halted the others to take in the shocking spectacle. "Wings? Really? Fucking wings now?"

The wings began to thrash, slinging viscous strands as they beat first the ground with a seismic force, and then the air.

Ana steadied her aim against the rush of foul wind.

Nell, Cassy, and Josie braced themselves against the forcible gust.

The great buffeting bore the demon's bulk, car and all, upward, out of the pit, freeing it into the cerise night.

Ana adjusted up and to the right and raised the monkey wrench. "Some motherfuckers just don't know when to quit." She brought the wrench down on the canister's exposed stem valve, bashing it clean off.

The sudden release of pressure propelled the canister rocket-like out of the pipe and directly at the risen demon.

Its legion heads turned as one to the sight of the onrushing canister.

Nell threw herself along with Josie and Cassy to the ground.

The world exploded. A sky-splitting boom momentarily muted all that was, then came a swell of upsurging flames so bright they lit up the entire camp like high-noon.

The roar ebbed and wavered through the swaying trees as the flames sank to a contented blaze. The entire side of the rec hall nearest the explosion was a blasted heap of smoking wood, with more crumbling away as an aftereffect.

Nell, Cassy, and Josie looked back from their prone positions, then covered their heads as fleshy chunks and scorched scraps and other burning debris rained down in a slapping, crashing torrent for a lingering moment.

Silvery moonlight crept through the scarlet pall, drawing Nell's eyes skyward. "Look." The others did. Above, the void was closing into itself, the colors and forms of normality returning by degrees as the thunderous clamor with which it came echoed across sky and land—the final sennet of this nightmare.

Order, such as it was, had been restored.

Ana rushed over. "Everybody okay?" She helped them each to their feet.

"Jury's still out on that one," said Cassy.

Nell brushed charred demon viscera off herself. "Yeah, I'm okay."

"You got a little—in your hair there," said Cassy, helping Nell to expel it.

Ana held Josie's face as she rose. "You okay?"

"Fuck—" Josie coughed harshly as she palmed her injured shoulder. "Fuck yeah."

Ana smiled as she pulled them all in for an embrace.

"This is nice," said Cassy.

"That was some MacGyver-level shit you pulled off back there," said Nell.

Cassy turned to Ana as they came apart. "Hey, yeah! What the shit was that?"

"You said I shoulda brought a bazooka." Ana shrugged. "So I made one."

Cassy looked dumbfounded. "You knew how to do that?"

"I guess."

"Woulda been great to know that earlier!"

"Cassy, you sure you're okay?" asked Nell, fully taking in the dire sight of her and the others.

Cassy raised her hands in a what-the-fuck gesture. "Seriously, if Ana knew how to make a bazooka, why didn't we use it right from the start?"

"She's fine," said Ana.

"That shit should've been plan-fucking-A!"

"Definitely fine," said Josie through coughs.

The group turned as one toward the flaming wreck, the air thick with the sulfurous stink of burning demon. Firelight flickered upon their blood and gore-matted forms as their minds approached the truth of Silas's eternal demise.

"Well, if this ain't a Kodak moment, I dunno what is," said Cassy.

"Did we just save the world?" asked Nell.

Ana looked uncertain. "Maybe?"

"Is he dead?" asked Josie with understandable uncertainty. "Really dead?"

"After all that, he fucking better be," said Cassy.

Nell gave a firm exhale. "Well, if he comes back, we'll be waiting, right?"

She got a "Right" and a "Damn right" from Josie and Ana, whereas Cassy merely mumbled something while giving a noncommittal shrug.

Intuition told Nell that it was over, conveyed via a lightness that blood loss alone couldn't account for. It was greater than a burdensome weight having been lifted, more profound than a dissipating dark sky. The world itself felt anew, and she born again within it.

Given the night's fantastical twists, she half expected to see the spirits of her old friends emerging from the forest, along with Silas's other victims, all of them able to rest in peace at last now that the monster had been slain. That didn't happen.

Instead, her imagination exercised its usual anxious reflex, asking, *What if it isn't over?* but Nell remained serene and resolute in the knowledge that even if it wasn't, or if some new monster were to rear its ugly head in her life—and she knew the world had plenty of them to go around—that she'd be able to handle it, not least because of her newfound friends, her sisters.

She turned and limped in the direction of the SUV. "Let's get outta here."

Josie put her good arm over Nell's shoulders for support. "This'll make a helluva sequel to your book."

"I am *well* and truly done with this story."

Ana carefully took Josie's other arm across her shoulders. "Here fucking here."

Cassy continued to stare at the fire. "This is gonna take some serious—" A surprise burp brought up a lingering maggot, which she spat aside. "Serious therapy to process."

Ana looped an arm around her waist, pulling her along. "C'mon, *Scorpio*."

A limping Cassy slung her arm over Ana's shoulders. "Like *a lot* of therapy!"

The bone-weary four ambled toward the SUV, leaning on one another for much-needed support as the adrenaline that had helped to hold their sundry pains at bay wore off, making each step an excruciating ordeal.

Nell couldn't help but laugh at the state they were in. "We're so fucked up." The others joined in her pained mirth.

"Did anybody else have that this is what you want song in their head like, the whole time?" asked Cassy.

Nell chuckled. "Really? The whole time?"

"Even when I almost got melted into that big ugly blob thing."

"What's that sound?" asked Josie, aware of a recurrent whistling noise.

A flaming, malformed hand crawled after the four like a lame tarantula.

Cassy touched lightly at her broken nose. "My busted schnoz. That's gonna cost me a pretty penny to fix."

The monstrous hand continued in its determined advance.

"Didn't your husband die tonight?" asked Ana.

"I know . . . God knows what I'm gonna tell the kids . . . and Krista."

The hand persisted toward its targets.

"Hey, did you all hear me when I was like, '*Consume this, motherfucker!*'?"

Nos all around.

"Aw man, that was like, my bestest moment."

Josie hissed at a particularly painful step. "I'm gonna feel *every* part of me in the morning, and every morning for a long, *long* time."

"I have a first-aid kit in the trunk," said Cassy.

"I'm thinking we need something stronger than band-aids," said Nell. "An ER, for example."

Ana bent down to retrieve—"Grimthorn!"

Cassy laughed. "What?"

"I mean—"

"I knew you named it! Nerd!"

"Don't make me laugh!" said Nell, doing just that through a pain-strained face.

"Ah, shut up," said a weary Ana.

Cassy stopped everyone to retrieve some of the cultists' athames. "Ooh, grab one of these fancy knives." She handed one to each of the others.

Nell turned the dagger over, admiring the way the radiant blade coruscated beneath the moonlight. "Real fancy."

"Probably worth something," said Josie.

Ana fixed hers in her belt. "Another one for the collection."

They continued.

They came to a stop by the SUV. Cassy patted herself for the keys. "Shit, don't tell me I—Oh, here they are."

"Want me to drive?" asked Nell.

"Probably best. My foot's fucked, plus my eyes are mostly swollen shut."

Nell and Cassy limpingly swapped sides, the keys passing hands as they crossed.

Noting she was veering helplessly off course, Cassy called, "Help. My body won't let me turn." Ana came to her aid, guiding her to the passenger side.

The four of them climbed in with a chorus of pained hisses.

Cassy looked at herself. "Ugh, I need a towel." She tried in vain to fling off some of the varied muck that coated her. "Maybe try to wipe your—Ah, fuck it."

Ana settled herself in the back. "Damn right, fuck it."

Nell and Josie chuckled as they took their seats.

Ana removed her tank top and pressed it to Josie's shoulder wound. "Keep pressure on it."

"Thanks," said a wincing Josie, surprising Ana by taking her hand. Smiling, Ana held it tight.

Shifting and groaning in their search for comfort, the exhausted four stared again at the ruined camp before them.

"That . . . was fucking in-sane," said Cassy. The others nodded in silence. "Should we like, call somebody or something?" asked Cassy. "Let them know about this?"

An uncaring Nell shrugged. "Be my guest."

Cassy deliberated for a lengthy moment. "Fuck it."

Nell keyed the ignition. The headlights and stereo came alive, lighting up the creeping hand while blaring out "We Belong" by Pat Benatar.

"Oh-ho-ho!" said Cassy.

"No, c'mon, seriously?" Ana moaned. "This fucking music again?"

"After what we've been through, I've earned the right." Cassy cranked up the '80s ballad.

The vengeful demon hand continued toward the SUV.

"She's not wrong," said Nell, setting the vehicle into motion.

"Yas!" Cassy took the lead in a singalong.

Nell joined in as the distance between the hand and SUV shrank.

"Don't encourage her!" Ana fumed.

Nell and Cassy sang with greater gusto.

The appendage sprouted tiny tentacles from its severed wrist stump, which it reared back upon as the fingers stretched and wriggled like small snakes, growing longer inch-by-inch.

Josie squeezed Ana's hand. "C'mon. Victory karaoke," she said, urging her to join in as she unified with Nell and Cassy.

Compelled by the others and roused by the song as it swelled toward its powerful chorus, Ana began to feel the pull.

The SUV drove right over the demon hand, squishing it with an unceremonious splat of finality.

Ana smiled and shook the notion from her head. "Fuck that."

Acknowledgements

Thank you to all those who supported and provided feedback on this book, in particular my brother, not only for the great cover, but for his tireless help throughout, even when he was very, very tired. Thanks also to Karmen Wells, owner of Shelf Made Creative Services, and Rachel Oestreich, owner of The Wallflower Editing, for elevating the book and my writing in general with their editing expertise. And lastly, thank you to you for choosing and reading this book. If you enjoyed it, please consider leaving a review on whatever platforms you use.

About the Author

Pardeep Aujla is an award-winning screenwriter, and narrative writer for video games. This is his first novel.

Printed in Great Britain
by Amazon